PENGUIN BO

My Oedipus C
and Other Stories

Frank O'Connor was the pseudonym of Michael O'Donovan who was born at Cork in 1903. Largely self-educated, he began to prepare a collected edition of his works at the age of twelve and later worked as a librarian, translator and journalist. When quite young he learned to speak Irish and saturated himself in Gaelic poetry, music and legend. When he was interned by the Free State Government he took the opportunity to learn several languages, but it was in Irish that he wrote a prize-winning study of Turgenev on his release. 'A.E.' began to publish his poems, stories and translations in the *Irish Statesman*. Meanwhile a local clergyman remarked of him, when he produced plays by Ibsen and Chekhov in Cork, that: 'Mike the moke would go down to posterity at the head of the pagan Dublin muses.' Frank O'Connor lived in Dublin and had an American wife, two sons and two daughters. He published *Guests of the Nation*, his first book, in 1931, and then followed over thirty volumes, largely of short stories, in addition to plays. Frank O'Connor died in 1966.

FRANK O'CONNOR

My Oedipus Complex and Other Stories

PENGUIN BOOKS
IN ASSOCIATION WITH HAMISH HAMILTON

PENGUIN BOOKS

Published by the Penguin Group
Penguin Books Ltd, 80 Strand, London WC2R 0RL, England
Penguin Putnam Inc., 375 Hudson Street, New York, New York 10014, USA
Penguin Books Australia Ltd, Ringwood, Victoria, Australia
Penguin Books Canada Ltd, 10 Alcorn Avenue, Toronto, Ontario, Canada M4V 3B2
Penguin Books India (P) Ltd, 11 Community Centre, Panchsheel Park, New Delhi – 110 017, India
Penguin Books (NZ) Ltd, Cnr Rosedale and Airborne Roads, Albany, Auckland, New Zealand
Penguin Books (South Africa) (Pty) Ltd, 24 Sturdee Avenue, Rosebank 2196 South Africa

Penguin Books Ltd, Registered Offices: 80 Strand, London WC2R 0RL, England

www.penguin.com

The texts used in this edition are taken from *The Stories of Frank O'Connor*,
first published by Hamish Hamilton 1953, and from *Domestic Relations*,
first published by Hamish Hamilton 1957

This selection published in Penguin Books 1963
Reprinted in Penguin Classics 2001

2

Copyright © Frank O'Connor, 1953, 1957
All rights reserved

Set in Imprint Monotype
Printed in England by Clays Ltd, St Ives plc

Contents

The Genius

SOME kids are cissies by nature but I was a cissy by conviction. Mother had told me about geniuses; I wanted to be one, and I could see for myself that fighting, as well as being sinful, was dangerous. The kids round the Barrack where I lived were always fighting. Mother said they were savages, that I needed proper friends, and that once I was old enough to go to school I would meet them.

My way, when someone wanted to fight and I could not get away, was to climb on the nearest wall and argue like hell in a shrill voice about Our Blessed Lord and good manners. This was a way of attracting attention, and it usually worked because the enemy, having stared incredulously at me for several minutes, wondering if he would have time to hammer my head on the pavement before someone came out to him, yelled something like 'blooming cissy' and went away in disgust. I didn't like being called a cissy but I preferred it to fighting. I felt very like one of those poor mongrels who slunk through our neighbourhood and took to their heels when anyone came near them, and I always tried to make friends with them.

I toyed with games, and enjoyed kicking a ball gently before me along the pavement till I discovered that any boy who joined me grew violent and started to shoulder me out of the way. I preferred little girls because they didn't fight so much, but otherwise I found them insipid and lacking in any solid basis of information. The only women I cared for were grown-ups, and my most intimate friend was an old washerwoman called Miss Cooney who had been in the lunatic asylum and was very religious. It was she who had told me all about dogs. She would run a mile after anyone she saw hurting an animal, and even went to the police about them, but the police knew she was mad and paid no attention.

She was a sad-looking woman with grey hair, high cheek-bones and toothless gums. While she ironed, I would sit for hours in the hot, steaming, damp kitchen, turning over the pages of her religious books. She was fond of me too, and told me she was sure I would be a priest. I agreed that I might be a bishop, but she didn't seem to think so highly of bishops. I told her there were so many other things I might be that I couldn't make up my mind, but she only smiled at this. Miss Cooney thought there was only one thing a genius could be and that was a priest.

On the whole I thought an explorer was what I would be. Our house was in a square between two roads, one terraced above the other, and I could leave home, follow the upper road for a mile past the Barrack, turn left on any of the intervening roads and lanes, and return almost without leaving the pavement. It was astonishing what valuable information you could pick up on a trip like that. When I came home I wrote down my adventures in a book called *The Voyages of Johnson Martin*, 'with many Maps and Illustrations, Irishtown University Press, 3s. 6d. nett'. I was also compiling *The Irishtown University Song Book for Use in Schools and Institutions by Johnson Martin*, which had the words and music of my favourite songs. I could not read music yet but I copied it from anything that came handy, preferring staff to solfa because it looked better on the page. But I still wasn't sure what I would be. All I knew was that I intended to be famous and have a statue put up to me near that of Father Matthew, in Patrick Street. Father Matthew was called the Apostle of Temperance, but I didn't think much of temperance. So far our town hadn't a proper genius and I intended to supply the deficiency.

But my work continued to bring home to me the great gaps in my knowledge. Mother understood my difficulty and worried herself endlessly finding answers to my questions, but neither she nor Miss Cooney had a great store of the sort of information I needed, and Father was more a hindrance than a help. He was talkative enough about subjects that interested himself but they did not greatly interest me. 'Ballybeg,' he would say brightly. 'Market town. Population 648. Nearest station, Rathkeale.' He was also forthcoming enough about other things, but later, Mother would take me aside and explain that he was only joking again. This made me mad, because I never knew when he was joking and when he wasn't.

I can see now, of course, that he didn't really like me. It was not the poor man's fault. He had never expected to be the father of a genius and it filled him with forebodings. He looked round him at all his contemporaries who had normal, blood-thirsty, illiterate children, and shuddered at the thought that I would never be good for anything but being a genius. To give him his due, it wasn't himself he worried about, but there had never been anything like it in the family before and he dreaded the shame of it. He would come in from the front door with his cap over his eyes and his hands in his trouser pockets and stare moodily at me while I sat at the kitchen table, surrounded by papers, producing fresh maps and illustrations for my book of voyages, or copying the music of 'The Minstrel Boy'.

'Why can't you go out and play with the Horgans?' he would ask wheedlingly, trying to make it sound attractive.

'I don't like the Horgans, Daddy,' I would reply politely.

'But what's wrong with them?' he would ask testily. 'They're fine manly young fellows.'

'They're always fighting, Daddy.'

'And what harm is fighting? Can't you fight them back?'

'I don't like fighting, Daddy, thank you,' I would say, still with perfect politeness.

'The dear knows, the child is right,' Mother would say, coming to my defence. 'I don't know what sort those children are.'

'Ah, you have him as bad as yourself,' Father would snort, and stalk to the front door again, to scald his heart with thoughts of the nice natural son he might have had if only he hadn't married the wrong woman. Granny had always said Mother was the wrong woman for him and now she was being proved right.

She was being proved so right that the poor man couldn't keep his eyes off me, waiting for the insanity to break out in me. One of the things he didn't like was my Opera House. The Opera House was a cardboard box I had mounted on two chairs in the dark hallway. It had a proscenium cut in it, and I had painted some back-drops of mountain and sea, with wings that represented trees and rocks. The characters were pictures cut out, mounted and coloured, and moved on bits of stick. It was lit with candles, for which I had made coloured screens, greased so that they were transparent, and I made up operas from story-books and bits of songs. I was singing a passionate duet for two of the characters while twiddling the screens to produce the effect of moonlight when one of the screens caught fire and everything went up in a mass of flames. I screamed and Father came out to stamp out the blaze, and he cursed me till even Mother lost her temper with him and told him he was worse than six children, after which he wouldn't speak to her for a week.

Another time I was so impressed with a lame teacher I knew that I decided to have a lame leg myself, and there was hell in the home for days because Mother had no difficulty at all in seeing that my foot was already out of shape while Father only looked at it and sniffed contemptuously. I was furious with him, and Mother decided he wasn't much better than a monster. They quarrelled for days over that until it became quite an embarrassment to me because, though I was bored stiff with limping, I felt I should be letting her down by getting better. When I went down the Square, lurching from side to side, Father stood at the gate, looking after me with a malicious knowing smile, and when I had discarded my limp, the way he mocked Mother was positively disgusting.

2

As I say, they squabbled endlessly about what I should be told. Father was for telling me nothing.

'But, Mick,' Mother would say earnestly, 'the child must learn.'

'He'll learn soon enough when he goes to school,' he snarled. 'Why do you be always at him, putting ideas into his head? Isn't he bad enough? I'd sooner the boy would grow up a bit natural.'

But either Mother didn't like children to be natural or she thought I was natural enough as I was. Women, of course, don't object to geniuses half as much as men do. I suppose they find them a relief.

Now one of the things I wanted badly to know was where babies came from, but this was something that no one seemed to be able to explain to me. When I asked Mother she got upset and talked about birds and flowers, and I decided that if she had ever known she must have forgotten it and was ashamed to say so. Miss Cooney only smiled wistfully when I asked her and said, 'You'll know all about it soon enough, child.'

'But, Miss Cooney,' I said with great dignity, 'I have to know now. It's for my work, you see.'

'Keep your innocence while you can, child,' she said in the same tone. 'Soon enough the world will rob you of it, and once 'tis gone 'tis gone for ever.'

But whatever the world wanted to rob me of, it was welcome to it from my point of view, if only I could get a few facts to work on. I appealed to Father and he told me that babies were dropped out of aeroplanes and if you caught one you could keep it. 'By parachute?' I asked, but he only looked pained and said, 'Oh, no, you don't want to begin by spoiling them.' Afterwards, Mother took me aside again and explained that he was only joking. I went quite dotty with rage and told her that one of these days he would go too far with his jokes.

All the same, it was a great worry to Mother. It wasn't every mother who had a genius for a son, and she dreaded that she might be wronging me. She suggested timidly to Father that he should tell me something about it and he danced with rage. I heard them because I was supposed to be playing with the Opera House upstairs at the time. He said she was going out of her mind, and that she was driving me out of my mind at the same time. She was very upset because she had considerable respect for his judgement.

At the same time when it was a matter of duty she could be very, very obstinate. It was a heavy responsibility, and she

disliked it intensely – a deeply pious woman who never mentioned the subject at all to anybody if she could avoid it – but
it had to be done. She took an awful long time over it – it was
a summer day, and we were sitting on the bank of a stream in
the Glen – but at last I managed to detach the fact that mum-
mies had an engine in their tummies and daddies had a
starting-handle that made it work, and once it started it went
on until it made a baby. That certainly explained an awful lot of
things I had not understood up to this – for instance, why fathers
were necessary and why Mother had buffers on her chest
while Father had none. It made her almost as interesting as a
locomotive, and for days I went round deploring my own rotten
luck that I wasn't a girl and couldn't have an engine and buffers
of my own instead of a measly old starting-handle like Father.

Soon afterwards I went to school and disliked it intensely.
I was too small to be moved up to the big boys and the other
'infants' were still at the stage of spelling 'cat' and 'dog'. I
tried to tell the old teacher about my work, but she only smiled
and said, 'Hush, Larry!' I hated being told to hush. Father
was always saying it to me.

One day I was standing at the playground gate, feeling very
lonely and dissatisfied, when a tall girl from the Senior Girls'
school spoke to me. She was a girl with a plump, dark face and
black pigtails.

'What's your name, little boy?' she asked.

I told her.

'Is this your first time at school?' she asked.

'Yes.'

'And do you like it?'

'No, I hate it,' I replied gravely. 'The children can't spell
and the old woman talks too much.'

Then I talked myself for a change and she listened attentively while I told her about myself, my voyages, my books and
the time of the trains from all the city stations. As she seemed
so interested I told her I would meet her after school and tell
her some more.

I was as good as my word. When I had eaten my lunch,
instead of going on further voyages I went back to the Girls'

School and waited for her to come out. She seemed pleased to see me because she took my hand and brought me home with her. She lived up Gardiner's Hill, a steep, demure suburban road with trees that overhung the walls at either side. She lived in a small house on top of the hill and was one of a family of three girls. Her little brother, John Joe, had been killed the previous year by a car. 'Look at what I brought home with me!' she said when we went into the kitchen, and her mother, a tall, thin woman made a great fuss of me and wanted me to have my dinner with Una. That was the girl's name. I didn't take anything, but while she ate I sat by the range and told her mother about myself as well. She seemed to like it as much as Una, and when dinner was over Una took me out in the fields behind the house for a walk.

When I went home at teatime, Mother was delighted.

'Ah,' she said, 'I knew you wouldn't be long making nice friends at school. It's about time for you, the dear knows.'

I felt much the same about it, and every fine day at three I waited for Una outside the school. When it rained and Mother would not let me out I was miserable.

One day while I was waiting for her there were two senior girls outside the gate.

'Your girl isn't out yet, Larry,' said one with a giggle.

'And do you mean to tell me Larry has a girl?' the other asked with a shocked air.

'Oh, yes,' said the first. 'Una Dwyer is Larry's girl. He goes with Una, don't you, Larry?'

I replied politely that I did, but in fact I was seriously alarmed. I had not realized that Una would be considered my girl. It had never happened to me before, and I had not understood that my waiting for her would be regarded in such a grave light. Now, I think the girls were probably right anyhow, for that is always the way it has happened to me. A woman has only to shut up and let me talk long enough for me to fall head and ears in love with her. But then I did not recognize the symptoms. All I knew was that going with somebody meant you intended to marry them. I had always planned on marrying Mother; now it seemed as if I was expected to marry someone else, and I wasn't sure if I should like it or if, like football, it would prove to be one of those games that two people could not play without pushing.

A couple of weeks later I went to a party at Una's house. By this time it was almost as much mine as theirs. All the girls liked me and Mrs Dwyer talked to me by the hour. I saw nothing peculiar about this except a proper appreciation of geniuses. Una had warned me that I should be expected to sing, so I was ready for the occasion. I sang the Gregorian *Credo*, and some of the little girls laughed, but Mrs Dwyer only looked at me fondly.

'I suppose you'll be a priest when you grow up, Larry?' she asked.

'No, Mrs Dwyer,' I replied firmly. 'As a matter of fact, I intend to be a composer. Priests can't marry, you see, and I want to get married.'

That seemed to surprise her quite a bit. I was quite prepared to continue discussing my plans for the future, but all the children talked together. I was used to planning discussions so that they went on for a long time, but I found that whenever I began one in the Dwyers', it was immediately interrupted so that I found it hard to concentrate. Besides, all the children shouted, and Mrs Dwyer, for all her gentleness, shouted with them and at them. At first, I was somewhat alarmed, but I soon saw that they meant no particular harm, and when the party ended I was jumping up and down on the sofa, shrieking louder than anyone while Una, in hysterics of giggling, encouraged me. She seemed to think I was the funniest thing ever.

It was a moonlit November night, and lights were burning in the little cottages along the road when Una brought me home. On the road outside she stopped uncertainly and said, 'This is where little John Joe was killed.'

There was nothing remarkable about the spot, and I saw no chance of acquiring any useful information.

'Was it a Ford or a Morris?' I asked, more out of politeness than anything else.

'I don't know,' she replied with smouldering anger. 'It was

Donegan's old car. They can never look where they're going, the old shows!'

'Our Lord probably wanted him,' I said perfunctorily.

'I dare say He did,' Una replied, though she showed no particular conviction. 'That old fool, Donegan – I could kill him whenever I think of it.'

'You should get your mother to make you another,' I suggested helpfully.

'Make me a what?' Una exclaimed in consternation.

'Make you another brother,' I repeated earnestly. 'It's quite easy, really. She has an engine in her tummy, and all your daddy has to do is to start it with his starting-handle.'

'Cripes!' Una said, and clapped her hand over her mouth in an explosion of giggles. 'Imagine me telling her that!'

'But it's true, Una,' I said obstinately. 'It only takes nine months. She could make you another little brother by next summer.'

'Oh, Jay!' exclaimed Una in another fit of giggles. 'Who told you all that?'

'Mummy did. Didn't your mother tell you?'

'Oh, she says you buy them from Nurse Daly,' said Una, and began to giggle again.

'I wouldn't really believe that,' I said with as much dignity as I could muster.

But the truth was I felt I had made a fool of myself again. I realized now that I had never been convinced by Mother's explanation. It was too simple. If there was anything that woman could get wrong she did so without fail. And it upset me, because for the first time I found myself wanting to make a really good impression. The Dwyers had managed to convince me that whatever else I wanted to be I did not want to be a priest. I didn't even want to be an explorer, a career which would take me away for long periods from my wife and family. I was prepared to be a composer and nothing but a composer.

That night in bed I sounded Mother on the subject of marriage. I tried to be tactful because it had always been agreed between us that I should marry her and I did not wish her to see that my feelings had changed.

'Mummy,' I asked, 'if a gentleman asks a lady to marry him, what does he say?'

'Oh,' she replied shortly, 'some of them say a lot. They say more than they mean.'

She was so irritable that I guessed she had divined my secret and I felt really sorry for her.

'If a gentleman said, "Excuse me, will you marry me?" would that be all right?' I persisted.

'Ah, well, he'd have to tell her first that he was fond of her,' said Mother who, no matter what she felt, could never bring herself to deceive me on any major issue.

But about the other matter I saw that it was hopeless to ask her any more. For days I made the most pertinacious inquiries at school and received some startling information. One boy had actually come floating down on a snowflake, wearing a bright blue dress, but to his chagrin and mine, the dress had been given away to a poor child in the North Main Street. I grieved long and deeply over this wanton destruction of evidence. The balance of opinion favoured Mrs Dwyer's solution, but of the theory of engines and starting-handles no one in the school had ever heard. That theory might have been all right when Mother was a girl but it was now definitely out of fashion.

And because of it I had been exposed to ridicule before the family whose good opinion I valued most. It was hard enough to keep up my dignity with a girl who was doing algebra while I hadn't got beyond long division without falling into childish errors that made her laugh. That is another thing I still cannot stand, being made fun of by women. Once they begin on it they never stop. Once when we were going up Gardiner's Hill together after school she stopped to look at a baby in a pram. The baby grinned at her and she gave him her finger to suck. He waved his fists and sucked like mad, and she went off into giggles again.

'I suppose that was another engine?' she said.

Four times at least she mentioned my silliness, twice in front of other girls and each time, though I pretended to ignore it, I was pierced to the heart. It made me determined not to be exposed again. Once Mother asked Una and her younger sister, Joan, to tea, and all the time I was in an agony of self-consciousness, dreading what she would say next. I felt that a woman who had said such things about babies was capable of anything. Then the talk turned on the death of little John Joe, and it all flowed back into my mind on a wave of mortification. I made two efforts to change the conversation, but Mother returned to it. She was full of pity for the Dwyers, full of sympathy for the little boy and had almost reduced herself to tears. Finally I got up and ordered Una and Joan to play with me. Then Mother got angry.

'For goodness' sake, Larry, let the children finish their tea!' she snapped.

'It's all right, Mrs Delaney,' Una said good-naturedly. 'I'll go with him.'

'Nonsense, Una!' Mother said sharply. 'Finish your tea and go on with what you were saying. It's a wonder to me your poor mother didn't go out of her mind. How can they let people like that drive cars?'

At this I set up a loud wail. At any moment now I felt she was going to get on to babies and advise Una about what her mother ought to do.

'Will you behave yourself, Larry!' Mother said in a quivering voice. 'Or what's come over you in the past few weeks? You used to have such nice manners, and now look at you! A little corner boy! I'm ashamed of you!'

How could she know what had come over me? How could she realize that I was imagining the family circle in the Dwyers' house and Una, between fits of laughter, describing my old-fashioned mother who still talked about babies coming out of people's stomachs? It must have been real love, for I have never known true love in which I wasn't ashamed of Mother.

And she knew it and was hurt. I still enjoyed going home with Una in the afternoons and while she ate her dinner, I sat at the piano and pretended to play my own compositions, but whenever she called at our house for me I grabbed her by the hand and tried to drag her away so that she and Mother shouldn't start talking.

'Ah, I'm disgusted with you,' Mother said one day. 'One

would think you were ashamed of me in front of that little girl. I'll engage she doesn't treat her mother like that.'

Then one day I was waiting for Una at the school gate as usual. Another boy was waiting there as well – one of the seniors. When he heard the screams of the school breaking up he strolled away and stationed himself at the foot of the hill by the crossroads. Then Una herself came rushing out in her wide-brimmed felt hat, swinging her satchel, and approached me with a conspiratorial air.

'Oh, Larry, guess what's happened!' she whispered. 'I can't bring you home with me today. I'll come down and see you during the week though. Will that do?'

'Yes, thank you,' I said in a dead cold voice. Even at the most tragic moment of my life I could be nothing but polite. I watched her scamper down the hill to where the big boy was waiting. He looked over his shoulder with a grin, and then the two of them went off together.

Instead of following them I went back up the hill alone and stood leaning over the quarry wall, looking at the roadway and the valley of the city beneath me. I knew this was the end. I was too young to marry Una. I didn't know where babies came from and I didn't understand algebra. The fellow she had gone home with probably knew everything about both. I was full of gloom and revengeful thoughts. I, who had considered it sinful and dangerous to fight, was now regretting that I hadn't gone after him to batter his teeth in and jump on his face. It wouldn't even have mattered to me that I was too young and weak and that he would have done all the battering. I saw that love was a game that two people couldn't play at without pushing, just like football.

I went home and, without saying a word, took out the work I had been neglecting so long. That too seemed to have lost its appeal. Moodily I ruled five lines and began to trace the difficult sign of the treble clef.

'Didn't you see Una, Larry?' Mother asked in surprise, looking up from her sewing.

'No, Mummy,' I said, too full for speech.

'Wisha, 'twasn't a falling-out ye had?' she asked in dismay, coming towards me. I put my head on my hands and sobbed. 'Wisha, never mind, childeen!' she murmured, running her hand through my hair. 'She was a bit old for you. You reminded her of her little brother that was killed, of course – that was why. You'll soon make new friends, take my word for it.'

But I did not believe her. That evening there was no comfort for me. My great work meant nothing to me and I knew it was all I would ever have. For all the difference it made I might as well become a priest. I felt it was a poor, sad, lonesome thing being nothing but a genius.

My Oedipus Complex

FATHER was in the army all through the war – the First War, I mean – so, up to the age of five, I never saw much of him, and what I saw did not worry me. Sometimes I woke and there was a big figure in khaki peering down at me in the candlelight. Sometimes in the early morning I heard the slamming of the front door and the clatter of nailed boots down the cobbles of the lane. These were Father's entrances and exits. Like Santa Claus he came and went mysteriously.

In fact, I rather liked his visits, though it was an uncomfortable squeeze between Mother and him when I got into the big bed in the early morning. He smoked, which gave him a pleasant musty smell, and shaved, an operation of astounding interest. Each time he left a trail of souvenirs – model tanks and Gurkha knives with handles made of bullet cases, and German helmets and cap badges and button-sticks, and all sorts of military equipment – carefully stowed away in a long box on top of the wardrobe, in case they ever came in handy. There was a bit of the magpie about Father; he expected everything to come in handy. When his back was turned, Mother let me get a chair and rummage through his treasures. She didn't seem to think so highly of them as he did.

The war was the most peaceful period of my life. The window of my attic faced south-east. My Mother had curtained it, but that had small effect. I always woke with the first light and, with all the responsibilities of the previous day melted, feeling myself rather like the sun, ready to illumine and rejoice. Life never seemed so simple and clear and full of possibilities as then. I put my feet out from under the clothes – I called them Mrs Left and Mrs Right – and invented dramatic situations for them in which they discussed the problems of the day. At least Mrs Right did; she was very demonstrative, but I hadn't the same control of Mrs Left, so she mostly contented herself with nodding agreement.

They discussed what Mother and I should do during the

day, what Santa Claus should give a fellow for Christmas, and what steps should be taken to brighten the home. There was that little matter of the baby, for instance. Mother and I could never agree about that. Ours was the only house in the terrace without a new baby, and Mother said we couldn't afford one till Father came back from the war because they cost seventeen and six. That showed how simple she was. The Geneys up the road had a baby, and everyone knew they couldn't afford seventeen and six. It was probably a cheap baby, and Mother wanted something really good, but I felt she was too exclusive. The Geneys' baby would have done us fine.

Having settled my plans for the day, I got up, put a chair under the attic window, and lifted the frame high enough to stick out my head. The window overlooked the front gardens of the terrace behind ours, and beyond these it looked over a deep valley to the tall, red-brick houses terraced up the opposite hillside, which were all still in shadow, while those at our side of the valley were all lit up, though with long strange shadows that made them seem unfamiliar; rigid and painted.

After that I went into Mother's room and climbed into the big bed. She woke and I began to tell her of my schemes. By this time, though I never seem to have noticed it, I was petrified in my nightshirt, and I thawed as I talked until, the last frost melted, I fell asleep beside her and woke again only when I heard her below in the kitchen, making the breakfast.

After breakfast we went into town; heard Mass at St Augustine's and said a prayer for Father, and did the shopping. If the afternoon was fine we either went for a walk in the country or a visit to Mother's great friend in the convent, Mother St Dominic. Mother had them all praying for Father, and every night, going to bed, I asked God to send him back safe from the war to us. Little, indeed, did I know what I was praying for!

One morning I got into the big bed, and there, sure enough, was Father in his usual Santa Claus manner, but later, instead of uniform, he put on his best blue suit, and Mother was as pleased as anything. I saw nothing to be pleased about, because, out of uniform, Father was altogether less interesting, but she only beamed, and explained that our prayers had been answered, and off we went to Mass to thank God for having brought Father safely home.

The irony of it! That very day when he came in to dinner he took off his boots and put on his slippers, donned the dirty old cap he wore about the house to save him from colds, crossed his legs, and began to talk gravely to Mother, who looked anxious. Naturally, I disliked her looking anxious, because it destroyed her good looks, so I interrupted him.

'Just a moment, Larry!' she said gently.

This was only what she said when we had boring visitors, so I attached no importance to it and went on talking.

'Do be quiet, Larry!' she said impatiently. 'Don't you hear me talking to Daddy?'

This was the first time I had heard those ominous words, 'talking to Daddy', and I couldn't help feeling that if this was how God answered prayers, he couldn't listen to them very attentively.

'Why are you talking to Daddy?' I asked with as great a show of indifference as I could muster.

'Because Daddy and I have business to discuss. Now don't interrupt again!'

In the afternoon, at Mother's request, Father took me for a walk. This time we went into town instead of out to the country, and I thought at first, in my usual optimistic way, that it might be an improvement. It was nothing of the sort. Father and I had quite different notions of a walk in town. He had no proper interest in trams, ships, and horses, and the only thing that seemed to divert him was talking to fellows as old as himself. When I wanted to stop he simply went on, dragging me behind him by the hand; when he wanted to stop I had no alternative but to do the same. I noticed that it seemed to be a sign that he wanted to stop for a long time whenever he leaned against a wall. The second time I saw him do it I got wild. He seemed to be settling himself forever. I pulled him by the coat and trousers, but, unlike Mother who, if you were too persistent, got into a wax and said: 'Larry, if you don't behave yourself, I'll give you a good slap,' Father had an extraordinary capacity for amiable inattention. I sized him up and wondered would I cry, but he seemed to be too remote to be annoyed even by that. Really, it was like going for a walk with a mountain! He either ignored the wrenching and pummelling entirely, or else glanced down with a grin of amusement from his peak. I had never met anyone so absorbed in himself as he seemed.

At teatime, 'talking to Daddy' began again, complicated this time by the fact that he had an evening paper, and every few minutes he put it down and told Mother something new out of it. I felt this was foul play. Man for man, I was prepared to compete with him any time for Mother's attention, but when he had it all made up for him by other people it left me no chance. Several times I tried to change the subject without success.

'You must be quiet while Daddy is reading, Larry,' Mother said impatiently.

It was clear that she either genuinely liked talking to Father better than talking to me, or else that he had some terrible hold on her which made her afraid to admit the truth.

'Mummy,' I said that night when she was tucking me up, 'do you think if I prayed hard God would send Daddy back to the war?'

She seemed to think about that for a moment.

'No, dear,' she said with a smile. 'I don't think he would.'

'Why wouldn't he, Mummy?'

'Because there isn't a war any longer, dear.'

'But, Mummy, couldn't God make another war, if He liked?'

'He wouldn't like to, dear. It's not God who makes wars, but bad people.'

'Oh!' I said.

I was disappointed about that. I began to think that God wasn't quite what he was cracked up to be.

Next morning I woke at my usual hour, feeling like a bottle of champagne. I put out my feet and invented a long conversation in which Mrs Right talked of the trouble she had with her own father till she put him in the Home. I didn't quite know what the Home was but it sounded the right place for Father. Then I got my chair and stuck my head out of the attic window. Dawn was just breaking, with a guilty air that made me feel I had caught it in the act. My head bursting with stories and schemes, I stumbled in next door, and in the half-darkness scrambled into the big bed. There was no room at Mother's side so I had to get between her and Father. For the time being I had forgotten about him, and for several minutes I sat bolt upright, racking my brains to know what I could do with him. He was taking up more than his fair share of the bed, and I couldn't get comfortable, so I gave him several kicks that made him grunt and stretch. He made room all right, though. Mother waked and felt for me. I settled back comfortably in the warmth of the bed with my thumb in my mouth.

'Mummy!' I hummed, loudly and contentedly.

'Sssh! dear,' she whispered. 'Don't wake Daddy!'

This was a new development, which threatened to be even more serious than 'talking to Daddy'. Life without my early-morning conferences was unthinkable.

'Why?' I asked severely.

'Because poor Daddy is tired.'

This seemed to me a quite inadequate reason, and I was sickened by the sentimentality of her 'poor Daddy'. I never liked that sort of gush; it always struck me as insincere.

'Oh!' I said lightly. Then in my most winning tone: 'Do you know where I want to go with you today, Mummy?'

'No, dear,' she sighed.

'I want to go down the Glen and fish for thornybacks with my new net, and then I want to go out to the Fox and Hounds, and – '

'Don't-wake-Daddy!' she hissed angrily, clapping her hand across my mouth.

But it was too late. He was awake, or nearly so. He grunted and reached for the matches. Then he stared incredulously at his watch.

'Like a cup of tea, dear?' asked Mother in a meek, hushed voice I had never heard her use before. It sounded almost as though she were afraid.

'Tea?' he exclaimed indignantly. 'Do you know what the time is?'

'And after that I want to go up the Rathcooney Road,' I said loudly, afraid I'd forget something in all those interruptions.

'Go to sleep at once, Larry!' she said sharply.

I began to snivel. I couldn't concentrate, the way that pair went on, and smothering my early-morning schemes was like burying a family from the cradle.

Father said nothing, but lit his pipe and sucked it, looking out into the shadows without minding Mother or me. I knew he was mad. Every time I made a remark Mother hushed me irritably. I was mortified. I felt it wasn't fair; there was even something sinister in it. Every time I had pointed out to her the waste of making two beds when we could both sleep in one, she had told me it was healthier like that, and now here was this man, this stranger, sleeping with her without the least regard for her health!

He got up early and made tea, but though he brought Mother a cup he brought none for me.

'Mummy,' I shouted, 'I want a cup of tea, too.'

'Yes, dear,' she said patiently. 'You can drink from Mummy's saucer.'

That settled it. Either Father or I would have to leave the house. I didn't want to drink from Mother's saucer; I wanted to be treated as an equal in my own home, so, just to spite her, I drank it all and left none for her. She took that quietly, too.

But that night when she was putting me to bed she said gently:

'Larry, I want you to promise me something.'

'What is it?' I asked.

'Not to come in and disturb poor Daddy in the morning. Promise?'

'Poor Daddy' again! I was becoming suspicious of everything involving that quite impossible man.

'Why?' I asked.

'Because poor Daddy is worried and tired and he doesn't sleep well.'

'Why doesn't he, Mummy?'

'Well, you know, don't you, that while he was at the war Mummy got the pennies from the Post Office?'

'From Miss MacCarthy?'

'That's right. But now, you see, Miss MacCarthy hasn't any more pennies, so Daddy must go out and find us some. You know what would happen if he couldn't?'

'No,' I said, 'tell us.'

'Well, I think we might have to go out and beg for them like the poor old woman on Fridays. We wouldn't like that, would we?'

'No,' I agreed. 'We wouldn't.'

'So you'll promise not to come in and wake him?'

'Promise.'

Mind you, I meant that. I knew pennies were a serious matter, and I was all against having to go out and beg like the old woman on Fridays. Mother laid out all my toys in a complete ring round the bed so that, whatever way I got out, I was bound to fall over one of them.

When I woke I remembered my promise all right. I got up and sat on the floor and played – for hours, it seemed to me. Then I got my chair and looked out the attic window for more hours. I wished it was time for Father to wake; I wished someone would make me a cup of tea. I didn't feel in the least like the sun; instead, I was bored and so very, very cold! I simply longed for the warmth and depth of the big featherbed.

At last I could stand it no longer. I went into the next room. As there was still no room at Mother's side I climbed over her and she woke with a start.

'Larry,' she whispered, gripping my arm very tightly, 'what did you promise?'

'But I did, Mummy,' I wailed, caught in the very act. 'I was quiet for ever so long.'

'Oh, dear, and you're perished!' she said sadly, feeling me all over. 'Now, if I let you stay will you promise not to talk?'

'But I want to talk, Mummy,' I wailed.

'That has nothing to do with it,' she said with a firmness that was new to me. 'Daddy wants to sleep. Now, do you understand that?'

I understood it only too well. I wanted to talk, he wanted to sleep – whose house was it, anyway?

'Mummy,' I said with equal firmness, 'I think it would be healthier for Daddy to sleep in his own bed.'

That seemed to stagger her, because she said nothing for a while.

'Now, once for all,' she went on, 'you're to be perfectly quiet or go back to your own bed. Which is it to be?'

The injustice of it got me down. I had convicted her out of her own mouth of inconsistency and unreasonableness, and she hadn't even attempted to reply. Full of spite, I gave Father a kick, which she didn't notice but which made him grunt and open his eyes in alarm.

'What time is it?' he asked in a panic-stricken voice, not looking at Mother but at the door, as if he saw someone there.

'It's early yet,' she replied soothingly. 'It's only the child. Go to sleep again. . . . Now, Larry,' she added, getting out of bed, 'you've wakened Daddy and you must go back.'

This time, for all her quiet air, I knew she meant it, and knew that my principal rights and privileges were as good as lost unless I asserted them at once. As she lifted me, I gave a screech, enough to wake the dead, not to mind Father. He groaned.

'That damn child! Doesn't he ever sleep?'

'It's only a habit, dear,' she said quietly, though I could see she was vexed.

'Well, it's time he got out of it,' shouted Father, beginning to heave in the bed. He suddenly gathered all the bedclothes about him, turned to the wall, and then looked back over his shoulder with nothing showing only two small, spiteful, dark eyes. The man looked very wicked.

To open the bedroom door, Mother had to let me down, and I broke free and dashed for the farthest corner, screeching. Father sat bolt upright in bed.

'Shut up, you little puppy!' he said in a choking voice.

I was so astonished that I stopped screeching. Never, never had anyone spoken to me in that tone before. I looked at him incredulously and saw his face convulsed with rage. It was only then that I fully realized how God had codded me, listening to my prayers for the safe return of this monster.

'Shut up, you!' I bawled, beside myself.

'What's that you said?' shouted Father, making a wild leap out of the bed.

'Mick, Mick!' cried Mother. 'Don't you see the child isn't used to you?'

'I see he's better fed than taught,' snarled Father, waving his arms wildly. 'He wants his bottom smacked.'

All his previous shouting was as nothing to these obscene words referring to my person. They really made my blood boil.

'Smack your own!' I screamed hysterically. 'Smack your own! Shut up! Shut up!'

At this he lost his patience and let fly at me. He did it with the lack of conviction you'd expect of a man under Mother's horrified eyes, and it ended up as a mere tap, but the sheer indignity of being struck at all by a stranger, a total stranger who had cajoled his way back from the war into our big bed as a result of my innocent intercession, made me completely dotty. I shrieked and shrieked, and danced in my bare feet, and Father, looking awkward and hairy in nothing but a short grey army shirt, glared down at me like a mountain out for murder. I think it must have been then that I realized he was jealous too. And there stood Mother in her nightdress, looking as if her heart was broken between us. I hoped she felt as she looked. It seemed to me that she deserved it all.

From that morning out my life was a hell. Father and I were enemies, open and avowed. We conducted a series of skirmishes against one another, he trying to steal my time with Mother and I his. When she was sitting on my bed, telling me a story, he took to looking for some pair of old boots which he alleged he had left behind him at the beginning of the war. While he talked to Mother I played loudly with my toys to show my total lack of concern. He created a terrible scene one evening when he came in from work and found me at his box, playing with his regimental badges, Gurkha knives, and button-sticks. Mother got up and took the box from me.

'You mustn't play with Daddy's toys unless he lets you, Larry,' she said severely. 'Daddy doesn't play with yours.'

For some reason Father looked at her as if she had struck him and then turned away with a scowl.

'Those are not toys,' he growled, taking down the box again to see had I lifted anything. 'Some of those curios are very rare and valuable.'

But as time went on I saw more and more how he managed

to alienate Mother and me. What made it worse was that I couldn't grasp his method or see what attraction he had for Mother. In every possible way he was less winning than I. He had a common accent and made noises at his tea. I thought for a while that it might be the newspapers she was interested in, so I made up bits of news of my own to read to her. Then I thought it might be the smoking, which I personally thought attractive, and took his pipes and went round the house dribbling into them till he caught me. I even made noises at my tea, but Mother only told me I was disgusting. It all seemed to hinge round that unhealthy habit of sleeping together, so I made a point of dropping into their bedroom and nosing round, talking to myself, so that they wouldn't know I was watching them, but they were never up to anything that I could see. In the end it beat me. It seemed to depend on being grown-up and giving people rings, and I realized I'd have to wait.

But at the same time I wanted him to see that I was only waiting, not giving up the fight. One evening when he was being particularly obnoxious, chattering away well above my head, I let him have it.

'Mummy,' I said, 'do you know what I'm going to do when I grow up?'

'No, dear,' she replied. 'What?'

'I'm going to marry you,' I said quietly.

Father gave a great guffaw out of him, but he didn't take me in. I knew it must only be pretence. And Mother, in spite of everything, was pleased. I felt she was probably relieved to know that one day Father's hold on her would be broken.

'Won't that be nice?' she said with a smile.

'It'll be very nice,' I said confidently. 'Because we're going to have lots and lots of babies.'

'That's right, dear,' she said placidly. 'I think we'll have one soon, and then you'll have plenty of company.'

I was no end pleased about that because it showed that in spite of the way she gave in to Father she still considered my wishes. Besides, it would put the Geneys in their place.

It didn't turn out like that, though. To begin with, she was very preoccupied – I supposed about where she would get the seventeen and six – and though Father took to staying out late in the evenings it did me no particular good. She stopped taking me for walks, became as touchy as blazes, and smacked me for nothing at all. Sometimes I wished I'd never mentioned the confounded baby – I seemed to have a genius for bringing calamity on myself.

And calamity it was! Sonny arrived in the most appalling hullabaloo – even that much he couldn't do without a fuss – and from the first moment I disliked him. He was a difficult child – so far as I was concerned he was always difficult – and demanded far too much attention. Mother was simply silly about him, and couldn't see when he was only showing off. As company he was worse than useless. He slept all day, and I had to go round the house on tiptoe to avoid waking him. It wasn't any longer a question of not waking Father. The slogan now was 'Don't-wake-Sonny!' I couldn't understand why the child wouldn't sleep at the proper time, so whenever Mother's back was turned I woke him. Sometimes to keep him awake I pinched him as well. Mother caught me at it one day and gave me a most unmerciful flaking.

One evening, when Father was coming in from work, I was playing trains in the front garden. I let on not to notice him; instead, I pretended to be talking to myself, and said in a loud voice: 'If another bloody baby comes into this house, I'm going out.'

Father stopped dead and looked at me over his shoulder.

'What's that you said?' he asked sternly.

'I was only talking to myself,' I replied, trying to conceal my panic. 'It's private.'

He turned and went in without a word. Mind you, I intended it as a solemn warning, but its effect was quite different. Father started being quite nice to me. I could understand that, of course. Mother was quite sickening about Sonny. Even at mealtimes she'd get up and gawk at him in the cradle with an idiotic smile, and tell Father to do the same. He was always polite about it, but he looked so puzzled you could see he didn't know what she was talking about. He complained of the way Sonny cried at night, but she only got cross and said that Sonny never cried except when there was something up with him – which was a flaming lie, because Sonny never had anything up with him, and only cried for attention. It was really painful to see how simple-minded she was. Father wasn't attractive, but he had a fine intelligence. He saw through Sonny, and now he knew that I saw through him as well.

One night I woke with a start. There was someone beside me in the bed. For one wild moment I felt sure it must be Mother, having come to her senses and left Father for good, but then I heard Sonny in convulsions in the next room, and Mother saying: 'There! There! There!' and I knew it wasn't she. It was Father. He was lying beside me, wide awake, breathing hard and apparently as mad as hell.

After a while it came to me what he was mad about. It was his turn now. After turning me out of the big bed, he had been turned out himself. Mother had no consideration now for anyone but that poisonous pup, Sonny. I couldn't help feeling sorry for Father. I had been through it all myself, and even at that age I was magnanimous. I began to stroke him down and say: 'There! There!' He wasn't exactly responsive.

'Aren't you asleep either?' he snarled.

'Ah, come on and put your arm around us, can't you?' I said, and he did, in a sort of way. Gingerly, I suppose, is how you'd describe it. He was very bony but better than nothing.

At Christmas he went out of his way to buy me a really nice model railway.

The Study of History

THE discovery of where babies came from filled my life with excitement and interest. Not in the way it's generally supposed to of course. Oh, no! I never seem to have done anything like a natural child in a standard textbook. I merely discovered the fascination of history. Up to this I had lived in a country of my own that had no history, and accepted my parents' marriage as an event ordained from the creation; now, when I considered it in this new, scientific way, I began to see it merely as one of the turning-points of history; one of those apparently trivial events that are little more than accidents, but have the effect of changing the destiny of humanity. I had not heard of Pascal, but I would have approved his remark about what would have happened if Cleopatra's nose had been a bit longer.

It immediately changed my view of my parents. Up to this they had been principles, not characters, like a chain of mountains guarding a green horizon. Suddenly a little shaft of light, emerging from behind a cloud, struck them, and the whole mass broke up into peaks, valleys, and foothills; you could even see whitewashed farmhouses and fields where people worked in the evening light, a whole world of interior perspective. Mother's past was the richer subject for study. It was extraordinary the variety of people and settings that woman had in her background. She had been an orphan, a parlour-maid, a companion, a traveller; and had been proposed to by a plasterer's apprentice, a French chef who had taught her to make superb coffee, and a rich elderly shopkeeper in Sunday's Well. Because I liked to feel myself different, I thought a great deal about the chef and the advantages of being a Frenchman, but the shopkeeper was an even more vivid figure in my imagination because he had married someone else and died soon after – of disappointment, I had no doubt – leaving a large fortune. The fortune was to me what Cleopatra's nose was to Pascal; the ultimate proof that things might have been different.

'How much was Mr Riordan's fortune, Mummy?' I asked thoughtfully.

'Ah, they said he left eleven thousand,' Mother replied doubtfully, 'but you couldn't believe everything people say.'

That was exactly what I could do. I was not prepared to minimize a fortune that I might so easily have inherited.

'And weren't you ever sorry for poor Mr Riordan?' I asked severely.

'Ah, why would I be sorry, child?' she asked with a shrug. 'Sure, what use would money be where there was no liking?'

That, of course, was not what I meant at all. My heart was full of pity for poor Mr Riordan who had tried to be my father; but, even on the low level at which Mother discussed it, money would have been of great use to me. I was not so fond of Father as to think he was worth eleven thousand pounds, a hard sum to visualize but more than twenty-seven times greater than the largest salary I had ever heard of – that of a Member of Parliament. One of the discoveries I was making at the time was that Mother was not only rather hard-hearted but very impractical as well.

But Father was the real surprise. He was a brooding, worried man who seemed to have no proper appreciation of me, and was always wanting me to go out and play or go upstairs and read, but the historical approach changed him like a character in a fairy-tale. 'Now let's talk about the ladies Daddy nearly married,' I would say; and he would stop whatever he was doing and give a great guffaw. 'Oh, ho, ho!' he would say, slapping his knee and looking slyly at Mother, 'you could write a book about them.' Even his face changed at such moments. He would look young and extraordinarily mischievous. Mother, on the other hand, would grow black.

'You could,' she would say, looking into the fire. 'Daisies!'

'"The handsomest man that walks Cork!"' Father would quote with a wink at me. 'That's what one of them called me.'

'Yes,' Mother would say, scowling. 'May Cadogan!'

'The very girl!' Father would cry in astonishment. 'How did I forget her name? A beautiful girl! 'Pon my word, a most remarkable girl! And still is, I hear.'

'She should be,' Mother would say in disgust. 'With six of them!'

'Oh, now, she'd be the one that could look after them! A fine head that girl had.'

'She had. I suppose she ties them to a lamp-post while she goes in to drink and gossip.'

That was one of the peculiar things about history. Father and Mother both loved to talk about it but in different ways. She would only talk about it when we were together somewhere, in the park or down the Glen, and even then it was very hard to make her stick to the facts, because her whole face would light up and she would begin to talk about donkey-carriages or concerts in the kitchen, or oil-lamps, and though nowadays I would probably value it for atmosphere, in those days it sometimes drove me mad with impatience. Father, on the other hand, never minded talking about it in front of her, and it made her angry. Particularly when he mentioned May Cadogan. He knew this perfectly well and he would wink at me and make me laugh outright, though I had no idea of why I laughed, and anyway, my sympathy was all with her.

'But, Daddy,' I would say, presuming on his high spirits, 'if you liked Miss Cadogan so much why didn't you marry her?'

At this, to my great delight, he would let on to be filled with doubt and distress. He would put his hands in his trousers pockets and stride to the door leading into the hallway.

'That was a delicate matter,' he would say, without looking at me. 'You see, I had your poor mother to think of.'

'I was a great trouble to you,' Mother would say, in a blaze.

'Poor May said it to me herself,' he would go on as though he had not heard her, 'and the tears pouring down her cheeks. "Mick," she said, "that girl with the brown hair will bring me to an untimely grave."'

'She could talk of hair!' Mother would hiss. 'With her carroty mop!'

'Never did I suffer the way I suffered then, between the two of them,' Father would say with deep emotion as he returned to his chair by the window.

'Oh, 'tis a pity about ye!' Mother could cry in an exasperated tone and suddenly get up and go into the front room with her book to escape his teasing. Every word that man said she took literally. Father would give a great guffaw of delight, his hands on his knees and his eyes on the ceiling and wink at me again. I would laugh with him of course, and then grow wretched because I hated Mother's sitting alone in the front room. I would go in and find her in her wicker-chair by the window in the dusk, the book open on her knee, looking out at the Square. She would always have regained her composure when she spoke to me, but I would have an uncanny feeling of unrest in her and stroke her and talk to her soothingly as if we had changed places and I were the adult and she the child.

But if I was excited by what history meant to them, I was even more excited by what it meant to me. My potentialities were double theirs. Through Mother I might have been a French boy called Laurence Armady or a rich boy from Sunday's Well called Laurence Riordan. Through Father I might, while still remaining a Delaney, have been one of the six children of the mysterious and beautiful Miss Cadogan. I was fascinated by the problem of who I would have been if I hadn't been me, and, even more, by the problem of whether or not I would have known that there was anything wrong with the arrangement. Naturally I tended to regard Laurence Delaney as the person I was intended to be, and so I could not help wondering whether as Laurence Riordan I would not have been aware of Laurence Delaney as a real gap in my make-up.

I remember that one afternoon after school I walked by myself all the way up to Sunday's Well which I now regarded as something like a second home. I stood for a while at the garden gate of the house where Mother-had been working when she was proposed to by Mr Riordan, and then went and studied the shop itself. It had clearly seen better days, and the cartons and advertisements in the window were dusty and sagging. It wasn't like one of the big stores in Patrick Street, but at the same time, in size and fittings it was well above the level of a village shop. I regretted that Mr Riordan was dead because I would like to have seen him for myself instead of relying on Mother's impressions which seemed to me to be biased. Since he had, more or less, died of grief on Mother's account, I conceived of him as a really nice man; lent him the countenance and manner of an old gentleman who always spoke to me when he met me on the road, and felt I could have become really attached to him as a father. I could imagine it all: Mother reading in the parlour while she waited for me to come home up Sunday's Well in a school cap and blazer, like the boys from the Grammar School, and with an expensive leather satchel instead of the old cloth school-bag I carried over my shoulder. I could see myself walking slowly and with a certain distinction, lingering at gateways and looking down at the river; and later I would go out to tea in one of the big houses with long gardens sloping to the water, and maybe row a boat on the river along with a girl in a pink frock. I wondered only whether I would have any awareness of the National School boy with the cloth school-bag who jammed his head between the bars of a gate and thought of me. It was a queer, lonesome feeling that all but reduced me to tears.

But the place that had the greatest attraction of all for me was the Douglas Road where Father's friend, Miss Cadogan, lived, only now she wasn't Miss Cadogan but Mrs O'Brien. Naturally, nobody called Mrs O'Brien could be as attractive to the imagination as a French chef and an elderly shopkeeper with eleven thousand pounds, but she had a physical reality that the other pair lacked. As I went regularly to the library at Parnell Bridge, I frequently found myself wandering up the road in the direction of Douglas and always stopped in front of the long row of houses where she lived. There were high steps up to them, and in the evening the sunlight fell brightly on the house-fronts till they looked like a screen. One evening as I watched a gang of boys playing ball in the street outside, curiosity overcame me. I spoke to one of them. Having been always a child of solemn and unnatural politeness, I probably scared the wits out of him.

'I wonder if you could tell me which house Mrs O'Brien lives in, please?' I asked.

'Hi, Gussie!' he yelled to another boy. 'This fellow wants to know where your old one lives.'

This was more than I had bargained for. Then a thin, good-looking boy of about my own age detached himself from the group and came up to me with his fists clenched. I was feeling distinctly panicky, but all the same I studied him closely. After all, he was the boy I might have been.

'What do you want to know for?' he asked suspiciously.

Again, this was something I had not anticipated.

'My father was a great friend of your mother,' I explained carefully, but, so far as he was concerned, I might as well have been talking a foreign language. It was clear that Gussie O'Brien had no sense of history.

'What's that?' he asked incredulously.

At this point we were interrupted by a woman I had noticed earlier, talking to another over the railing between the two steep gardens. She was a small, untidy-looking woman who occasionally rocked the pram in an absent-minded way as though she only remembered it at intervals.

'What is it, Gussie?' she cried, raising herself on tiptoe to see us better.

'I don't really want to disturb your mother, thank you,' I said, in something like hysterics, but Gussie anticipated me, actually pointing me out to her in a manner I had been brought up to regard as rude.

'This fellow wants you,' he bawled.

'I don't really,' I murmured, feeling that now I was in for it. She skipped down the high flight of steps to the gate with a laughing, puzzled air, her eyes in slits and her right hand arranging her hair at the back. It was not carroty as Mother described it, though it had red lights when the sun caught it.

'What is it, little boy?' she asked coaxingly, bending forward.

'I didn't really want anything, thank you,' I said in terror. 'It was just that my daddy said you lived up here, and, as I was changing my book at the library I thought I'd come up and inquire. You can see,' I added, showing her the book as proof, 'that I've only just been to the library.'

'But who is your daddy, little boy?' she asked, her grey eyes still in long, laughing slits. 'What's your name?'

'My name is Delaney,' I said, 'Larry Delaney.'

'Not *Mike* Delaney's boy?' she exclaimed wonderingly. 'Well, for God's sake! Sure, I should have known it from that big head of yours.' She passed her hand down the back of my head and laughed. 'If you'd only get your hair cut I wouldn't be long recognizing you. You wouldn't think I'd know the feel of your old fellow's head, would you?' she added roguishly.

'No, Mrs O'Brien,' I replied meekly.

'Why, then indeed I do, and more along with it,' she added in the same saucy tone though the meaning of what she said was not clear to me. 'Ah, come in and give us a good look at you! That's my eldest, Gussie, you were talking to,' she added, taking my hand. Gussie trailed behind us for a purpose I only recognized later.

'Ma-a-a-a, who's dat fella with you?' yelled a fat little girl who had been playing hop-scotch on the pavement.

'That's Larry Delaney,' her mother sang over her shoulder. I don't know what it was about that woman but there was something about her high spirits that made her more like a regiment than a woman. You felt that everyone should fall into step behind her. 'Mick Delaney's son from Barrackton. I nearly married his old fellow once. Did he ever tell you that, Larry?' she added slyly. She made sudden swift transitions from brilliance to intimacy that I found attractive.

'Yes, Mrs O'Brien, he did,' I replied, trying to sound as roguish as she, and she went off into a delighted laugh, tossing her red head.

'Ah, look at that now! How well the old divil didn't forget me! You can tell him I didn't forget him either. And if I married him, I'd be your mother now. Wouldn't that be a queer old three and fourpence? How would you like me for a mother, Larry?'

'Very much, thank you,' I said complacently.

'Ah, go on with you, you would not,' she exclaimed, but she was pleased all the same. She struck me as the sort of woman it would be easy enough to please. 'Your old fellow always said it: your mother was a *most* superior woman, and you're a *most* superior child. Ah, and I'm not too bad myself either,' she added with a laugh and a shrug, wrinkling up her merry little face.

In the kitchen she cut me a slice of bread, smothered it with jam, and gave me a big mug of milk. 'Will you have some, Gussie?' she asked in a sharp voice as if she knew only too well what the answer would be. 'Aideen,' she said to the horrible little girl who had followed us in, 'aren't you fat and ugly enough without making a pig of yourself? Murder the Loaf we call her,' she added smilingly to me. 'You're a polite little boy, Larry, but damn the politeness you'd have if you had to deal with them. Is the book for your mother?'

'Oh, no, Mrs O'Brien,' I replied. 'It's my own.'

'You mean you can read a big book like that?' she asked incredulously, taking it from my hands and measuring the length of it with a puzzled air.

'Oh, yes, I can.'

'I don't believe you,' she said mockingly. 'Go on and prove it!'

There was nothing I asked better than to prove it. I felt that as a performer I had never got my due, so I stood in the middle of the kitchen, cleared my throat and began with great feeling to enunciate one of those horribly involved opening paragraphs you found in children's books of the time. 'On a fine evening in spring, as the setting sun was beginning to gild the blue peaks with its lambent rays, a rider, recognizable as a student by certain niceties of attire, was slowly, and perhaps regretfully making his way . . .' It was the sort of opening sentence I loved.

'I declare to God!' Mrs O'Brien interrupted in astonishment. 'And that fellow there is one age with you, and he can't spell house. How well you wouldn't be down at the library, you caubogue you! . . . That's enough now, Larry,' she added hastily as I made ready to entertain them further.

'Who wants to read that blooming old stuff?' Gussie said contemptuously.

Later, he took me upstairs to show me his air rifle and model aeroplanes. Every detail of the room is still clear to me: the view into the back garden with its jungle of wild plants where Gussie had pitched his tent (a bad site for a tent as I patiently explained to him, owing to the danger from wild beasts); the three cots still unmade, the scribbles on the walls, and Mrs O'Brien's voice from the kitchen calling to Aideen to see what was wrong with the baby who was screaming his head off from the pram outside the front door. Gussie, in particular, fascinated me. He was spoiled, clever, casual; good-looking, with his mother's small clean features; gay and calculating. I saw that when I left and his mother gave me sixpence. Naturally I refused it politely, but she thrust it into my trousers pocket, and Gussie dragged at her skirt, noisily demanding something for himself.

'If you give him a tanner you ought to give me a tanner,' he yelled.

'I'll tan you,' she said laughingly.

'Well, give us a lop anyway,' he begged, and she did give him a penny to take his face off her, as she said herself, and after that he followed me down the street and suggested we should go to the shop and buy sweets. I was simple-minded, but I wasn't an out-and-out fool, and I knew that if I went to a sweet-shop with Gussie I should end up with no sixpence and very few sweets. So I told him I could not buy sweets without Mother's permission, at which he gave me up altogether as a cissy or worse.

It had been an exhausting afternoon but a very instructive one. In the twilight I went back slowly over the bridges, a little regretful for that fast-moving, colourful household, but with a new appreciation of my own home. When I went in the lamp was lit over the fireplace and Father was at his tea.

'What kept you, child?' Mother asked with an anxious air, and suddenly I felt slightly guilty, and I played it as I usually did whenever I was at fault in a loud, demonstrative, grown-up way. I stood in the middle of the kitchen with my cap in my hand and pointed it first at one, then at the other.

'You wouldn't believe who I met!' I said dramatically.

'Wisha, who, child?' Mother asked.

'Miss Cadogan,' I said, placing my cap squarely on a chair

and turning on them both again. 'Miss May Cadogan. Mrs
O'Brien as she is now.'

'Mrs O'Brien?' Father exclaimed, putting down his cup. 'But
where did you meet Mrs O'Brien?'

'I said you wouldn't believe it. It was near the library.
I was talking to some fellows, and what do you think but one
of them was Gussie O'Brien, Mrs O'Brien's son. And he
took me home with him, and his mother gave me bread and
jam, and she gave me THIS.' I produced the sixpence with
a real flourish.

'Well, I'm blowed!' Father gasped, and first he looked at
me, and then he looked at Mother and burst into a loud guffaw.

'And she said to tell you she remembers you too, and that
she sent her love.'

'Oh, by the jumping bell of Athlone!' Father crowed and
clapped his hands on his knees. I could see he believed the
story I had told and was delighted with it, and I could see too
that Mother did not believe it and that she was not in the least
delighted. That, of course, was the trouble with Mother.
Though she would do anything to help me with an intellectual
problem, she never seemed to understand the need for experi-
ment. She never opened her mouth while Father cross-
questioned me, shaking his head in wonder and storing it up
to tell the men in the factory. What pleased him most was
Mrs O'Brien's remembering the shape of his head, and later,
while Mother was out of the kitchen, I caught him looking in
the mirror and stroking the back of his head.

But I knew too that for the first time I had managed to
produce in Mother the unrest that Father could produce, and
I felt wretched and guilty and didn't know why. That was an
aspect of history I only studied later.

That night I was really able to indulge my passion. At last I
had the material to work with. I saw myself as Gussie O'Brien,
standing in the bedroom, looking down at my tent in the garden, and Aideen as my sister, and Mrs O'Brien as my mother
and, like Pascal, I re-created history. I remembered Mrs
O'Brien's laughter, her scolding and the way she stroked my
head. I knew she was kind – casually kind – and hot-tempered,

and recognized that in dealing with her I must somehow be a different sort of person. Being good at reading would never satisfy her. She would almost compel you to be as Gussie was; flattering, impertinent, and exacting. Though I couldn't have expressed it in those terms, she was the sort of woman who would compel you to flirt with her.

Then, when I had had enough, I deliberately soothed myself as I did whenever I had scared myself by pretending that there was a burglar in the house or a wild animal trying to get in the attic window. I just crossed my hands on my chest, looked up at the window and said to myself: 'It is not like that. I am not Gussie O'Brien. I am Larry Delaney, and my mother is Mary Delaney, and we live in Number 8 Wellington Square. To-morrow I'll go to school at the Cross, and first there will be prayers, and then arithmetic and after that composition.'

For the first time the charm did not work. I had ceased to be Gussie all right, but somehow I had not become myself again, not any self that I knew. It was as though my own identity was a sort of sack I had to live in, and I had deliberately worked my way out of it, and now I couldn't get back again because I had grown too big for it. I practised every trick I knew to reassure myself. I tried to play a counting game; then I prayed, but even the prayer seemed different as though it didn't belong to me at all. I was away in the middle of empty space, divorced from my mother and home and everything permanent and familiar. Suddenly I found myself sobbing. The door opened and Mother came in in her nightdress, shivering, her hair over her face.

'You're not sleeping, child,' she said in a wan and complaining voice.

I snivelled, and she put her hand on my forehead.

'You're hot,' she said. 'What ails you?'

I could not tell her of the nightmare in which I was lost. Instead, I took her hand, and gradually the terror retreated, and I became myself again, shrank into my little skin of identity, and left infinity and all its anguish behind.

'Mummy,' I said, 'I promise I never wanted anyone but you.'

First Confession

ALL the trouble began when my grandfather died and my grandmother – my father's mother – came to live with us. Relations in the one house are a strain at the best of times, but, to make matters worse, my grandmother was a real old country-woman and quite unsuited to the life in town. She had a fat, wrinkled old face, and, to Mother's great indignation, went round the house in bare feet – the boots had her crippled, she said. For dinner she had a jug of porter and a pot of potatoes with – sometimes – a bit of salt fish, and she poured out the potatoes on the table and ate them slowly, with great relish, using her fingers by way of a fork.

Now, girls are supposed to be fastidious, but I was the one who suffered most from this. Nora, my sister, just sucked up to the old woman for the penny she got every Friday out of the old-age pension, a thing I could not do. I was too honest, that was my trouble; and when I was playing with Bill Connell, the sergeant-major's son, and saw my grandmother steering up the path with the jug of porter sticking out from beneath her shawl, I was mortified. I made excuses not to let him come into the house, because I could never be sure what she would be up to when we went in.

When Mother was at work and my grandmother made the dinner I wouldn't touch it. Nora once tried to make me, but I hid under the table from her and took the bread-knife with me for protection. Nora let on to be very indignant (she wasn't, of course, but she knew Mother saw through her, so she sided with Gran) and came after me. I lashed out at her with the bread-knife, and after that she left me alone. I stayed there till Mother came in from work and made my dinner, but when Father came in later Nora said in a shocked voice: 'Oh, Dadda, do you know what Jackie did at dinner-time?' Then, of course, it all came out; Father gave me a flaking; Mother interfered, and for days after that he didn't speak to me and Mother barely spoke to Nora. And all because of that old woman! God knows, I was heart-scalded.

Then, to crown my misfortunes, I had to make my first confession and communion. It was an old woman called Ryan who prepared us for these. She was about the one age with Gran; she was well-do-to, lived in a big house on Montenotte, wore a black cloak and bonnet, and came every day to school at three o'clock when we should have been going home, and talked to us of hell. She may have mentioned the other place as well, but that could only have been by accident, for hell had the first place in her heart.

She lit a candle, took out a new half-crown, and offered it to the first boy who would hold one finger – only one finger! – in the flame for five minutes by the school clock. Being always very ambitious I was tempted to volunteer, but I thought it might look greedy. Then she asked were we afraid of holding one finger – only one finger! – in a little candle flame for five minutes and not afraid of burning all over in roasting hot furnaces for all eternity. 'All eternity! Just think of that! A whole lifetime goes by and it's nothing, not even a drop in the ocean of your sufferings.' The woman was really interesting about hell, but my attention was all fixed on the half-crown. At the end of the lesson she put it back in her purse. It was a great disappointment; a religious woman like that, you wouldn't think she'd bother about a thing like a half-crown.

Another day she said she knew a priest who woke one night to find a fellow he didn't recognize leaning over the end of his bed. The priest was a bit frightened – naturally enough – but he asked the fellow what he wanted, and the fellow said in a deep, husky voice that he wanted to go to confession. The priest said it was an awkward time and wouldn't it do in the morning, but the fellow said that last time he went to confession, there was one sin he kept back, being ashamed to mention it, and now it was always on his mind. Then the priest knew it was a bad case, because the fellow was after making a bad confession and committing a mortal sin. He got up to dress, and just then the cock crew in the yard outside, and – lo and behold! – when the priest looked round there was no sign of the fellow, only a smell of burning timber, and when the priest looked at his bed didn't he see the print of two hands burned in it? That was because the fellow had made a bad confession. This story made a shocking impression on me.

But the worst of all was when she showed us how to examine our conscience. Did we take the name of the Lord, our God, in vain? Did we honour our father and our mother? (I asked her did this include grandmothers and she said it did.) Did we love our neighbours as ourselves? Did we covet our neighbour's goods? (I thought of the way I felt about the penny that Nora got every Friday.) I decided that, between one thing and another, I must have broken the whole ten commandments, all on account of that old woman, and so far as I could see, so long as she remained in the house I had no hope of ever doing anything else.

I was scared to death of confession. The day the whole class went I let on to have a toothache, hoping my absence wouldn't be noticed; but at three o'clock, just as I was feeling safe, along comes a chap with a message from Mrs Ryan that I was to go to confession myself on Saturday and be at the chapel for communion with the rest. To make it worse, Mother couldn't come with me and sent Nora instead.

Now, that girl had ways of tormenting me that Mother never knew of. She held my hand as we went down the hill, smiling sadly and saying how sorry she was for me, as if she were bringing me to the hospital for an operation.

'Oh, God help us!' she moaned. 'Isn't it a terrible pity you weren't a good boy? Oh, Jackie, my heart bleeds for you! How will you ever think of all your sins? Don't forget you have to tell him about the time you kicked Gran on the shin.'

'Lemme go!' I said, trying to drag myself free of her. 'I don't want to go to confession at all.'

'But sure, you'll have to go to confession, Jackie,' she replied in the same regretful tone. 'Sure, if you didn't, the parish priest would be up to the house, looking for you. 'Tisn't, God knows, that I'm not sorry for you. Do you remember the time you tried to kill me with the bread-knife under the table? And the language you used to me? I don't know what he'll do with you at all, Jackie. He might have to send you up to the bishop.'

I remember thinking bitterly that she didn't know the

half of what I had to tell – if I told it. I knew I couldn't tell it, and understood perfectly why the fellow in Mrs Ryan's story made a bad confession; it seemed to me a great shame that people wouldn't stop criticizing him. I remember that steep hill down to the church, and the sunlit hillsides beyond the valley of the river, which I saw in the gaps between the houses like Adam's last glimpse of Paradise.

Then, when she had manoeuvred me down the long flight of steps to the chapel yard, Nora suddenly changed her tone. She became the raging malicious devil she really was.

'There you are!' she said with a yelp of triumph, hurling me through the church door. 'And I hope he'll give you the penitential psalms, you dirty little caffler.'

I knew then I was lost, given up to eternal justice. The door with the coloured-glass panels swung shut behind me, the sunlight went out and gave place to deep shadow, and the wind whistled outside so that the silence within seemed to crackle like ice under my feet. Nora sat in front of me by the confession box. There were a couple of old women ahead of her, and then a miserable-looking poor devil came and wedged me in at the other side, so that I couldn't escape even if I had the courage. He joined his hands and rolled his eyes in the direction of the roof, muttering aspirations in an anguished tone, and I wondered had he a grandmother too. Only a grandmother could account for a fellow behaving in that heart-broken way, but he was better off than I, for he at least could go and confess his sins; while I would make a bad confession and then die in the night and be continually coming back and burning people's furniture.

Nora's turn came, and I heard the sound of something slamming, and then her voice as if butter wouldn't melt in her mouth, and then another slam, and out she came. God, the hypocrisy of women! Her eyes were lowered, her head was bowed, and her hands were joined very low down on her stomach, and she walked up the aisle to the side altar looking like a saint. You never saw such an exhibition of devotion; and I remembered the devilish malice with which she had tormented me all the way from our door, and wondered were all religious people like that, really. It was my turn now. With the fear of damnation in my soul I went in, and the confessional door closed of itself behind me.

It was pitch-dark and I couldn't see priest or anything else. Then I really began to be frightened. In the darkness it was a matter between God and me, and He had all the odds. He knew what my intentions were before I even started; I had no chance. All I had ever been told about confession got mixed up in my mind, and I knelt to one wall and said: 'Bless me, father, for I have sinned; this is my first confession.' I waited for a few minutes, but nothing happened, so I tried it on the other wall. Nothing happened there either. He had me spotted all right.

It must have been then that I noticed the shelf at about one height with my head. It was really a place for grown-up people to rest their elbows, but in my distracted state I thought it was probably the place you were supposed to kneel. Of course, it was on the high side and not very deep, but I was always good at climbing and managed to get up all right. Staying up was the trouble. There was room only for my knees, and nothing you could get a grip on but a sort of wooden moulding a bit above it. I held on to the moulding and repeated the words a little louder, and this time something happened all right. A slide was slammed back; a little light entered the box, and a man's voice said: 'Who's there?'

''Tis me, father,' I said for fear he mightn't see me and go away again. I couldn't see him at all. The place the voice came from was under the moulding, about level with my knees, so I took a good grip of the moulding and swung myself down till I saw the astonished face of a young priest looking up at me. He had to put his head on one side to see me, and I had to put mine on one side to see him, so we were more or less talking to one another upside-down. It struck me as a queer way of hearing confessions, but I didn't feel it my place to criticize.

'Bless me, father, for I have sinned; this is my first confession,' I rattled off all in one breath, and swung myself down the least shade more to make it easier for him.

'What are you doing up there?' he shouted in an angry voice; and the strain the politeness was putting on my hold of the moulding, and the shock of being addressed in such an uncivil tone, were too much for me. I lost my grip, tumbled, and hit the door an unmerciful wallop before I found myself flat on my back in the middle of the aisle. The people who had been waiting stood up with their mouths open. The priest opened the door of the middle box and came out, pushing his biretta back from his forehead; he looked something terrible. Then Nora came scampering down the aisle.

'Oh, you dirty little caffler!' she said. 'I might have known you'd do it. I might have known you'd disgrace me. I can't leave you out of my sight for one minute.'

Before I could even get to my feet to defend myself she bent down and gave me a clip across the ear. This reminded me that I was so stunned I had even forgotten to cry, so that people might think I wasn't hurt at all, when in fact I was probably maimed for life. I gave a roar out of me.

'What's all this about?' the priest hissed, getting angrier than ever and pushing Nora off me. 'How dare you hit the child like that, you little vixen?'

'But I can't do my penance with him, father,' Nora cried, cocking an outraged eye up at him.

'Well, go and do it, or I'll give you some more to do,' he said, giving me a hand up. 'Was it coming to confession you were, my poor man?' he asked me.

''Twas, father,' said I with a sob.

'Oh,' he said respectfully, 'a big hefty fellow like you must have terrible sins. Is this your first?'

''Tis, father,' said I.

'Worse and worse,' he said gloomily. 'The crimes of a lifetime. I don't know will I get rid of you at all today. You'd better wait now till I'm finished with these old ones. You can see by the looks of them they haven't much to tell.'

'I will, father,' I said with something approaching joy.

The relief of it was really enormous. Nora stuck out her tongue at me from behind his back, but I couldn't even be bothered retorting. I knew from the very moment that man opened his mouth that he was intelligent above the ordinary. When I had time to think, I saw how right I was. It only stood to reason that a fellow confessing after seven years would have more to tell than people that went every week. The crimes of a lifetime, exactly as he said. It was only what he expected, and the rest was the cackle of old women and girls with their talk of hell, the bishop, and the penitential psalms. That was all they knew. I started to make my examination of conscience, and barring the one bad business of my grandmother it didn't seem so bad.

The next time, the priest steered me into the confession box himself and left the shutter back the way I could see him get in and sit down at the further side of the grille from me.

'Well, now,' he said, 'what do they call you?'

'Jackie, father,' said I.

'And what's a-trouble to you, Jackie?'

'Father,' I said, feeling I might as well get it over while I had him in good humour, 'I had it all arranged to kill my grandmother.'

He seemed a bit shaken by that, all right, because he said nothing for quite a while.

'My goodness,' he said at last, 'that'd be a shocking thing to do. What put that into your head?'

'Father,' I said, feeling very sorry for myself, 'she's an awful woman.'

'Is she?' he asked. 'What way is she awful?'

'She takes porter, father,' I said, knowing well from the way Mother talked of it that this was a mortal sin, and hoping it would make the priest take a more favourable view of my case.

'Oh, my!' he said, and I could see he was impressed.

'And snuff, father,' said I.

'That's a bad case, sure enough, Jackie,' he said.

'And she goes round in her bare feet, father,' I went on in a rush of self-pity, 'and she know I don't like her, and she gives pennies to Nora and none to me, and my da sides with her and flakes me, and one night I was so heart-scalded I made up my mind I'd have to kill her.'

'And what would you do with the body?' he asked with great interest.

'I was thinking I could chop that up and carry it away in a barrow I have,' I said.

'Begor, Jackie,' he said, 'do you know you're a terrible child?'

'I know, father,' I said, for I was just thinking the same thing myself. 'I tried to kill Nora too with a bread-knife under the table, only I missed her.'

'Is that the little girl that was beating you just now?' he asked.

'"Tis, father.'

'Someone will go for her with a bread-knife one day, and he won't miss her,' he said rather cryptically. 'You must have great courage. Between ourselves, there's a lot of people I'd like to do the same to but I'd never have the nerve. Hanging is an awful death.'

'Is it, father?' I asked with the deepest interest – I was always very keen on hanging. 'Did you ever see a fellow hanged?'

'Dozens of them,' he said solemnly. 'And they all died roaring.'

'Jay!' I said.

'Oh, a horrible death!' he said with great satisfaction. 'Lots of the fellows I saw killed their grandmothers too, but they all said 'twas never worth it.'

He had me there for a full ten minutes talking, and then walked out the chapel yard with me. I was genuinely sorry to part with him, because he was the most entertaining character I'd ever met in the religious line. Outside, after the shadow of the church, the sunlight was like the roaring of waves on a beach; it dazzled me; and when the frozen silence melted and I heard the screech of trams on the road my heart soared. I knew now I wouldn't die in the night and come back, leaving marks on my mother's furniture. It would be a great worry to her, and the poor soul had enough.

Nora was sitting on the railing, waiting for me, and she put on a very sour puss when she saw the priest with me. She was mad jealous because a priest had never come out of the church with her.

'Well,' she asked coldly, after he left me, 'what did he give you?'

'Three Hail Marys,' I said.

'Three Hail Marys,' she repeated incredulously. 'You mustn't have told him anything.'

'I told him everything,' I said confidently.

'About Gran and all?'

'About Gran and all.'

(All she wanted was to be able to go home and say I'd made a bad confession.)

'Did you tell him you went for me with the bread-knife?' she asked with a frown.

'I did to be sure.'

'And he only gave you three Hail Marys?'

'That's all.'

She slowly got down from the railing with a baffled air. Clearly, this was beyond her. As we mounted the steps back to the main road she looked at me suspiciously.

'What are you sucking?' she asked.

'Bullseyes.'

'Was it the priest gave them to you?'

''Twas.'

'Lord God,' she wailed bitterly, 'some people have all the luck! 'Tis no advantage to anybody trying to be good. I might just as well be a sinner like you.'

The Duke's Children

TILL I was a grown man I could never see precisely what was supposed to be exaggerated in the plots of novelists like Dickens. To this day I can still read about some mysterious street-urchin, brought up to poverty and vice by a rag-picker, who turns out to be the missing heir to an earldom and see nothing peculiar about it. To me it all seems the most natural thing in the world.

Having always been Mother's pet, I was comparatively grown-up when the truth about my own birth broke on me first. In fact I was already at work as a messenger boy on the railway. Naturally, I had played with the idea as I had played with scores of other ideas, but suddenly, almost in a day, every other possibility disappeared, and I knew I had nothing whatever in common with the two commonplace creatures with whom my fate had become so strangely linked.

It wasn't their poverty only that repelled me, though that was bad enough, or the tiny terrace house we lived in with its twelve-foot square of garden in front, its crumbling stumps of gate-posts and low wall that had lost its railing. It was their utter commonness, their squabbles about money, their low friends and fatuous conversations. You could see that no breath of fineness had ever touched them. They seemed like people who had been crippled from birth and never known what it was to walk or run or dance. Though I might be – for the moment at least – only a messenger, I had those long spells when by some sort of instinct I knew who I really was, could stand aside and watch myself come up the road after my day's work with relaxed and measured steps, turning my head slowly to greet some neighbour and raising my cap with a grace and charm that came of centuries of breeding. Not only could I see myself like that; there were even times when I could hear an interior voice that preceded and dictated each movement as though it were a fragment of a story-book – 'He raised his cap gracefully while his face broke into a thoughtful smile.'

And then, as I turned the corner I would see Father at the gate in his house clothes, a ragged trousers and vest, an old cap that came down over his eyes, and boots cut into something that resembled sandals and that he insisted on calling his 'slippers'. Father was a creature of habit. No sooner was he out of his working clothes than he was peppering for his evening paper, and if the newsboy were five minutes late, Father muttered 'I don't know what's coming over that boy at all!' and drifted down to the main road to listen for him. When the newsboy did at last appear, Father would grab the paper from his hand and almost run home, putting on his spectacles awkwardly as he ran and triumphantly surveying the promised treat of the headlines.

And suddenly everything would go black on me, and I would take the chair by the open back door while Father, sitting at the other end, uttered little exclamations of joy or rage and Mother asked anxiously how I had got on during the day. Most of the time I could reply only in monosyllables. How could I tell her that nothing had happened at work that was not as common as the things that happened at home; nothing but those moments of blinding illumination when I was alone in the station yard on a spring morning with sunlight striking the cliffs above the tunnel, and, picking my way between the rails and the trucks, I realized that it was not for long, that I was a duke or earl, lost, stolen or strayed from my proper home and that I had only to be discovered for everything to fall into its place. Illumination came only when I had escaped; most often when I crossed the yard on my way from work and dawdled in the passenger station before the bookstall or watched a passenger train go out on its way to Queenstown or Dublin and realized that one day some train like that would take me back to my true home and patrimony.

These gloomy silences used to make Father mad. He was a talkative man, and every little incident of his day turned into narrative and drama for him. He seemed forever to be meeting old comrades of his army days whom he had not met for fifteen years, and astounding changes had always taken place in them in the meantime. When one of his old friends called, or even when some woman from across the square dropped in for a cup of tea, he would leave everything, even his newspaper, to talk. His corner by the window permitting him no room for drama, he would stamp about the tiny kitchen, pausing at the back door to glance up at the sky or by the other door into the little hallway to see who was passing outside in the Square. It irritated him when I got up in the middle of all this, took my cap and went quietly out. It irritated him even more if I read while he and the others talked, and when some question was addressed to me put down my book and gazed at him blankly. He was so coarse in grain that he regarded it as insolence. He had no experience of dukes, and had never heard that interior voice which dictated my movements and words. 'Slowly the lad lowered the book in which he had been immersed and gazed wonderingly at the man who called himself his father.'

One evening I was coming home from work when a girl spoke to me. Her name was Nancy Harding, and I knew her elder brother slightly. I had never spoken to her – indeed, there were not many girls I did speak to. I was too conscious of the fact that though my jacket was good enough, my trousers were an old blue pair of Father's cut down and with a big patch in the seat. But Nancy, emerging from a house near the quarry, hailed me as if we were old friends and walked with me up the road. She was a slim, dark-haired girl with an eager and inconsequent manner, and her chatter bewildered and charmed me. My own conversation was of a rather portentous sort.

'I was down with Madge Regan, getting the answers for my homework,' she explained. 'I don't know what's wrong with me, but I can't do those blooming old sums. Where were you?'

'Oh, I was at work,' I answered.

'At work?' she exclaimed in astonishment. 'Till this hour?'

'I have to work from eight to seven,' I said modestly.

'But, Cripes, aren't they terrible hours?' she said.

'Ah, I'm only filling in time,' I explained lightly. 'I don't expect to be there long.'

This was prophetic, because I was sacked a couple of months later, but at the time I just wanted to make it clear that if there was any exploitation being done it was I and not the railway company that was doing it. We walked slowly, and she stood under the gas-lamp at the end of the Square with me. Darkness or day, it was funny how people made a rendezvous of gas-lamps. They were our playrooms when we were kids and our clubs as we became older. And then for the first time I heard the words running through my head as though they were dictating to someone else besides myself. 'Pleased with his quiet conversation and well-bred voice, she wondered if he could really be the son of the Delaneys at all.' Up to this, the voice had paid no attention to other people; now that it had begun to expand its activities it took on a new reality, and I longed to repeat the experience.

I had several opportunities because we met like that a couple of times when I was coming home from work. I was not observant, and it wasn't until years after that it struck me that she might have been waiting for me. And one evening when we were standing under our old gas-lamp I talked a little too enthusiastically about some story-book and Nancy asked for the loan of it. I was pleased with her attention but alarmed at the thought of her seeing where I lived.

'I'll bring it with me tomorrow,' I said.

'Ah, come on and get it for me now,' she said coaxingly, and I glanced over my shoulder and saw Father at the gate, his head cocked listening for the newsboy. I felt suddenly sick. I knew such a nice girl couldn't possibly want to meet Father, but I didn't see how I was to get the book without introducing them. We went up the little uneven avenue together.

'This is Nancy Harding, Dad,' I said in an off-hand tone. 'I just want to get a book for her.'

'Oh, come in, girl, come in,' he said, smiling amiably. 'Sit down, can't you, while you're waiting.' Father's sociability almost caused him to forget the newsboy. 'Min,' he called to Mother, 'you keep an eye on the paper,' and he set a chair in the middle of the kitchen floor. As I searched in the front room for the book, which in my desperation I could not find, I heard Mother go for the paper and Father talking away like mad to Nancy, and when I went into the kitchen, there he was in his favourite chair, the paper lying unopened on the table beside him while he told an endless, pointless story about old times in the neighbourhood. Father had been born in the neighbourhood which he seemed to think a matter for pride, but if there was one of Father's favourite subjects I could not stand it was the still wilder and more sordid life people had lived there when he was growing up. This story was about a wake – all his juiciest stories were about wakes – and a tired woman getting jealous of the corpse in the bed. He was so pleased with Nancy's attention that he was dramatizing even more than usual, and I stood silent in the kitchen door for several minutes with a ducal air of scorn before he even noticed me. As I saw Nancy to the road I felt humiliated to the depths of my being. I noticed that the hallway was streaming with damp, that our gate was only a pair of brick stumps from which the cement had fallen away and that the Square, which had never been adopted by the Council, was full of washing. There were two washerwomen on the terrace, each with a line of her own.

But that wasn't the worst. One evening when I came home Mother said joyously:

'Oh, your dad ran into that nice little Harding girl on his way home.'

'Oh, did he?' I asked indifferently though feeling I had been kicked hard in the stomach.

'Oh, my goodness!' Father exclaimed, letting down his paper for a moment and crowing. 'The way that one talks! Spatter! spatter! spatter! And, by the way,' he added, looking at me over his glasses, 'her aunt Lil used to be a great friend of your mother's at one time. Her mother was a Clancy. I knew there was something familiar about her face.'

'I'd never have recognized it,' Mother said gravely. 'Such a quiet little woman as Miss Clancy used to be.'

'Oh, begor there's nothing quiet about that piece,' chortled Father but he did not sound disapproving. Father liked young people with something to say for themselves – not like me.

I was mortified. It was bad enough not seeing Nancy myself, but to have her meet Father like that in his working clothes coming from the manure factory down the Glen, and hear him – as I had no doubt she did hear him – talk in his ignorant way about me was too much. I could not help contrasting Father with Mr Harding whom I occasionally met coming from work and whom I looked at with a respect that bordered on reverence. He was a small man with a face like a clenched fist, always very neatly dressed, and he usually carried his newspaper rolled up like a baton and sometimes hit his thigh with it as he strode briskly home.

One evening when I glanced shyly at him he nodded in his brusque way. Everything about him was brusque, keen, and soldierly, and when I saw that he recognized me I swung into step beside him. He was like a military procession with a brass band, the way he always set the pace for anyone who accompanied him.

'Where are you working now?' he asked sharply with a side-glance at me.

'Oh, on the railway still,' I said. 'Just for a few months anyway.'

'And what are you doing there?'

'Oh, just helping in the office,' I replied lightly. I knew this was not exactly true but I hated to tell anybody that I was only a messenger boy. 'Of course I study in my spare time,' I added hastily. It was remarkable how the speeding up of my pace seemed to speed up my romancing as well. There was something breathless about the man that left me breathless too. 'I thought of taking the Indian Civil Service exam or something of the sort. There's no future in railways.'

'Isn't there?' he asked with some surprise.

'Not really,' I answered indifferently. 'Another few years and it will all be trucks. I really do it only as a stop-gap. I wouldn't like to take any permanent job unless I could travel. Outside Ireland I mean. You see, languages are my major interest.'

'Are they?' he asked in the same tone. 'How many do you know?'

'Oh, only French and German at the moment – I mean enough to get round with,' I said. The pace was telling on me. I felt I wasn't making the right impression. Maybe to be a proper linguist you needed to know a dozen languages. I mended my hand as best I could. 'I'm going to do Italian and Spanish this winter if I get time. You can't get anywhere in the modern world without Spanish. After English it's the most spoken of them all.'

'Go on!' he said.

I wasn't altogether pleased with the result of this conversation. The moment I had left him I slowed down to a gentle stroll, and this made me realize that the quick march had committed me further than I liked to go. All I really knew of foreign languages was a few odd words and phrases, like echoes of some dream of my lost fatherland, which I learned and repeated to myself with a strange vague pleasure. It was not prudent to pretend that I knew the languages thoroughly. After all, Mr Harding had three daughters, all well-educated. People were always being asked to his house, and I had even been encouraging myself with the prospect of being asked as well. But now, if I were invited it would mainly be because of my supposed knowledge of foreign languages, and when Nancy or one of her sisters burst into fluent French or German my few poetic phrases would not be much help. I needed something more practical, something to do with railways, for preference. I had an old French phrase-book which I had borrowed from somebody, and I determined to learn as much as I could of this by heart.

I worked hard, spurred on by an unexpected meeting with Nancy's eldest sister, Rita, who suddenly stopped and spoke to me on the road though to my astonishment and relief she spoke in English.

Then, one evening when I was on my usual walk, which in those days nearly always brought me somewhere near Nancy's house, I ran into her going in, and we stood at the street corner near her home. I was pleased with this because Rita came out soon afterwards and said in a conspiratorial tone 'Why don't ye grab the sofa before Kitty gets it?' which made Nancy blush, and then her father passed and nodded to us. I waved back to him, but Nancy had turned her back as he appeared so that she did not see him. I drew her attention to him striding down the road, but somehow this only put her in mind of my father.

'I saw him again the other day,' she said with a smile that hurt me.

'Did you?' I asked with a sniff. 'What was he talking about? His soldiering days?'

'No,' she said with interest. 'Does he talk about them?'

'Does he ever talk about anything else?' I replied wearily. 'I have that last war off by heart. It seems to have been the only thing that ever happened to him.'

'He knows a terrible lot, though, doesn't he?' she asked.

'He's managed to conceal it pretty well,' I replied. 'The man is an out-and-out failure, and he's managed to turn Mother into one as well. I suppose she had whatever brains there were between them – which wasn't much, I'm afraid.'

'Go on!' said Nancy with a bewildered air. 'Then why did she marry him?'

'"Echo answers why,"' I said with a laugh at being able to get in a phrase that had delighted me in some story-book. 'Oh, I suppose it was the usual thing.' And when I saw her gaping at me in wonderment I shrugged my shoulders and added contemptuously, 'Lust.'

Nancy blushed again and made to leave.

'Well, it's well to be you,' she said, 'knowing what's wrong with him. God alone knows what's wrong with mine.'

I was sorry she had to go in such a hurry but pleased with the impression of culture and sophistication I had managed to convey, and I looked forward to showing off a bit more when I went to one of their Sunday evening parties. With that, and some really practical French, I could probably get anywhere.

At the same time it struck me that they were very slow about asking me, and my evening walks past their house took on a sort of stubborn defiance. At least, I wouldn't let them ignore me. It wasn't until weeks later that the bitter truth dawned on me that I was not being invited because nobody wanted me there. Nancy had seen my home and talked to my parents; her sisters and father had seen me, and all of them had seen my cut-down trousers with the patch on the seat. It mattered nothing to them even if I spoke French and German like an angel, even if I were liable to be sent off to India in the next few months. They did not think I was their class.

Those were the bitterest weeks of my life. With a sort of despair I took my evening walk in the early winter days past their house but never saw anybody, and as I turned up the muddy lane behind it and heard the wind moaning in the branches, and looked down across the sloping field to their house, nestling in the hollow with the light shining brilliantly in the kitchen where the girls did their homework, it seemed to be full of all the beauty I would never know. Sometimes, leaning over the lane wall and watching it, it even seemed possible that I was what they thought, not the son of a Duke but the son of a labourer in the manure factory; but at other times, walking home by myself, tired and dispirited, the truth blazed up angrily in me again, and I knew that when it became known, the Hardings would be the first to regret their blindness. At such times I was always making brilliant loveless matches and then revealing coldly to Nancy that I had never cared for anyone but herself.

It was at the lowest depth of my misery that I was introduced to a girl called May Dwyer, and somehow, from the first moment, I found that there was no need for me to indulge in invention. Invention and May would never have gone together. She had a directness of approach I had never met with before in a girl. The very first evening I saw her home she asked me if I could afford the tram fare. That shocked me but afterwards I was grateful. Then she asked me in to see her parents which scared me stiff, but I promised to come in another night when it wasn't so late, and at once she told me which evenings she was free. It was not forwardness or lightness in her; it was all part of a directness that made her immediately both a companion and a sweetheart. I owe her a lot, for without her I might still be airing my French and German to any woman who attracted me.

Even when I did go in with her for a cup of tea I felt at home after the first few minutes. Of course, May asked me if I wanted to go upstairs, a thing no woman had ever suggested before to me, and I blushed, but by this time I was becoming used to her methods. Her father was a long, sad Civil Servant, and her mother a bright, direct little woman not unlike May herself, and whatever he said, the pair of them argued with and jeered him unmercifully. This only made him hang his head lower, but suddenly, after I had been talking for a while he began to argue with me about the state of the country, which seemed to cause him a lot of concern. In those days I was very optimistic on the subject, and I put my hands deep in my trousers pockets and answered him back politely but firmly. Then he caught me out on a matter of fact, and suddenly he gave a great crow of delight and went out to bring in two bottles of Guinness. By this time I was so much in my element that I accepted the Guinness; I always have loved a good argument.

'Cripes!' May said when I was leaving, 'do you ever stop once you start?'

'It's not so often I meet an intelligent talker,' I said loftily.

'When you've heard as much of my old fellow as I have, maybe you won't think he's so intelligent,' she said, but she did not sound indignant, and I had an impression that she was really quite pleased at having brought home a young fellow who could entertain her father. It gave her the feeling that she was really all the time an intellectual but had met the wrong sort of boy. In the years I was courting her we quarrelled like hell, but between her father and me it was a case of love at first sight. After I was fired from the railway, it was he who got me another job and insisted on my looking after it. The poor devil had always been pining for a man in the house.

Then one evening I ran into Nancy Harding whom I had not seen for some months. It was an embarrassing moment because I realized at once that my fantasy had all come true. If I had not actually made a brilliant match, I had as good as done so, and yet she was my first and purest love.

'I hear you and May Dwyer are very great these days,' she said and something in her tone struck me as peculiar. Afterwards I realized that it was the tone I was supposed to adopt when I broke the news to her.

'I've seen quite a lot of her,' I admitted.

'You weren't long getting hooked,' she went on with a smile that somehow did not come off.

'I don't know about being "hooked" as you call it,' I said, getting on my dignity at once. 'She asked me to her house and I went, that's all.'

'Oh, we know all about it,' said Nancy, and this time there was no mistaking the malice in her tone. 'You don't have to tell me anything.'

'Well, there isn't so much to tell,' I replied with a bland smile.

'And I suppose she talks French and German like a native?' asked Nancy.

This reference to the falsehoods I had told did hurt me. I had known they were indiscreet, but it hadn't occurred to me that they would become a joke in the Harding family.

'I don't honestly know what you're talking about, Nancy,' I said weakly. 'May asked me to her house and I went, just as I'd have gone to yours if you'd asked me. That's all there is to it.'

'Oh, is that all?' she asked in her commonest tone, and suddenly to my astonishment I saw tears in her eyes. 'And if you had a house like mine you wouldn't mind asking people there either, would you? And sisters like mine! And a father like mine! It's all very well for you to grouse about your old fellow, but if you had one like mine you'd have something to talk about. Blooming old pig, wouldn't open his mouth to you. 'Tis easy for you to talk, Larry Delaney! Damn easy!'

And then she shot away from me to conceal her tears, and I was left standing there on the pavement, stunned. Too stunned really to have done anything about it. It had all happened too suddenly, and been too great an intrusion on my fantasy for me to grasp it at all. I was so astonished and upset that though I was to have met May that night I didn't go. Instead I went for a lonely walk by myself over the hills to the river to think what I should do about it. In the end, of course, I did nothing at all; I had no experience to indicate to me what I could do; and it was not until years later that I even realized that the reason I had cared so much for Nancy was that she, like myself, was one of the Duke's children, one of those outcasts of a lost fatherland who go through life, living above and beyond themselves like some image of man's original aspiration.

First Love

PETER met Mick Dowling for the first time when he was six-teen and Mick was eighteen. The age-gap between them was wide but it was not the only thing that divided them. Mick was a university student and Peter an office boy. He called himself a junior clerk but that was only to save his face. And as well as that, Peter was moody and contrary, boastful and inclined to self-pity, unable to concentrate. Now it was a commercial career he proposed for himself, and he took up accountancy, but by the following week he had already tired of that and wanted to be a soldier, a man of action, to travel and see the world. Then he took up French and smoked French cigarettes. Mick already stood out among his contemporaries, a grown man, tall, well-built, and extremely sedate. He had an inex-pressive face, handsome in a rough-hewn way, which would have been dull but for the flush which occasionally lit it up and hinted at the depth of feeling beneath.

Their first meeting threw Peter into a perfect fever. He knew at once that Mick was the one man in the world he wanted to be. In the office he tried to imitate Mick's manners and way of speech; very slow, very serious, even dull except for an almost imperceptible streak of poker-faced humour. But either it did not suit the office or it didn't suit Peter, because several of the clerks looked at him in astonishment and said: 'What's wrong with you, Dwyer? Are you sick?' When they started to ridicule him he decided to reserve his imitation of Mick for more suitable company.

Unfortunately, Mick did not seem to like him at all. When they met he was usually with two friends of his own age, Con-way and Hynes, and Peter had to force his company on them. They treated him as a kid, and Peter, stung, talked well above his age and station, bragging and blustering, though at the same time he knew that he was behaving in a way the very opposite of Mick's. Sometimes he caught the calm grey eyes fixed searchingly on him for a moment and then a mask of reserve, like creeping paralysis, spread down Mick's handsome face.

Peter took his evening walk up the Western Road, and sometimes caught Mick, Conway, and Hynes when they were sitting on the river wall below the bridge and could not escape him. Their departure left him giddy and inclined to tears. As his bluster only roused their mockery he resolved to be profound, and for weeks spoke only in a deep voice on serious subjects, while to keep his face from betraying him he adopted the air of a man recovering from a serious illness. He thought he saw Mick give him that furtive puzzled look a little oftener, but then one evening Mick crushed him with a few words and in a way that showed he had found Peter out. Peter walked back by Sunday's Well in the moonlight, wept a little, and resolved not to speak to Mick again till he was a great and famous man and could show Mick how wrong he had been.

This mood lasted a whole day but, with the bottling-down effect of the office, enthusiasm returned towards evening, and it seemed to him that it was rather unjust to Mick to punish him so severely for a moment's ill humour, and his imagination got to work again. In the talk between Mick and his friends he had noticed that Mick was more deeply concerned about religion than they. They only chattered about priests being rich and having cars and being seen with girls – the usual envious talk of young men with salaries too small for their imaginations – but Mick always brought the talk back to fundamentals: Eternity, Hell, Purgatory, Limbo, Sin. Now Peter knew that fundamentals were his own strong point. He had studied them all and decided that they were grossly exaggerated. This, he felt, was the way to attract Mick's attention. He succeeded only too well. As he talked, Mick's face grew blacker and blacker.

'If you knew what you were talking about, Dwyer,' he said in a low voice, 'you'd want your backside kicked.'

Stung to tears, not so much by the rebuke as by the presence of Hynes and Conway, whom he despised, Peter retorted by calling Mick 'a crawthumper' and 'a bourgeois parasite', and stamped off, in real despair this time. How was he to have known that Mick's intellectual corns were so tender? He felt now that he had succeeded in making Mick his enemy for life and that even becoming a great and famous man would not wipe out the injury.

A week later he ran into the three of them on the Western Road. They were coming up as he was returning and he deliberately looked the other way. He didn't intend Mick to get away with the impression that he couldn't be done without. From the corner of his eye he saw Mick stare and then stop. The others stopped as well.

'Hullo, Peter,' he said.

'Oh, hullo, Mick,' Peter said with fictitious surprise.

'Come along back with us,' Mick said more by way of an order than an invitation.

Peter was so astonished that he was modest and almost silent for a quarter of an hour. He couldn't make it out. He didn't know whether Mick had recognized the justice of his charge about being 'a bourgeois parasite' or was so full of pity for his ignorance that he wanted to be kind. To be truthful with himself, he had to admit that he didn't give a damn. The main thing was that Mick had wiped out the injury.

But there were stranger things to come. On the way back Hynes stopped outside a pub and suggested a drink with something like a gangster air. As Peter had only a shilling and didn't know whether or not it would buy a round of drinks he pleaded an appointment. Mick didn't even ask whom the appointment was with. He merely took Peter firmly by the arm and pushed him in, laughing and uneasy. In a furtive whisper Hynes asked each what they'd have, and Peter, copying the others, said in a low voice: 'Stout, please.'

'Stout, right,' said Hynes with a nod.

'He's having ginger beer, Bill,' Mick said quietly, and Peter thrilled at the tone of quiet authority with which he spoke, said at once: 'All right. Ginger beer will do.'

He watched to see how much Hynes paid, and then stood up and said with a grown-up air: 'Same again, lads?' But before the others could reply Mick had chimed in with his poker-faced air.

'There's a bobby in plain clothes at the bar. Children under twelve aren't supposed to be here. I'd hide if I was you.'

Peter felt suddenly close to tears. It was not only a recognition that his position was privileged by the fact that he couldn't afford it; it was an admission that he was now, really and truly, one of the group.

Clearly, Hynes and Conway could not understand what Mick saw in him, and when they got Peter alone they ragged him unmercifully, but even their ragging was now on a different key; it was the ragging of a mascot whose extravagances provided them with entertainment, not the ragging of an outsider who tried to butt in. Even alone he was protected by his friendship with Mick. Mick called for him and Peter suffered endless embarrassment mingled with pride, knowing his visits were talked of. He in turn soon got to know Mick's people, who lived in a small house on a terrace. His father was a builder, his mother a tall, sugary, pious woman who was a sore trial to Mick. She was a hard-working woman but she had no method, was always losing or mislaying money, borrowing to make it up so that her husband wouldn't know, and then taking sips of whisky on the side to nerve her for the ordeal of 'telling Dowling'. If she worried about her husband and son, this was pure good-nature on her part, because she had cause enough to worry about herself. All the same it riled Mick, particularly when she made novenas for him to pass his examinations. When everyone in the university recognizes your industry and brilliance, it's not pleasant to have all the credit go to the Infant Jesus of Prague or St Rose of Lima. Mick argued with her and denounced her superstition, but she only looked at him with a pitying, good-natured smile and said: 'We're all smart when we're your age.' She was a plain woman who looked on heaven as a glorified extension of the County Council, where saints, with the faces of County Councillors, made it their business to look after the interests of relatives and constituents.

Though Mick was rather silent about his parents, he once confessed to Peter that it was largely because of her that he was so touchy about religion. He lived in dread of losing his faith. To Peter, strong on fundamentals, this did not seem such a serious loss, but Mick went on to explain that it was different for him because he was a man of ungovernable passions and religion was the only thing which stood between them and him. When he walked through town he averted his eyes from the shopwindows with their frillies and half-dressed tailors' dummies, and suffered agonies of conscience with Babiche Regan, the girl he walked out with, comparing his own gloomy fantasies of lust with her radiance and innocence. But Peter knew himself to be of coarser stuff altogether; though he had no Babiche Regan to act as a standard for judging himself, he was merely thrilled by the blast of inconsequence and frivolity that came from the nightdresses in shop windows and explained and humanized the frosty beauties who ignored him in the street; and though he now realized that Mick's quiet manner concealed passions stronger than his own, and continued to admire him as a marvel of self-control, he felt no conflict whatever in himself and thought that, if all he heard was true, sexual experience and losing one's faith were equally interesting and exhilarating.

But his own life continued to be bounded by home and the office, and whenever he met a girl he became impossible. It was just as with Mick only worse; the profound sense of his own inadequacy hit him like a gale of wind, and at once he began to rave about Tolstoy and his views of women. What was worse, he even did it to Babiche and Rosemary. One evening Mick and himself met them in town, and Mick, whose passions were probably giving him trouble, suggested that the four of them go for a walk over the hills to the river. It was an attractive suggestion; too attractive for Peter, because his panic grew to such an extent that within ten minutes his conversation had sent the two girls flying. It was a summer evening and Mick stood in an almost empty street, looking after them, his hands in his trousers pockets and as mad as ever Peter had seen him look.

'What the hell did Tolstoy say about women anyway?' he asked gruffly over his shoulder without even looking at Peter.

'Oh, about clothes,' stammered Peter, feeling only too well how unconvincing it sounded. 'That women are only interested in a man's clothes.'

'Sounds as if Tolstoy wanted his backside kicked too,' Mick said gloomily.

Peter's eyes suddenly filled with tears.

'It's only nerves, you know, Mick,' he said in a high, squeaky voice.

Mick thought about that for a moment and then gave a faint grin.

'I used to talk to Babiche about building,' he said.

Babiche was really pretty and attractive and unlike any other girl whom Peter had met. He was really quite satisfied that she escaped from Tolstoy's generalization. She was frank, inconsequent, and startlingly generous. When Mick took Peter to her house she insisted on showing him the bathroom herself, and when they met in town and he had the nerve to ask her to have coffee she wanted to force a ten-shilling note on him. She was the only girl Peter had met who seemed to have any intuition about the agonies of self-consciousness that young fellows went through, and Peter could well believe that she had cured Mick of talking about building technique.

He sometimes felt that if only he had been lucky enough to discover her for himself she could have cured him too, but as Mick's intended she could do nothing for him. For Mick's sake he tried hard to like her, but he couldn't like anyone who took Mick away from him so many nights in the week. When they were going to the theatre he spent a gloomy day in the office because of the lonesome evening which faced him. When they went for a walk he turned deliberately in the opposite direction, trying to say lightly to Hynes or Conway when they asked where Mick was: 'Oh, out with the doll as usual.' And then when Mick and he met he had to listen to Mick repeating her amusing remarks, all off at a tangent, and all, according to Mick, who seemed to brood over them as though they were oracles, peculiarly and even unnaturally apposite and witty, and pretend to be amused himself while wondering at the blindness of such a brilliant man. He wished to be just but he knew he was jealous.

Mick, who seemed to recognize it, tried bringing Peter with them but Peter talked so much that Babiche never got a chance.

Then she took a hand by bringing Rosemary as well. Babiche was convinced that Rosemary was an intellectual, and that, since Peter was intellectual too, they should hit it off. Actually Rosemary, gold to Babiche's black, though quite as pretty, was the silliest girl God ever put into the world. Mick had a very soft spot for her, but then Mick had what Peter lacked, a philosophic interest in the silliness of girls compared with the silliness of fellows. Rosemary attended the School of Art and fooled with amateur theatricals. Naturally Peter could not let her get away with this, and whenever she talked of some dim acquaintance in the School of Art who was supposed to draw well he said firmly that no modern could draw except perhaps Degas, knowing perfectly well that Rosemary would never have heard of Degas or remembered it if she had.

But though Peter could quench the girls' chatter in a way that made Mick sigh, they had ways of getting their own back on him against which he was defenceless. It didn't even have to be a joke; a glance or a smile could be sufficient. There were times after he had been out with them when he felt he had been scratched all over and wondered at Mick's lack of taste. Babiche was better than Rosemary, of course: Babiche at least was human, but all the same she was not good enough for Mick. It was not her fault that she was shallow, uneducated, and provincial, but there was more than that in it. Jealousy apart, he felt that she lacked Mick's nobility of character and that sooner or later she would be bound to betray his trust. Peter was too modest to lay claim to nobility himself, but he knew it when he saw it; he felt that Mick's crude passions might be less dangerous to their happiness than Babiche's good-natured commonness, and that the radiance and innocence against which Mick contrasted himself was probably no more than another of his illusions. There was tragedy in the situation. He saw it all coming, but was powerless to intervene. The disparity of ages made it impossible. With a younger man – indeed with anyone else except Mick – he would merely have said: 'You know, old man, Babiche is a very attractive girl but she isn't your weight.'

Mick left the university and took his first job, in a country town. For the first time Peter really knew what loneliness was. Mick wrote frequently and amusingly, and the whole life of the small town was revealed in his letters, but somehow the life of the city as Peter tried to bottle it in his own letters seemed cruelly dull; without Mick it seemed that it could be nothing but dull. He went down and spent a week-end at Mick's lodgings and this was wonderful, because Mick took him to the hotel and laid on all the characters whose amusing remarks had filled his letters, like the inspector of schools who said that the only thing he really missed in the Irish countryside was a nice dish of Romanian pie. They all seemed to drink a good deal, and Mick took bottle for bottle with them, but in the way in which he did everything else, without once losing control of the situation. Even in drink Mick remained himself.

Back in town, Peter's loneliness returned worse than ever. He began to feel that he couldn't continue there much longer. He too would have to break out, and if it was only as a labourer in an English town it would be better than hanging on as a clerk among people whom he despised. He went for walks only with Conway and Hynes, but since Mick's departure they had proved mediocre company. He talked of Mick to them, but they didn't seem to realize that they were talking of a man who was immeasurably their superior. Then he took to calling at Mick's house by way of inquiring if there was anything he could do for Mrs Dowling, but really to talk of him and get material for his letters. But Mrs Dowling too seemed to be unaware that there was anything remarkable about her son, and seemed inclined to credit it all to the account of the Infant Jesus of Prague and St Rose of Lima. Mick's father was an intelligent, excitable man who had no truck with saints, and Peter felt sure that he could tell him a lot about Mick if only he ever happened to think of him while Peter was there, but the visits and the occasions when he thought of Mick never seemed to synchronize, and all Peter got from him were reminiscences of the Civil War – a trifling affair, as Peter thought. There was nothing else for it. Babiche was the only one he could talk to about Mick, and to Babiche he went, Rosemary notwithstanding. With Mick absent and visited by them both only on occasional week-ends, he was prepared to call an armistice to jealousy.

Babiche seemed to like it too. At least she always lit up whenever he came, in a way quite different to her old watchful good-humoured air. It even struck Peter that she was probably a bit lonely herself, because even if you are not worthy of a man like Mick, he still leaves a gap in your life. It also seemed to have occurred to her that even if Rosemary was intellectual it was not in quite the same way as he, and whenever he called to bring her for a walk she always put on her hat and coat very firmly without hinting to Rosemary that she might join them. Rosemary giggled at them both with a malicious and knowing air.

'I hope Mick Dowling doesn't get to hear of this,' she said.

'I tell Mick about everything we do,' Peter said in a crushing tone, but Babiche only laughed and bit her underlip as she glanced in the mirror over the fireplace.

'Anyway, it's his own fault for leaving me in Peter's charge,' she said as she pulled on her belt, apparently not in the least put out by Rosemary's ragging.

Peter didn't altogether like her taking that tone with Rosemary; someone, he felt, should really tell the girl that she dragged down everything she touched to the level of her own sordid day-dreaming.

But Babiche was grand. She never seemed to weary talking of Mick. The walks they took were his favourite walks, along the river and up the hills; the things they admired were those that interested him, like the old Georgian houses behind their belts of trees; and, imagining how they would strike Mick, Peter imitated his gravity, his concentration, and his solemn poker-faced humour until Babiche shrieked with laughter, grabbed his arm and shouted: 'Stop!' She said he was the funniest thing she'd ever seen, and at home she insisted on his repeating it for her family and their guests. 'Go on, Peter!' she would say eagerly. 'Do Mick for us – he's a scream!' she would add inconsequently to anyone who happened to be there. And Peter would sit up stiff in his chair with unblinking inexpressive eyes and, apparently struggling for every word,

announce that mimicry was more suitable for children than for
adults, and Babiche would go into shrieks of laughter again till
she had everyone laughing with her. 'It's Mick!' she cried.
'Mick down to the ground! Do Mick at the races!' For the
first time Peter found himself a social success and stopped
talking of Tolstoy and Degas.

He was almost too successful. This was not the purpose for
which his imitation of Mick was intended at all. He had begun
it in the office, in the same way as he had begun imitating
Mick's handwriting, because he had at last discovered the
person he really wanted to be, and continued it because when
he was lonely it was a way of evoking Mick's personality so that
he could carry on interesting conversations with himself on his
solitary walks; but when he did it like this before strangers –
even before Babiche – it was not the same thing at all. It was
almost as though characteristics in himself which he didn't
even know of were crowding to it as a safety valve, and what
emerged was not glorification but ridicule. He always felt uneasy after it, as though he had exposed the more precious part
of himself to mockery, and he even resented the way Babiche
encouraged him. It only showed her even less worthy of Mick.

But at the same time he could not refuse her, could not even
check her. The truth was that as he grew accustomed to being
with her and to the chaffing of fellows in the office about her he
found himself becoming jealous of Mick as well as of her. His
mimicry, which had been a way of aspiring to Mick, was now
turning into a way of being superior to him. He wanted to be
Mick; he wanted to be well-balanced and serious, and because
in some way Mick's seriousness was connected with his love of
Babiche, Peter felt he must love her too. While he was with her,
though still professing to admire Mick, he found himself trying
to shake Babiche's confidence in him. Though he knew he was
behaving badly he repeated to her things that Mick had said to
him about the trouble he had with his ungovernable passions.
Alternatively and contradictorily he stressed Mick's preoccupation with religion and suggested that Mick would never
really be happy as anything but a monk – preferably a Trappist.
Whichever line he took it was to sympathize with her in having

to deal with such an unpredictable man. At the same time he was slightly annoyed because she didn't seem to mind.

One evening as they walked up a dark lane from the river Peter probed her like that – slyly as he thought. This time it was Mick's ungovernable passions that were uppermost.

'I suppose he must have another girl down there,' he said sadly.

'You didn't meet her?' she asked with interest.

'No, but you know how secretive Mick is. You wouldn't blame him, of course – a chap as elemental as that.'

'I'm not blaming him,' she said with a shrug. 'I suppose it's only natural. I don't mind.'

They emerged on to an open place above the roofs of a terrace. The valley of the river stretched up from them, the meadows flooded, the city in the background, spires peering out of brown mist. It was obvious that Babiche did not care greatly for Mick. What was worse, her standards of fidelity were as low as Peter had always suspected. But he didn't care about that.

'All right,' he said in a low voice. 'If he picks up with another girl, you take me and then we'll all be happy.'

She looked at him in surprise for a moment and shrugged herself again. She seemed more surprised than annoyed.

'Don't be silly!' she said. 'You'd never be satisfied with someone like me.'

'Don't be too sure of that,' he said earnestly, taking her hand. It was so small it almost frightened him into dropping it again, small and living and frightening like a bird the time you take it up. She didn't seem to mind his holding it. She didn't even seem to mind his kissing her, but she was alarmed at the way he did it.

'All right, all right,' she said with a grin. 'Don't make a show of us. Come in here where we won't be seen.'

After that they returned to her house and she made tea. She seemed quietly, snugly happy and without a shadow of guilt, and whenever her eye caught his she grinned and wriggled her shoulders contentedly. Peter, who would have plunged at once into a discussion of the difference the evening had made in the relations of both of them with Mick, felt it might be in bad taste while she continued in this humour.

Then the detestable Rosemary came in and seemed to understand it all at a glance. She stood in the doorway, tapping a theatre programme on her knee, and looked knowingly from one to the other.

'Sorry to intrude,' she said in a high, giggling, affected voice. 'You really should have a red light outside the studio. Babiche, have you been at my rouge again?'

Babiche tucked in her chin, grinned knowingly, and did something attractive and silly with her back hair. Peter sat and glowered in silence. It was as though Rosemary had been expecting and prophesying it for months and Babiche was amused at her shrewdness. She accompanied Peter to the gate and he kissed her good night in a tumult of emotion. In his arms she felt real, but she looked and spoke like something out of a fairy tale. Obviously, Tolstoy hadn't a clue. Peter felt suddenly as though he had become ten years older, full of power, peace, and self-confidence, never again to be shaken to the heart by some generalization out of a book. He had broken out of the magic circle of fantasy into the wide world of reality where Mick lived. He was Mick; he was loved by the girl Mick loved; what better proof could anyone ask for? The moon was high in the sky over the valley of the city, where now the mist was white, and he stood for a few moments in a gateway, looking down at it through the bars as though he had just given birth to it.

Then his mind reverted to the problem Babiche's nonchalance had deferred. What was to happen about Mick? He could, of course, take Babiche from Mick, but when it came to the point he felt that he needed Mick more than Babiche. His duty to Mick required him to see that nothing of the sort occurred again. This would be a strain, but nothing like the strain it would have continued to be unless it had happened. Since it had, and could not be denied, he was enabled to bear the thought of the future with equanimity. He would easily find another girl, since after Babiche the rest would be child's play. Nothing whatever could now stop him in a career of conquest.

But it occurred to him that it might be difficult to make Babiche take the same noble view. As Peter had always suspected, she was an impulsive, sensual girl who always needed a man about her. And again it astonished him that Mick, years older than he and so much more brilliant, had not realized it for himself. Babiche was a nice girl, a really delightful girl, but quite unworthy of his friend.

Unfortunately, this was something that Peter still could not tell him, even now. Particularly now. It would always have to remain a secret between Babiche and himself, and this would be made far more difficult by the malice of Rosemary who, to avenge the way he had humiliated her on the subject of Degas, would take any opportunity of injuring him with Mick. This time it was his own blindness that he wondered at. As a realist he should have seen that Rosemary expected what had happened merely because she knew her sister so much better than Mick or himself knew her, and had merely waited cynically for the moment when some man would give her an opportunity. Probably the only thing which had surprised them both was the length of time Peter had taken about it. There were depths of unworthiness in Babiche which even he had not suspected. She wouldn't do; she wouldn't do at all. It was madness to have endangered his friendship with Mick over such a woman.

But it was only in bed that the full madness of his conduct was revealed to him. He had indeed proved Babiche unworthy of Mick, but only at the cost of proving himself unworthy of him. Mick would forgive Babiche because unworthy women had the advantage of being forgiven. He wouldn't be forgiven, and all his ideas of covering it up were only fantasies. He couldn't lie to Mick because Mick was both inside and outside him; he was Mick, and he knew that the Mick within him would not let him rest. His mistake had been in trying to become Mick in the outside world as well, for in that process he had become something which the real Mick would despise.

He knew it was hopeless. He did not go to Babiche's again. She wrote asking him to tea – a cheerful, inconsequent, rattle-pated letter that showed her entirely devoid of any sense of guilt – but he didn't reply. Mick came home on holidays but didn't call to see him. Peter knew he had learned the whole story from herself, or worse, from Rosemary. All lies, he knew, but no lies could be worse than the truth. In sober moments he realized that it was only growing-pains. There would be other friends and other girls but never again anything like this. His treachery had made two parts of him. He had become a man. But the idea gave him singularly little comfort.

The Ugly Duckling

I

MICK COURTNEY had known Nan Ryan from the time he was fourteen or fifteen. She was the sister of his best friend, and youngest of a family of four in which she was the only girl. He came to be almost as fond of her as her father and brothers were; she had practically lost her mother's regard by inheriting her father's looks. Her ugliness indeed was quite endearing. She had a stocky, sturdy figure and masculine features all crammed into a feminine container till it bulged. None of her features was really bad, and her big, brown, twinkling eyes were delightful, but they made a group that was almost comic.

Her brothers liked her spirit; they let her play with them while any of them was of an age for play, and, though she suffered from night-panics and Dinny broke the maternal rule by letting her into his bed, they never told. He, poor kid, would be wakened in the middle of the night by Nan's pulling and shaking. 'Dinny, Dinny,' she would hiss fiercely, 'I have 'em again!' 'What are they this time?' Dinny would ask drowsily. 'Li-i-ons!' she would reply in a blood-curdling tone, and then lie for half an hour in his arms, contracting her toes and kicking spasmodically while he patted and soothed her.

She grew up a tomboy, fierce, tough, and tearless, fighting in Dinny's gang, which contested the old quarry on the road with the hill-tribes from the slum area above it; and this was how Mick was to remember her best; an ugly, stocky little Amazon, leaping from rock to rock, hurling stones in an awkward but effective way and screaming deadly insults at the enemy and encouragement to her own side.

He could not have said when she gave up fighting, but between twelve and fourteen she became the pious one in a family not remarkable for piety; always out at Mass or diving into church on her way from school to light candles and make novenas. Afterwards it struck Mick that it might have been an alternative to getting in Dinny's bed, for she still suffered from night-fears, only now when they came on she grabbed her rosary beads instead.

It amused him to discover that she had developed something of a crush on himself. Mick had lost his faith, which in Cork is rather similar to a girl's loss of her virtue and starts the same sort of flutterings among the quiet ones of the opposite sex. Nan would be waiting for him at the door in the evening, and when she saw him would begin to jump down the steps one by one with her feet together, her hands stiff at her sides, and her pigtail tossing.

'How are the novenas coming on, Nan?' he would ask with amusement.

'Fine!' she would reply in a shrill, expressionless voice. 'You're on your way.'

'I'll come quietly.'

'You think you won't, but I know better. I'm a fierce pray-er.'

Another stiff jump took her past him.

'Why don't you do it for the blacks, Nan?'

'I'm doing it for them too, sure.'

But though her brothers could ease the pangs of childhood for her, adolescence threw her on the mercy of life. Her mother, a roly-poly of a woman who went round a great deal with folded arms, thus increasing the impression of curves and rolls, was still a beauty, and did her best to disguise Nan's ugliness, a process that mystified her husband who could see nothing lacking in the child except her shaky mathematics.

'I'm no blooming beauty,' Nan would cry with an imitation of a schoolboy's toughness whenever her mother tried to get her out of the rough tweeds and dirty pullovers she fancied into something more feminine.

'The dear knows you're not,' her mother would say, folding her arms with an expression of resignation. 'I don't suppose you want to advertise it though.'

'Why wouldn't I advertise it?' Nan would cry, squaring up to her. 'I don't want any of your dirty old men.'

'You needn't worry, child. They'll let you well alone.'

'Let them!' Nan would say, scowling. 'I don't care. I want to be a nun.'

All the same it made her self-conscious about friendships with girls of her own age, even pious ones like herself. They too would have boys around, and the boys wanted nothing to do with Nan. Though she carefully avoided all occasion for a slight, even the hint of one was enough to make her brooding and resentful, and then she seemed to become hideous and shapeless and furtive. She slunk round the house with her shoulders up about her ears, her red-brown hair hanging loose and a cigarette glued loosely to her lower lip. Suddenly and inexplicably she would drop some quite nice girl she had been friendly with for years and never even speak of her again. It gave her the reputation of being cold and insincere, but as Dinny in his shrewd, old-mannish way observed to Mick, she made her real friends among older women and even sick people – 'all seventy or paralysed' as he put it. Yet, even with these she tended to be jealous and exacting.

Dinny didn't like this, and his mother thought it was awful, but Nan paid no attention to their views. She had become exceedingly obstinate in a way that did not suit either her age or her sex, and it made her seem curiously angular, almost masculine, as though it were the psychological aspect of her ugliness. She had no apparent shyness and stalked in and out of a room, swinging her arms like a boy. Her conversation changed too, and took on the tone of an older woman's. It was not dull – she was far too brainy to be dull – but it was too much on one key – 'crabbed' to use a local word – and it did not make the sharp distinctions young people's conversation makes between passion and boredom. Dinny and Mick could be very bored indeed in one another's company, but suddenly some topic would set flame to their minds, and they would walk the streets by the hour with their coats buttoned up, arguing.

Her father was disappointed when she refused to go to college. When she did go to work it was in a dress shop, a curious occupation for a girl whose only notions of dress were a trousers and jersey.

2

Then one night something happened that electrified Mick. It
was more like a transformation scene in a pantomime than anything in his experience. Later, of course, he realized that it
had not happened like that at all. It was just that, as usual with
those one has known too well, he had ceased to observe Nan,
had taken her too much for granted, and the change in her had
come about gradually and imperceptibly till it forced itself on
his attention in the form of a shock.

Dinny was upstairs and Mick and she were arguing. Though
without formal education, Mick was a well-read man, and he
had no patience with Nan's literary tastes which were those of
her aged and invalid acquaintances – popular novels and
biographies. As usual he made fun of her and as usual she
grew angry. 'You're so damn superior, Mick Courtney,' she
said with a scowl and went to search for the book they had
discussed in the big mahogany bookcase, which was one of the
handsome pieces of furniture her mother took pride in.
Laughing, Mick got up and stood beside her, putting his arm
round her shoulder as he would have done at any other time.
She misunderstood the gesture for she leaned back on his
shoulder and offered herself to be kissed. At that moment only
did he realize that she had turned into a girl of startling beauty.
He did not kiss her. Instead, he dropped his arm and looked at
her incredulously. She gave him a malicious grin and went on
with her search.

For the rest of the evening he could not take his eyes from
her. Now he could easily analyse the change for himself. He
remembered that she had been ill with some type of fever and
had come out of it white and thin. Then she had seemed to
shoot up, and now he saw that during her illness her face had
lengthened and one by one each of those awkward lumps of
feature had dropped into place and proportion till they formed
a perfect structure that neither age nor illness could any longer
quite destroy. It was not in the least like her mother's type of
beauty which was round and soft and eminently pattable. It
was like a translation of her father's masculinity, tight and
strained and almost harsh, and she had deliberately emphasized

it by the way she pulled her hair back in a tight knot, exposing the rather big ears. Already it had begun to affect her gait because she no longer charged about a room, swinging her arms like a sergeant-major. At the same time she had not yet learned to move gracefully, and she seemed to drift rather than walk, and came in and went out in profile as though afraid to face a visitor or turn her back on him. And he wondered again at the power of habit that causes us to live with people historically, with faults or virtues that have long disappeared to every eye but our own.

For twelve months Mick had been going steadily with a nice girl from Sunday's Well and in due course he would have married her. Mick was that sort; a creature of habit who controlled circumstances by simplifying them down to a routine – the same restaurant, the same table, the same waitress, and the same dish. It enabled him to go on with his own thoughts. But whenever anything did happen to disturb this routine it was like a convulsion of Nature for him; even his favourite restaurant became a burden and he did not know what to do with his evenings and week-ends. The transformation of Nan into a beauty had a similar effect on him. Gradually he dropped the nice girl from Sunday's Well without a word of explanation or apology and went more and more to the Ryans, where he had a feeling of not being particularly welcome to anyone but Dinny and – sometimes at least – to Nan herself.

She had plenty of admirers without him. Mr Ryan, a tall, bald, noisy man with an ape-like countenance of striking good nature, enjoyed it as proof that sensible men were not put off by a girl's mathematics – he, poor man, had noticed no change whatever in his daughter. Mrs Ryan had no such pleasure. Naturally, she had always cared more for her sons, but they had not brought home with them attractive young men who were compelled to flirt with her, and now Nan took an almost perverse delight in keeping the young men and her mother apart. Beauty had brought out what ugliness had failed to do – a deep resentment of her mother that at times went too far for Mick's taste. Occasionally he saw it in a reversion to a heavy, stolid, almost stupid air that harked back to her childhood, sometimes in a sparkle of wit that had malice in it. She made up for this by what Mick thought of as an undue consideration for her father. Whenever he came into the room, bellowing and cheerful, her face lit up.

She had ceased to wear the rough masculine tweeds she had always preferred and to Mick's eye it was not a change for the better. She had developed a passion for good clothes without an understanding of them, and she used powder and lipstick in the lavish tasteless manner of a girl of twelve.

But if he disapproved of her taste in dress, he hated her taste in men. What left Dinny bored made Mick mad. He and Nan argued about this in the same way they argued about books. 'Smoothies,' he called her admirers to her face. There was Joe Lyons, the solicitor, a suave, dark-haired young man with mysterious slit-like eyes who combined a knowledge of wines with an intellectual Catholicism, and Matt Healy, a little leprechaun of a butter merchant who had a boat and rattled on cheerfully about whisky and 'dames'. The pair of them could argue for a full half-hour about a particular make of car or a Dublin hotel without, so far as Mick could see, ever uttering one word of sense, and obviously Lyons despised Healy as a chatter-box and Healy despised Lyons as a fake, while both of them despised Mick. They thought he was a character, and whenever he tried to discuss religion or politics with them they listened with an amusement that made him furious.

'I stick to Mick against the day the Revolution comes,' said Healy with his leprechaun's laugh.

'No,' Lyons said, putting his arm patronizingly about Mick, 'Mick will have nothing to do with revolutions.'

'Don't be too sure,' said Healy, his face lit up with merriment. 'Mick is a *sans-culotte*. Isn't that the word, Mick?'

'I repeat no,' said Lyons with his grave smile. 'I know Mick. Mick is a wise man. Mind,' he added solemnly, raising his finger, 'I didn't say an intelligent man. I said a wise one. There's a difference.'

Mick could not help being angry. When they talked that way to Dinny he only blinked politely and drifted upstairs to his book or his gramophone, but Mick stayed and grew mad. He was hard-working but unambitious; too intelligent to value the things commonplace people valued, but too thin-skinned to ignore their scorn at his failure to do so.

Nan herself had no objection to being courted by Mick. She was still under the influence of her childish infatuation, and it satisfied her vanity to be able to indulge it. She was an excellent companion, active and intelligent, and would go off for long walks with him over the hills through the fields to the river. They would end up in a public house in Glanmire or Little Island, though she soon stopped him trying to be extravagant in the manner of Lyons and Healy. 'I'm a whisky drinker, Mick,' she would say with a laugh. 'You're not a whisky buyer.' She could talk for an hour over a glass of beer, but when Mick tried to give their conversation a sentimental turn she countered with a bluff practicality that shocked him.

'Marry you?' she exclaimed with a laugh. 'Who died and left you the fortune?'

'Why, do I have to have a fortune?' he asked quietly, though he was stung by her good-natured contempt.

'Well, it would be a help if you're thinking of getting married,' she replied with a laugh. 'As long as I remember my family, we never seem to have been worried by anything else.'

'Of course, if you married Joe Lyons, you wouldn't have to worry,' he said with a hint of a sneer.

'From my point of view, that would be a very good reason,' she said.

'A classy car and St Thomas Aquinas,' Mick went on, feeling like a small boy but unable to stop himself. 'What more could a girl ask?'

'You resent people having cars, don't you?' she asked, leaning her elbows on the table and giving him a nasty look. 'Don't you think it might help if you went and got one for yourself?'

The worldly, middle-aged tone, particularly when linked with the Ryan go-getting, could be exceedingly destructive. There was something else that troubled him, too, though he was not sure why. He had always liked to pose a little as a man of the world, but Nan could sometimes shock him badly. There seemed to be depths of sensuality in her that were out of character. He could not believe that she really intended it, but she could sometimes inflame him with some sudden violence or coarseness as no ordinary girl could do.

Then one evening when they were out together, walking in the Lee Fields, he noticed a change in her. She and another girl had been spending a few days in Glengarriffe with Lyons and Healy. She did not want to talk of it, and he had the feeling that something about it had disappointed her. She was different; brooding, affectionate, and intense. She pulled off her shoes and stockings and sat with her feet in the river, her hands joined between her knees while she gazed at the woods on the other side of the river.

'You think too much of Matt and Joe,' she said, splashing her feet. 'Why can't you feel sorry for them?'

'Feel sorry for them?' he repeated, so astonished that he burst into a laugh. She turned her head and her brown eyes rested on him with a strange innocence.

'If you weren't such an old agnostic, I'd say pray for them.'

'For what?' he asked, still laughing. 'Bigger dividends?'

'The dividends aren't much use to them,' she said. 'They're both bored. That's why they like me – I don't bore them. They don't know what to make of me. . . . Mind,' she added, laughing in her enthusiastic way, 'I love money, Mick Courtney. I love expensive clothes and flashy dinners and wines I can't pronounce the names of, but they don't take me in. A girl who was brought up as I was needs more than that to take her in.'

'What is it you need?' asked Mick.

'Why don't you go and do something?' she asked with sudden gravity.

'What?' he replied with a shrug.

'What?' she asked, waving her hands. 'What do I care? I don't even know what you care about. I don't mind if you make a mess of it. It's not failure I'm afraid of. It's just getting stuck in the mud, not caring for anything. Look at Daddy! You may not think so, but I know he's a brilliant man, and he's stuck. Now he hopes the boys will find out whatever secret there is and do all the things he couldn't do. That doesn't appeal to me.'

'Yes,' Mick agreed thoughtfully, lighting a cigarette and answering himself rather than her. 'I know what you mean. I dare say I'm not ambitious. I've never felt the need for being ambitious. But I fancy I could be ambitious for someone else. I'd have to get out of Cork though. Probably to Dublin. There's nothing here in my line.'

'Dublin would do me fine,' she said with satisfaction. 'Mother and I would get on much better at that distance.'

He said nothing for a few moments, and Nan went on splashing gaily with her feet.

'Is that a bargain then?' he asked.

'Oh, yes,' she said, turning her big soft eyes on him. 'That's a bargain. Don't you know I was always mad about you?'

Their engagement made a big change in Mick. He was, as I have said, a creature of habit, a man who lived by associations. He really knew the city in a way that few of us knew it, its interesting corners and queer characters, and the idea of having to exchange it for a place of no associations at all was more of a shock to him than it would have been to any of us; but though at certain times it left him with a lost feeling, at others it restored to him a boyish excitement and gaiety as though the trip he was preparing for was some dangerous voyage from which he might not return, and when he lit up like that he became more attractive, reckless, and innocent. Nan had always been attracted by him; now she really admired and loved him.

All the same she did not discontinue her outings with her other beaux. In particular, she remained friendly with Lyons, who was really fond of her and believed that she wasn't serious about marrying Mick. He was, as she said, a genuinely kind man, and was shocked at the thought that so beautiful a girl should even consider cooking and washing clothes on a clerk's income. He went to her father about it, and explained patiently to him that it would mean social extinction for Nan, and would even have gone to Mick himself but that Nan forbade it. 'But he can't do it, Nan,' he protested earnestly. 'Mick is a decent man. He can't do that to you.' 'He can't like hell,' said Nan, chuckling and putting her head on Lyons's chest. 'He'd send me out on the streets to keep himself in fags.'

These minor infidelities did not in the least worry Mick, who was almost devoid of jealousy. He was merely amused by her occasional lies and evasions and even more by the fits of conscience that followed them.

'Mick,' she asked between anger and laughter, 'why do I tell you all these lies? I'm not naturally untruthful, am I? I didn't go to confession on Saturday night. I went out with Joe Lyons instead. He still believes I'm going to marry him, and I would, too, if only he had a brain in his head. Mick, why can't you be attractive like that?'

But if Mick didn't resent it, Mrs Ryan resented it on his behalf, though she resented his complaisance even more. She was sufficiently feminine to know she might have done the same herself, and to feel that if she had, she would need correction. No man is ever as anti-feminist as a really feminine woman.

No, it was Nan's father who exasperated Mick, and he was sensible enough to realize that he was being exasperated without proper cause. When Joe Lyons lamented Nan's decision to Tom Ryan as though it were no better than suicide, the old man was thunderstruck. He had never mixed in society himself which might be the reason that he had never got anywhere in life.

'You really think it would come to that, Joe?' he asked, scowling.

'But consider it for yourself, Mr Ryan,' pleaded Joe, raising that warning finger of his. 'Who is going to receive them? They can always come to my house, but I'm not everybody. Do you think they'll be invited to the Healys? I say, the moment they marry, Matt will drop them, and I won't blame him. It's a game, admitted, but you have to play it. Even I have to play it, and my only interest is in philosophy.'

By the end of the evening Tom Ryan had managed to persuade himself that Mick was almost a ne'er-do-well and certainly an adventurer. The prospect of the Dublin job did not satisfy him in the least. He wanted to know what Mick proposed to do then. Rest on his oars? There were examinations he could take which would ensure his chances of promotion. Tom would arrange it all and coach him himself.

At first Mick was amused and patient; then he became sarcastic, a great weakness of his whenever he was forced on the defensive. Tom Ryan, who was as incapable as a child of understanding sarcasm, rubbed his bald head angrily and left the room in a flurry. If Mick had only hit him over the head, as his wife did whenever he got on her nerves, Tom would have understood that he was only relieving his feelings, and liked him the better for it. But sarcasm was to him a sort of silence, a denial of attention that hurt him bitterly.

'I wish you wouldn't speak to Daddy like that,' Nan said one night when her father had been buzzing about Mick with syllabuses he had refused even to look at.

'I wish Daddy would stop arranging my life for me,' Mick said wearily.

'He only means it in kindness.'

'I didn't think he meant it any other way,' Mick said stiffly. 'But I wish he'd get it into his head that I'm marrying you, not him.'

'I wouldn't be too sure of that either, Mick,' she said angrily.

'Really, Nan!' he said reproachfully. 'Do you want me to be pushed round by your old man?'

'It's not only that,' she said, rising and crossing the room to the fireplace. He noticed that when she lost her temper, she suddenly seemed to lose command of her beauty. She scowled, bowed her head, and walked with a heavy guardsman's tread. 'It's just as well we've had this out, because I'd have had to tell you anyway. I've thought about it enough, God knows. I can't possibly marry you.'

Her tone was all that was necessary to bring Mick back to his own tolerant, reasonable self.

'Why not?' he asked gently.

'Because I'm scared, if you want to know.' And just then, looking down at him, she seemed scared.

'Of marriage?'

'Of marriage as well.' He noticed the reservation.

'Of me, so?'

'Oh, of marriage and you and myself,' she said explosively. 'Myself most of all.'

'Afraid you may kick over the traces?' he asked with affectionate mockery.

'You think I wouldn't?' she hissed, with clenched fists, her eyes narrowing and her face looking old and grim. 'You don't understand me at all, Mick Courtney,' she added, with a sort of boyish braggadocio that made her seem again like the little tomboy he had known. 'You don't even know the sort of things I'm capable of. You're wrong for me. I always knew you were.'

Mick treated the scene lightly as though it were merely another of their disagreements, but when he left the house he was both hurt and troubled. Clearly there was a side of her character that he did not understand, and he was a man who liked to understand things, if only so that he could forget about them and go on with his own thoughts. Even on the familiar hill-street with the gas-lamp poised against the night sky, he seemed to be walking a road without associations. He knew Nan was unhappy and felt it had nothing to do with the subject of their quarrel. It was unhappiness that had driven her into his arms in the first place, and now it was as though she were being driven out again by the same wind. He had assumed rather too complacently that she had turned to him in the first place because she had seen through Lyons and Healy, but now he felt that her unhappiness had nothing to do with them either. She was desperate about herself rather than them. It struck him that she might easily have been tempted too far by Lyons's good looks and kindness. She was the sort of passionate girl who could very easily be lured into an indiscretion and who would then react from it in loathing and self-disgust. The very thought that this might be the cause moved him to a passion of protective tenderness, and before he went to bed he wrote and posted an affectionate letter, apologizing for his rudeness to her father and promising to consider her feelings more in the future.

In reply, he got a brief note, delivered at his house while he was at work. She did not refer at all to his letter, and told him that she was marrying Lyons. It was a dry note, and, for him, full of suppressed malice. He left his own house and met Dinny on the way up to call for him. From Dinny's gloomy air Mick saw that he knew all about it. They went for one of their usual country walks, and only when they were sitting in a country pub over their beer did Mick speak of the breach.

Dinny was worried and his worry made him rude, and through the rudeness Mick seemed to hear the voices of the Ryans discussing him. They hadn't really thought much of him as a husband for Nan but had been prepared to put up with him on her account. At the same time there was no question in their minds but that she didn't really care for Lyons and was marrying him only in some mood of desperation induced by Mick. Obviously, it was all Mick's fault.

'I can't really imagine what I did,' Mick said reasonably. 'Your father started bossing me and I was rude to him. I know that, and I told Nan I was sorry.'

'Oh, the old man bosses us all, and we're all rude,' said Dinny. 'It's not that.'

'Then it's nothing to do with me,' Mick said doggedly.

'Maybe not,' replied Dinny without conviction. 'But whatever it is, the harm is done. You know how obstinate Nan is when she takes an idea into her head.'

'And you don't think I should see her and ask her?'

'I wouldn't,' said Dinny, looking at Mick directly for the first time. 'I don't think Nan will marry you, old man, and I'm not at all sure but that it might be the best thing for you. You know I'm fond of her but she's a curious girl. I think you'll only hurt yourself worse than you're hurt already.'

Mick realized that Dinny, for whatever reasons, was advising him to quit, and for once he was in a position to do so. With the usual irony of events, the job in Dublin he had been seeking only on her account had been offered to him, and he would have to leave at the end of the month.

This, which had seemed an enormous break with his past, now turned out to be the very best solace for his troubled mind. Though he missed old friends and familiar places more than most people, he had the sensitiveness of his type to any sort of novelty, and soon ended by wondering how he could ever have stuck Cork for so long. Within twelve months he had met a nice girl called Eilish and married her. And though Cork people might be parochial, Eilish believed that anything that didn't happen between Glasnevin and Terenure had not happened at all. When he talked to her of Cork her eyes simply glazed over.

So entirely did Cork scenes and characters fade from his memory that it came as a shock to him to meet Dinny one fine day in Grafton Street. Dinny was on his way to his first job in England, and Mick at once invited him home. But before they left town they celebrated their reunion in Mick's favourite pub off Grafton Street. Then he could ask the question that had sprung to his mind when he caught sight of Dinny's face.

'How's Nan?'

'Oh, didn't you hear about her?' Dinny asked with his usual air of mild surprise. 'Nan's gone into a convent, you know.'

'Nan?' repeated Mick. 'Into a convent?'

'Yes,' said Dinny. 'Of course, she used to talk of it when she was a kid, but we never paid much attention. It came as a surprise to us. I fancy it surprised the convent even more,' he added dryly.

'For God's sake!' exclaimed Mick. 'And the fellow she was engaged to – Lyons?'

'Oh, she dropped him inside a couple of months,' said Dinny with distaste. 'I never thought she was serious about him anyway. The fellow is a damned idiot.'

Mick went on with his drink, suddenly feeling embarrassed and strained. A few minutes later he asked with the pretence of a smile.

'You don't think if I'd hung on she might have changed her mind?'

'I dare say she might,' Dinny replied sagaciously. 'I'm not so sure it would have been the best thing for you though,' he added kindly. 'The truth is, I don't think Nan is the marrying kind.'

'I dare say not,' said Mick, but he did not believe it for an instant. He was quite sure that Nan was the marrying kind, and that nothing except the deep unhappiness that had first united and then divided them had kept her from marrying. But what that unhappiness was about he still had no idea, and he saw that Dinny knew even less than he did.

Their meeting had brought it all back, and at intervals during the next few years it returned again to his mind, disturbing him. It was not that he was unhappy in his own married life – a man would have to have something gravely wrong with him to be unhappy with a girl like Eilish – but sometimes in the morning when he kissed her at the gate and went swinging down the ugly modern avenue towards the sea, he would think of the river or the hills of Cork and of the girl who had seemed to have none of his pleasure in simple things, whose decisions seemed all to have been dictated by some inner torment.

3

Then, long after, he found himself alone in Cork, tidying up things after the death of his father, his last relative there, and was suddenly plunged back into the world of his childhood and youth, wandering like a ghost from street to street, from pub to pub, from old friend to old friend, resurrecting other ghosts in a mood that was half anguish, half delight. He walked out to Blackpool and up Goulding's Glen only to find that the big mill-pond had all dried up, and sat on the edge remembering winter days when he was a child and the pond was full of skaters, and summer nights when it was full of stars. His absorption in the familiar made him peculiarly susceptible to the poetry of change. He visited the Ryans and found Mrs Ryan almost as good-looking and pattable as ever, though she moaned sentimentally about the departure of the boys, her disappointment with Nan and her husband's growing crankiness.

When she saw him to the door she folded her arms and leaned against the jamb.

'Wisha, Mick, wouldn't you go and see her?' she asked reproachfully.

'Nan?' said Mick. 'You don't think she'd mind?'

'Why would she mind, boy?' Mrs Ryan said with a shrug. 'Sure the girl must be dead for someone to talk to! Mick, boy, I was never one for criticizing religion, but God forgive me, that's not a natural life at all. I wouldn't stand it for a week. All those old hags!'

Mick, imagining the effect of Mrs Ryan on any well-organized convent, decided that God would probably not hold it too much against her, but he made up his mind to visit Nan. The convent was on one of the steep hills outside the city with a wide view of the valley from its front lawn. He was expecting a change but her appearance in the ugly convent parlour startled him. The frame of white linen and black veil gave her strongly marked features the unnatural relief of a fifteenth-century German portrait. And the twinkle of the big brown eyes convinced him of an idea that had been forming slowly in his mind through the years.

'Isn't it terrible I can't kiss you, Mick?' she said with a chuckle. 'I suppose I could really, but our old chaplain is a terror. He thinks I'm the New Nun. He's been hearing about her all his life, but I'm the first he's run across. Come into the garden where we can talk,' she added with an awed glance at the holy pictures on the walls. 'This place would give you the creeps. I'm at them the whole time to get rid of that Sacred Heart. It's Bavarian, of course. They love it.'

Chattering on, she rustled ahead of him on to the lawn with her head bowed. He knew from the little flutter in her voice and manner that she was as pleased to see him as he was to see her. She led him to a garden seat behind a hedge that hid them from the convent and then grabbed in her enthusiastic way at his hand.

'Now, tell me all about you,' she said. 'I heard you were married to a very nice girl. One of the sisters went to school with her. She says she's a saint. Has she converted you yet?'

'Do I look as if she had?' he asked with a pale smile.

'No,' she replied with a chuckle. 'I'd know that agnostic look of yours anywhere. But you needn't think you'll escape me all the same.'

'You're a fierce pray-er,' he quoted, and she burst into a delighted laugh.

'It's true,' she said. 'I am. I'm a terror for holding on.'

'Really?' he asked mockingly. 'A girl that let two men slip in – what was it? a month?'

'Ah, that was different,' she said with sudden gravity. 'Then there were other things at stake. I suppose God came first.' Then she looked at him slyly out of the corner of her eye. 'Or do you think I'm only talking nonsense?'

'Don't you? What else is it?' he asked.

'I'm not really,' she said. 'Though I sometimes wonder myself how it all happened,' she added with a rueful shrug. 'And it's not that I'm not happy here. You know that?'

'Yes,' he said quietly. 'I've suspected that for quite a while.'

'My,' she said with a laugh, 'you *have* changed!'

He had not needed her to say that she was happy, nor did he need her to tell him why. He knew that the idea that had been forming in his mind for the last year or two was the true one, and that what had happened to her was not something unique and inexplicable. It was something that happened to others in different ways. Because of some inadequacy in themselves – poverty or physical weakness in men, poverty or ugliness in women – those with the gift of creation built for themselves a rich interior world; and when the inadequacy disappeared and the real world was spread before them with all its wealth and beauty, they could not give their whole heart to it. Uncertain of their choice, they wavered between goals; were lonely in crowds, dissatisfied amid noise and laughter, unhappy even with those they loved best. The interior world called them back, and for some it was a case of having to return there or die.

He tried to explain this to her, feeling his own lack of persuasiveness and at the same time aware that she was watching him keenly and with amusement, almost as though she did not take him seriously. Perhaps she didn't, for which of us can feel, let alone describe, another's interior world? They sat there for close on an hour, listening to the convent bells calling one sister or another, and Mick refused to stay for tea. He knew convent tea parties, and had no wish to spoil the impression that their meeting had left on him.

'Pray for me,' he said with a smile as they shook hands.

'Do you think I ever stopped?' she replied with a mocking laugh, and he strode quickly down the shady steps to the lodge-gate in a strange mood of rejoicing, realizing that however the city might change, that old love-affair went on unbroken in a world where disgust or despair would never touch it, and would continue to do so till both of them were dead.

Don Juan's Temptation

AGAINST the Gussie Leonards of the world, we poor whores have no defences. Sons of bitches to a man, we can't like them, we can't even believe them, and still we must listen to them because deep down in every man jack of us there is the feeling that our own experience of life is insufficient. Humanly we understand our wives and girls and daughters; we put up with their tantrums and consider what we imagine are their wishes, but then the moment comes and we realize that that fat sleeky rascal understands them at a level where we can never even meet them, as if they put off their ordinary humanity as they put off their clothes, and went wandering through the world invisible except to the men like Gussie whose eyes are trained only to see them that way. The only consolation we have is that they too have their temptations – or so at least they say. The sons of bitches! Even that much you can't believe from them.

Anyhow, Gussie met this girl at a party in the Green and picked her out at once. She was young, tall, dark, good-looking, but it wasn't so much her looks that appealed to Gussie as the naturalness with which she moved among all those wooden dolls in nightdresses. She was a country-town girl who had never learned to dress up and pose, and however she moved or whatever she said it always seemed to be natural and right.

They left together and she took Gussie's arm with a boyish camaraderie that delighted him. It was a lovely night with the moon nearly at the full. Gussie's flat was in a Georgian house on the street which ran through the Green; she had a room in Pembroke Road, and as they passed the house Gussie halted and asked her in. She gave a slight start, but Gussie, having a few drinks in, didn't notice that until later.

'For what?' she asked gaily.

'Oh, for the night if you like,' Gussie replied in the same tone and felt like biting off his tongue when he heard it. It sounded so awkward, like a schoolboy the first time he goes with a girl.

'No, thanks,' she said shortly. 'I have a room of my own.'

'Oh, please, Helen, please!' he moaned, taking her hand and squeezing it in the way of an old friend of the family. 'You're not taking offence at my harmless little joke. Now you'll have to come up and have a drink, just to show there's no ill-feeling.'

'Some other night,' she said, 'when it's not so late.'

He let it go at that because he knew that anything further he said would only frighten her more. He knew perfectly well what had happened. The Sheehans, mischief-makers and busybodies, had warned her against him, and he had walked straight into the trap. She still held on to his arm, but that was only not to make a fuss. Inside she was as hurt as anything. Hurt and surprised. In spite of the Sheehans' warnings she had taken him at his face value, not believing him to be that sort at all. Or rather, as Gussie, whose eyes were differently focused from ours, phrased it to himself, knowing damn well he was that sort but hoping that he would reveal it gradually so that she wouldn't be compelled to take notice.

She stopped at the canal bridge and leaned over to look at the view. It was beautiful there in the moonlight with the still water, the trees, the banked houses with odd windows caught in the snowy light, but Gussie knew it was not the moonlight she was thinking of. She was getting over her fright and now it was her pride that was hurt.

'Tell us,' she said, letting on to be very light-hearted and interested in the subject, as it were, only from the psychological standpoint, 'do you ask all the girls you meet the same thing?'

'But my goodness, didn't I tell you it was only a joke?' Gussie asked reproachfully.

She rested her head on her arms and looked back at him over her shoulder, the cloche hat shading her face to the chin. It was a natural, beautiful pose but Gussie knew she wasn't aware of it.

'Now you're not being honest,' she said.

'Are you?' Gussie asked with a faint smile.

'Am I what?' she replied with a start.

'Can't you admit that you were warned against me?' he said.

'As a matter of fact I was,' she replied candidly, 'but I didn't pay much attention. I take people as I find them.'

'Now you're talking sensibly,' said Gussie and thought in a fatherly way: 'The girl is nice. She's a bit shocked but she'll have to learn sooner or later and it would be better for her to learn from someone who knows.' The awkwardness of Irish husbands was a theme-song of Gussie's. The things their wives told you were almost incredible.

'You probably wouldn't believe me if I told you how few women interest me enough for that,' he said.

'But the ones you do ask,' she went on, sticking to her point, though pretending to be quite detached as though she really were only looking for information, 'do they come?'

'Some,' he said, smiling at her innocence. 'Sometimes you meet a difficult girl who makes a hullabaloo and won't even come and have a drink with you afterwards.'

'Married women or girls?' she asked in the tone of an official filling up a form, but the quaver in her voice gave her away.

'Both,' said Gussie. If he had been perfectly honest he would have had to admit that at that time there was only one of the former and not exactly a queue of the latter but he had decided, purely in Helen's own interest, that since she needed to have her mind broadened there was no use doing it by halves. It was better to get it over and be done with it, like having a tooth out. 'Why?'

'Oh, nothing,' she said casually. 'but I'm not surprised you have such a poor opinion of women if you can pick them up as easily as that.'

This view of the matter came as a real surprise to Gussie, who would never have described his conduct in that way.

'But my dear young lady,' he said offering her a cigarette, 'whoever said I have a poor opinion of women? What would I be doing with women if I had? On the contrary, I have a very high opinion of women, and the more I see of them the more I like them.'

'Have you?' she asked, stooping low over the match-flame so that he shouldn't see her face. He guessed that it was very flushed. 'It must be a poor opinion of me so.'

'What an extraordinary idea!' said Gussie, still genuinely trying to fathom it. 'How can you make out that wanting to see more of you means I have a poor opinion of you. Even if I do want to make love to you. As a matter of fact, if it's any news to you, I do.'

'You want it rather easy, don't you?' she asked with a trace of resentment.

'Why?' he asked blandly. 'Do you think it should be made difficult?'

'I thought it was the usual thing to ask a girl to go to the pictures with you first,' she said with a brassy air that wouldn't have taken in a child.

'I wouldn't know,' murmured Gussie in amusement. 'Anyway, I suppose I thought you weren't the usual sort of girl.'

'But if you get it as easy as that, how do you know if it's the real thing or not?' she asked.

'How do you know anything is the real thing?' he retorted. 'As you say yourself, you have to take things as you find them.'

'Taking them as you find them doesn't mean swallowing them whole,' she said. 'It would be rather late in the day to change your mind about a thing like that.'

'But what difference does it make?' he asked wonderingly. 'It happens every day of the week. You do it yourself with boys you go out walking with. You spoon with them till you find they bore you and then you drop them. There's no difference. You don't suddenly change your character. People don't say when they meet you in the street: "How different that girl is looking! You can see she has a man." Of course, if you attach so much importance to the physical side of it – '

'I do,' she said quickly. By this time Gussie noticed to his surprise that she was almost laughing. She had got over her fright and hurt and felt that in argument she was more than a match for him. 'Isn't it awful?' she added brightly. 'But I'm very queer like that.'

'Oh, there's nothing queer about it,' Gussie said, determined on keeping control of the situation and not letting her away with anything. 'It's just ordinary schoolgirl romanticism.'

'Is that all?' she asked lightly, and though she pretended not to care he saw she was stung. 'You have an answer for everything, haven't you?'

'If you call that everything, my dear child,' he replied paternally patting her on the shoulder. 'I call it growing-pains. I don't know, with that romantic nature of yours, whether you've noticed that there's a nasty wind coming up the canal.'

'No,' she said archly, 'I hadn't,' and then turned to face him, resting her elbows on the coping of the bridge. 'Anyhow, I like it. Go on with what you were saying. Being romantic is thinking you ought to stick to someone you're fond of, isn't that it?'

Gussie was amused again. The girl was so transparent. It was clear now that she was in love with some young fellow who couldn't afford to marry her and that they were scarifying one another in the usual adolescent rough-and-tumble without knowing what ailed them.

'No, my dear, it isn't,' said Gussie. 'Being romantic is thinking you're very fond of someone you really don't give a damn about, and imagining on that account that you're never going to care for anyone else. It goes with your age. Come on now, or you'll be catching something worse.'

'You don't mean you were ever like that?' she asked, taking his arm again as they went on down Pembroke Road. Even her tone revealed her mingled fascination and loathing. It didn't worry Gussie. He was used to it.

'Oh,' he said sentimentally, 'we all go through it.'

There were a lot of contradictions in Gussie. Despising youth and its illusions, he could scarcely ever think of his own youth without self-pity. He had been lonely enough; sometimes he felt no one had ever been so lonely. He had woken up from a nice, well-ordered, intelligible world to find eternity stretching all round him and no one, priest or scientist, who could explain it to him. And with that awakening had gone the longing for companionship and love which he had not known how to satisfy, and often he had walked for hours, looking up at the stars and thinking that if only he could meet an understanding girl it would all explain itself naturally. The picture of Gussie's youth seemed to amuse Helen.

'Go on!' she said gaily, her face turned to his, screwed up

with mischief. 'I could have sworn you must have been born like that. How did you get sense so young?'

'Quite naturally,' Gussie said with a grave priestly air. 'I saw I was only making trouble for myself, as you're doing now, and as there seemed to be quite enough trouble in the world without that, I gave it up.'

'And lived happy ever after?' she said mockingly. 'And the women you knock round with? Aren't they romantic either?'

'Not since they were your age,' he said mockingly.

'You needn't rub it in about the age,' she said without taking umbrage. 'It'll cure itself soon enough. Tell us more about your girls – the married ones, for instance.'

'That's easy,' he said. 'There's only one at the moment.'

'And her husband? Does he know?'

'I never asked him,' Gussie said slyly. 'But I dare say he finds it more convenient not to.'

'Obliging sort of chap,' she said. 'I could do with a man like that myself.'

Gussie stopped dead. As I say there were contradictions in Gussie, and for some reason her scorn of Francie's husband filled him with indignation. It was so uncalled-for, so unjust!

'Now you are talking like a schoolgirl,' he said reproachfully.

'Am I?' she asked doubtfully, noticing the change in him. 'How?'

'What business have you talking in that tone about a man you never even met?' Gussie went on, growing quite heated. 'He isn't a thief or a blackguard. He's a decent, good-natured man. It's not his fault if after seventeen or eighteen years of living together his wife and himself can't bear the living sight of one another. That's a thing that happens to everybody. He only does what he thinks is the best thing for his family. You think, I suppose, that he should take out a gun to defend his wife's honour?'

'I wasn't thinking of her honour,' she protested quietly.

'His own then?' Gussie cried mockingly. 'At the expense of his wife and children? He's to drag her name in the mud all because some silly schoolgirl might think his position undignified. Ah, for goodness' sake, child, have sense! His wife would have something to say to that. Besides, don't you see that at his age it would be a very serious thing if she was to leave him?'

'More serious than letting her go to your flat – how often did you say?'

'Now you're talking like a little cat,' he snapped, and went on. He really was furious. 'But as a matter of fact it would,' he went on in a more reasonable tone. 'Where she goes in the evenings is nobody's business. Whether the meals are ready is another matter. They have two daughters at school – one nearly the one age with yourself.'

'I wonder if he lets them out at night,' she said dryly. 'And what sort of woman is their mother?'

'You wouldn't believe me if I told you,' said Gussie, 'but she's a great sort; a woman who'd give you her heart out.'

'I wonder what she'd say if she heard you asking another girl in to spend the night,' she added in the same casual tone. Gussie was beginning to conceive a considerable respect for her tongue.

'Ah,' he said without conviction, 'I don't suppose she has many illusions left,' but the girl had scored and she knew it. The trouble with Francie was that she had far too many illusions left, even about Gussie. And the greatest illusion of all was that if only she had married a man whose intelligence she respected as she respected his, she could have been faithful to him.

'She can't have,' said Helen, 'but I still have a few.'

'Oh, you!' Gussie said with a jolly laugh which had got him out of many tight corners. 'You're walking with them.'

'They must be in the family,' she said. 'Daddy died five years ago and Mum still thinks he was the one really great man that walked the world.'

'I dare say,' Gussie said wearily. 'And they were probably often sick to death of one another.'

'They were,' she agreed. 'They used to fight like mad and not talk for a week, and then Dad would go on the booze and Mum would take it out of me. Cripes, I used to go up to him with my bottom so sore I could hardly sit down and there he'd be sprawled in his big chair with his arms hanging down, looking into the grate as if 'twas the end of the world, and he'd just beckon me to come on his knee. We'd stop like that for hours without opening our gobs, just thinking what a bitch of hell Mum was. . . . But the thing is, young man, they stuck it out, and when 'tis her turn to go, she won't regret it because she's certain the Boss will be waiting for her. She goes to Mass every morning but that's only not to give God any excuse for making distinctions. Do you think he will?'

'Who will?' asked Gussie. In a curious way the story had gripped him. A woman could bawl her heart out on Gussie, and he'd only think her a nuisance, but he was exceedingly vulnerable to indirect sentiment.

'The Boss,' she explained. 'Meet her, I mean?'

'Well,' Gussie said feebly, 'there's nothing like optimism.' At the same time he knew he was not being altogether truthful, because orthodoxy was one of Gussie's strongest lines.

'I know,' the girl said quickly. 'That's the lousy part of it. But I suppose she's lucky even to be able to kid herself about it. Death doesn't frighten her the way it frightens me. . . . But that's what I mean by love, Mr L.,' she added light-heartedly.

'I hope you get it, Miss C.,' replied Gussie in the same tone.

'I don't suppose I'm likely to,' she said with resignation. 'There doesn't seem to be much of it round. I suppose it's the shortage of optimists.'

When they reached her flat, she leaned against the railings with her legs crossed and her hands behind her back – again a boyish attitude which attracted Gussie.

'Well, good night, Miss Romantic,' he said ceremoniously, taking her hand and kissing it.

'Good night, Don Juan,' she replied to Gussie's infinite delight. Nobody had ever called Gussie that before.

'When do I see you again?'

'Are you sure you want to see me?' she asked with light mockery. 'An old-fashioned girl like me!'

'I still have hopes of converting you,' said Gussie.

'That's marvellous,' she said. 'I love being converted. I was nearly converted by a parson once. Give us a ring-up some time.'

'I will to be sure,' said Gussie, and it was not until he reached the canal bridge that he realized he had really meant: 'What a fool you think I am!' He felt sore all over. 'The trouble with me is that I'm getting things too easy,' he thought.

He felt exactly like a man with a thousand a year whom some-body wanted to push back into the thirty-shillings-a-week class. Thirty shillings a week was all right when you had never been accustomed to anything else, but to Gussie it meant only one thing – destitution. He knew exactly what he would be letting himself in for if he took the girl on her own terms; the same thing that some poor devil of a boy was enduring with her now; park benches and canal banks with a sixty-mile-an-hour gale blowing round the corner, and finally she would be detained at the office – by a good-looking chap in uniform. 'What a fool I am!' he thought mockingly.

But even to find himself summing up the odds like this was a new experience for Gussie. He was attracted by the girl; he couldn't deny that. Instead of crossing the bridge he turned up the moonlit walk by the canal. This was another new thing and he commented ironically on it to himself. 'Now this, Gussie,' he said, 'is what you'll be letting yourself in for if you're not careful.' He suddenly realized what it was that attracted him. It was her resemblance to Joan, a girl who had crossed for a moment his lonely boyhood. He had haunted the roads at night, trying to catch even a glimpse of her as she passed. She was a tall, thin, reedy girl, and, though Gussie did not know it, already far gone with the disease which killed her. On the night before she left for the sanatorium he had met her coming from town, and as they came up the hill she had suddenly slipped her hand into his. So she too, it seemed, had been lonely. He had been too shy to look for more; he hadn't even wished to ask for more. Perfectly happy, he had held her hand the whole way home and neither had spoken a word. It had been some-thing complete and perfect, for in six months' time she was dead. He still dreamt of her sometimes. Once he dreamt that she came into the room where he was sitting with Francie, and sat on the other side of him and spoke to Francie in French, but Francie was too indignant to reply.

And now, here he was fifteen years later feeling the same sort of thing about another girl who merely reminded him of her, and though he knew Helen was talking rubbish he understood perfectly what she wanted; what Joan had wanted that night before she went to the sanatorium; something bigger than life that would last beyond death. He felt himself a brute for trying to deprive her of her illusions. Perhaps people couldn't do without illusions. Walking by the canal in the moonlight, Gussie felt he would give anything to be able to feel like that about a woman again. Even a sixty-mile-an-hour gale would not have put him off.

Then, as he came back up the street from the opposite direction, he noticed how the moonlight fell on the doctors' houses at the other side. His was in darkness. He put his key in the lock and then started, feeling frightened and weak. There was a figure by the door, leaning back against the railings, her hands by her side, her face very white. She stood there as though hoping he would pass without noticing her. 'It's Joan' was his first thought, and then: 'She's come back,' and finally, with a growing feeling of incredulity: 'So it does last.' He looked again and saw who it really was.

'My goodness, Helen,' he said almost petulantly, 'what are you doing here?'

'Well,' she said in a low voice, doing her best to smile, 'you see I was converted after all.'

He led her silently up the stairs with a growing feeling of relief, but it wasn't until they were in his own flat that he really knew how overjoyed he was. It was all over now, but he felt he had been through a really terrible temptation, the temptation of a lifetime. Only that people might interpret it wrongly, and he was really a most decorous man, he would have said his guardian angel had been looking after him.

Sons of bitches! That's what they are, to a man.

The Bridal Night

IT was sunset, and the two great humps of rock made a twilight in the cove where the boats were lying high up the strand. There was one light only in a little whitewashed cottage. Around the headland came a boat and the heavy dipping of its oars was like a heron's flight. The old woman was sitting on the low stone wall outside her cottage.

''Tis a lonesome place,' said I.

''Tis so,' she agreed, 'a lonesome place, but any place is lonesome without one you'd care for.'

'Your own flock are gone from you, I suppose?' I asked.

'I never had but the one,' she replied, 'the one son only,' and I knew because she did not add a prayer for his soul that he was still alive.

'Is it in America he is?' I asked. (It is to America all the boys of the locality go when they leave home.)

'No, then,' she replied simply. 'It is in the asylum in Cork he is on me these twelve years.'

I had no fear of trespassing on her emotions. These lonesome people in wild places, it is their nature to speak; they must cry out their sorrows like the wild birds.

'God help us!' I said. 'Far enough!'

'Far enough,' she sighed. 'Too far for an old woman. There was a nice priest here one time brought me up in his car to see him. All the ways to this wild place he brought it, and he drove me into the city. It is a place I was never used to, but it eased my mind to see poor Denis well-cared-for and well-liked. It was a trouble to me before that, not knowing would they see what a good boy he was before his madness came on him. He knew me; he saluted me, but he said nothing until the superintendent came to tell me the tea was ready for me. Then poor Denis raised his head and says: "Leave ye not forget the toast. She was ever a great one for her bit of toast." It seemed to give him ease and he cried after. A good boy he was and is. It was like him after seven long years to think of his old mother and her little bit of toast.'

'God help us,' I said for her voice was like the birds', hurrying high, immensely high, in the coloured light, out to sea to the last islands where their nests were.

'Blessed be His holy will,' the old woman added, 'there is no turning aside what is in store. It was a teacher that was here at the time. Miss Regan her name was. She was a fine big jolly girl from the town. Her father had a shop there. They said she had three hundred pounds to her own cheek the day she set foot in the school, and – 'tis hard to believe but 'tis what they all said: I will not belie her – 'twasn't banished she was at all but she came here of her own choice, for the great liking she had for the sea and the mountains. Now, that is the story, and with my own eyes I saw her, day in day out, coming down the little pathway you came yourself from the road and sitting beyond there in a hollow you can hardly see, out of the wind. The neighbours could make nothing of it, and she being a stranger, and with only the book Irish, they left her alone. It never seemed to take a peg out of her, only sitting in that hole in the rocks, as happy as the day is long, reading her little book or writing her letters. Of an odd time she might bring one of the little scholars along with her to be picking posies.

'That was where my Denis saw her. He'd go up to her of an evening and sit on the grass beside her, and off and on he might take her out in the boat with him. And she'd say with that big laugh of hers: "Denis is my beau." Those now were her words and she meant no more harm by it than the child unborn, and I knew it and Denis knew it, and it was a little joke we had, the three of us. It was the same way she used to joke about her little hollow. "Mrs Sullivan," she'd say, "leave no one near it. It is my nest and my cell and my little prayer-house, and maybe I would be like the birds and catch the smell of the stranger and then fly away from ye all." It did me good to hear her laugh, and whenever I saw Denis moping or idle I would say it to him myself: "Denis, why wouldn't you go out and pay your attentions to Miss Regan and all saying you are her intended?" It was only a joke. I would say the same thing to her face, for Denis was such a quiet boy, no way rough or accustomed to the girls at all – and how would he in this lonesome place?

'I will not belie her; it was she saw first that poor Denis was after more than company, and it was not to this cove she came at all then but to the little cove beyond the headland, and 'tis hardly she would go there itself without a little scholar along with her. "Ah," I says, for I missed her company, "isn't it the great stranger Miss Regan is becoming?" and Denis would put on his coat and go hunting in the dusk till he came to whatever spot she was. Little ease that was to him, poor boy, for he lost his tongue entirely, and lying on his belly before her, chewing an old bit of grass, is all he would do till she got up and left him. He could not help himself, poor boy. The madness was on him, even then, and it was only when I saw the plunder done that I knew there was no cure for him only to put her out of his mind entirely. For 'twas madness in him and he knew it, and that was what made him lose his tongue – he that was maybe without the price of an ounce of 'baccy – I will not deny it: often enough he had to do without it when the hens would not be laying, and often enough stirabout and praties was all we had for days. And there was she with money to her name in the bank! And that wasn't all, for he was a good boy; a quiet, good-natured boy, and another would take pity on him, knowing he would make her a fine steady husband, but she was not the sort, and well I knew it from the first day I laid eyes on her, that her hand would never rock the cradle. There was the madness out and out.

'So here was I, pulling and hauling, coaxing him to stop at home, and hiding whatever little thing was to be done till evening the way his hands would not be idle. But he had no heart in the work, only listening, always listening, or climbing the cnuceen to see would he catch a glimpse of her coming or going. And, oh, Mary, the heavy sigh he'd give when his bit of supper was over and I bolting the house for the night, and he with the long hours of darkness forninst him – my heart was broken thinking of it. It was the madness, you see. It was on him. He could hardly sleep or eat, and at night I would hear him, turning and groaning as loud as the sea on the rocks.

'It was then when the sleep was a fever to him that he took to walking in the night. I remember well the first night I heard him lift the latch. I put on my few things and went out after him. It was standing here I heard his feet on the stile. I went back and latched the door and hurried after him. What else could I do, and this place terrible after the fall of night with rocks and hills and water and streams, and he, poor soul, blinded with the dint of sleep. He travelled the road a piece, and then took to the hills and I followed him with my legs all torn with briars and furze. It was over beyond by the new house that he gave up. He turned to me then the way a little child that is running away turns and clings to your knees; he turned to me and said: "Mother, we'll go home now. It was the bad day for you ever you brought me into the world." And as the day was breaking I got him back to bed and covered him up to sleep.

'I was hoping that in time he'd wear himself out, but it was worse he was getting. I was a strong woman then, a mayen-strong woman. I could cart a load of seaweed or dig a field with any man, but the night-walking broke me. I knelt one night before the Blessed Virgin and prayed whatever was to happen, it would happen while the light of life was in me, the way I would not be leaving him lonesome like that in a wild place.

'And it happened the way I prayed. Blessed be God, he woke that night or the next night on me and he roaring. I went in to him but I couldn't hold him. He had the strength of five men. So I went out and locked the door behind me. It was down the hill I faced in the starlight to the little house above the cove. The Donoghues came with me: I will not belie them; they were fine powerful men and good neighbours. The father and the two sons came with me and brought the rope from the boats. It was a hard struggle they had of it and a long time before they got him on the floor, and a longer time before they got the ropes on him. And when they had him tied they put him back into bed for me, and I covered him up, nice and decent, and put a hot stone to his feet to take the chill of the cold floor off him.

'Sean Donoghue spent the night sitting beside the fire with me, and in the morning he sent one of the boys off for the doctor. Then Denis called me in his own voice and I went into him. "Mother," says Denis, "will you leave me this way against the time they come for me?" I hadn't the heart. God knows I hadn't. "Don't do it, Peg," says Sean. "If 'twas a hard job trussing him before, it will be harder the next time, and I won't answer for it."

'"You're a kind neighbour, Sean," says I, "and I would never make little of you, but he is the only son I ever reared and I'd sooner he'd kill me now than shame him at the last."

'So I loosened the ropes on him and he lay there very quiet all day without breaking his fast. Coming on to evening he asked me for the sup of tea and he drank it, and soon after the doctor and another man came in the car. They said a few words to Denis but he made them no answer and the doctor gave me the bit of writing. "It will be tomorrow before they come for him," says he, "and 'tisn't right for you to be alone in the house with the man." But I said I would stop with him and Sean Donoghue said the same.

'When darkness came on there was a little bit of a wind blew up from the sea and Denis began to rave to himself, and it was her name he was calling all the time. "Winnie," that was her name, and it was the first time I heard it spoken. "Who is that he is calling?" says Sean. "It is the schoolmistress," says I, "for though I do not recognize the name, I know 'tis no one else he'd be asking for." "That is a bad sign," says Sean. "He'll get worse as the night goes on and the wind rises. 'Twould be better for me go down and get the boys to put the ropes on him again while he's quiet." And it was then something struck me, and I said: "Maybe if she came to him herself for a minute he would be quiet after." "We can try it anyway," says Sean, "and if the girl has a kind heart she will come."

'It was Sean that went up for her. I would not have the courage to ask her. Her little house is there on the edge of the hill; you can see it as you go back the road with the bit of garden before it the new teacher left grow wild. And it was a true word Sean said for 'twas worse Denis was getting, shouting out against the wind for us to get Winnie for him. Sean was a long time away or maybe I felt it long, and I thought it might be the way she was afeared to come. There are many like that, small blame to them. Then I heard her step that I knew so well on the boreen beside the house and I ran to the door, meaning to say I was sorry for the trouble we were giving her, but when I opened the door Denis called out her name in a loud voice, and the crying fit came on me, thinking how light-hearted we used to be together.

'I couldn't help it, and she pushed in apast me into the bedroom with her face as white as that wall. The candle was lighting on the dresser. He turned to her roaring with the mad look in his eyes, and then went quiet all of a sudden, seeing her like that overright him with her hair all rumbled in the wind. I was coming behind her. I heard it. He put up his two poor hands and the red mark of the ropes on his wrists and whispered to her: "Winnie, asthore, isn't it the long time you were away from me?"

'"It is, Denis, it is indeed," says she, "but you know I couldn't help it."

'"Don't leave me any more now, Winnie," says he, and then he said no more, only the two eyes lighting out on her as she sat by the bed. And Sean Donoghue brought in the little stooleen for me, and there we were, the three of us, talking, and Denis paying us no attention, only staring at her.

'"Winnie," says he, "lie down here beside me."

'"Oye," says Sean, humouring him, "don't you know the poor girl is played out after her day's work? She must go home to bed."

'"No, no, no," says Denis and the terrible mad light in his eyes. "There is a high wind blowing and 'tis no night for one like her to be out. Leave her sleep here beside me. Leave her creep in under the clothes to me the way I'll keep her warm."

'"Oh, oh, oh, oh," says I, "indeed and indeed, Miss Regan, 'tis I'm sorry for bringing you here. 'Tisn't my son is talking at all but the madness in him. I'll go now," says I, "and bring Sean's boys to put the ropes on him again."

'"No, Mrs Sullivan," says she in a quiet voice. "Don't do that at all. I'll stop here with him and he'll go fast asleep. Won't you, Denis?"

'"I will, I will," says he, "but come under the clothes to

me. There does a terrible draught blow under that door."

'"I will indeed, Denis," says she, "if you'll promise me to go to sleep."

'"Oye, whisht, girl," says I. "'Tis you that's mad. While you're here you're in my charge, and how would I answer to your father if you stopped in here by yourself?"

'"Never mind about me, Mrs Sullivan," she said. "I'm not a bit in dread of Denis. I promise you there will no harm come to me. You and Mr Donoghue can sit outside in the kitchen and I'll be all right here."

'She had a worried look but there was something about her there was no mistaking. I wouldn't take it on myself to cross the girl. We went out to the kitchen, Sean and myself, and we heard every whisper that passed between them. She got into the bed beside him: I heard her. He was whispering into her ear the sort of foolish things boys do be saying at that age, and then we heard no more only the pair of them breathing. I went to the room door and looked in. He was lying with his arm about her and his head on her bosom, sleeping like a child, sleeping like he slept in his good days with no worry at all on his poor face. She did not look at me and I did not speak to her. My heart was too full. God help us, it was an old song of my father's that was going through my head: "Lonely Rock is the one wife my children will know."

'Later on, the candle went out and I did not light another. I wasn't a bit afraid for her then. The storm blew up and he slept through it all, breathing nice and even. When it was light I made a cup of tea for her and beckoned her from the room door. She loosened his hold and slipped out of bed. Then he stirred and opened his eyes.

'"Winnie," says he, "where are you going?"

'"I'm going to work, Denis," says she. "Don't you know I must be at school early?"

'"But you'll come back to me tonight, Winnie?" says he.

'"I will, Denis," says she. "I'll come back, never fear."

'And he turned on his side and went fast asleep again.

'When she walked into the kitchen I went on my two knees before her and kissed her hands. I did so. There would no words come to me, and we sat there, the three of us, over our tea, and I declare for the time being I felt 'twas worth it all, all the troubles of his birth and rearing and all the lonesome years ahead.

'It was a great ease to us. Poor Denis never stirred, and when the police came he went along with them without commotion or handcuffs or anything that would shame him, and all the words he said to me was: "Mother, tell Winnie I'll be expecting her."

'And isn't it a strange and wonderful thing? From that day to the day she left us there did no one speak a bad word about what she did, and the people couldn't do enough for her. Isn't it a strange thing and the world as wicked as it is, that no one would say the bad word about her?'

Darkness had fallen over the Atlantic, blank grey to its farthest reaches.

A Salesman's Romance

My friend, Charlie Ford, was a commercial traveller in the office-equipment business, and one of the nicest commercials I have known. And, in spite of all the propaganda against them, you meet some very nice commercials. At their best, they are artists in their own right; people who make something out of nothing.

Charlie had only one drawback from my point of view, which was that he could never resist trying to sell me things, just for practice. And they did not have to be office chairs or any other sort of commodity. That is the sign of the true salesman; it isn't the money alone that appeals to him; it is salesmanship for its own sweet sake.

Charlie, for instance, was from Connemara, and wild horses wouldn't have dragged him back to it, but I could not mention Connemara over a drink without Charlie's trying to sell it to me, and the tears would come in his eyes and a catch would come in his voice, and the Mother Machrees and the evening rosaries would get so colourful that nothing but blasphemy would put a stop to them. Then he would smile sadly at me, put a fat hand firmly on my shoulder, and tell me in a deep voice that he wished I did not talk like a wrecker. I wasn't a real wrecker, of course, not at heart. Other people might think so but he knew that at heart I loved all those beautiful things as much as he did, and concealed it only out of modesty. And I declare to my God, before I knew where I was, Charlie would be selling me a substitute self with a heart of gold that the manufacturers would replace within two years unless it gave perfect satisfaction. All the same Charlie liked me. I was a sort of laboratory for him, and whenever he succeeded in selling me anything like a new movie or a funny story, it set him up for a week.

Charlie was engaged to a girl called Celia Halligan. Celia was handsome, she had a dirty tongue and an attitude of cynical but good-humoured contempt for men, yet even she could not resist the coloured enlargement of herself that Charlie presented to her in a gilt frame, and he had only to give her a sweet, sad smile to make her skip demurely back into it.

Now, one night the two of them were motoring back from a pub outside Rathfarnham, cruising gently down the mountainside, admiring the toylike, whitewashed cottages above them and the valley of the city far below with the lamplit prow of Howth thrusting out into Dublin Bay, when all at once as they turned a corner, there was a jaunting car ahead of them, going hoppity-bump with no lights on the wrong side of the road. Charlie was a first-rate driver and boasted that he had been driving for fifteen years without an accident. He did not rush his car into the ditch or try to pass out. Instead, he put his brakes on hard and ran the bonnet of his car under the well of the jaunting car without doing any more damage than to raise the driver and pitch him gently forward on the back of his old horse. The bump was so slight that the jarvey's bowler hat still remained on his head, and the horse, who had all the sense of responsibility required by the situation, stopped dead with the jarvey plastered affectionately across his back, and waited for somebody to do something.

Then presence of mind came to the jarvey's assistance: he judged the road and the steadiness of the horse and the intentions of the driver behind him, and slid gently to the ground. It was as neat a bit of work as Charlie had seen in years. By the time Charlie reached him, he was doing a convincing take-off of unconsciousness that deceived even Celia.

'Is that fellow dead, Cha?' she asked anxiously.

'No, dear, only stunned,' Charlie replied comfortingly, but it was he who felt stunned. He knew he had a ripe and subtle intelligence to deal with. Then he cursed softly because he heard two cyclists talking as they pushed their bikes up the hill. The jarvey heard them too, and lay doggo till all the proper questions had been asked. Then he opened his red-rimmed eyes and asked feebly:

'Where am I?'

'In the presence of witnesses,' retorted Charlie who couldn't resist it. The jarvey, a small man with a thin, mournful face that had the blue glaze of the confirmed alcoholic all over it, looked at him reproachfully. Charlie could smell the whisky off him from the side of the road.

When they had found a farm-labourer to look after the horse and car the jarvey, whose name turned out to be Clarke, permitted himself to be driven to hospital, and an over-conscientious medical student decided to detain him for the night, while Charlie went off to report the accident to the guards with a certain sour satisfaction at the thought of the presence of mind that enabled a boozy little man like that to seize on a moment's opportunity and turn it into a career.

And a career it looked like becoming. The solicitor for the insurance company, an old friend of Charlie's called Cronin, agreed to defend the case, but this was mainly on Charlie's account because Charlie felt about his driving as good women feel about their reputation. You could call Charlie a sex-fiend and he only smiled; you could call him a swindler and he positively chortled, but suggest that he hadn't taken proper precautions at a corner and you were in danger of losing a friend.

As the weeks went by, the jarvey's case grew like a masterpiece in the mind of a great artist. It looked as if it would never stop. After months he was still in bed, because, according to himself, he got reelings when he rose.

'Ah, it's the girl,' said Cronin, a cheerful, noisy little man who was never depressed about anything except the law.

'What has Celia to do with it?' Charlie asked sternly.

'You'll soon see when they ask you what you were doing with her in the car,' said Cronin gloomily. 'I told you to let the case go.'

'But that's scandalous,' Charlie said hotly. 'I'm not the man to do that sort of thing when I'm driving.'

'You're not like hell,' said Cronin cynically, leaving Charlie uncertain whether to take it as a compliment or not.

Altogether it was a shocking experience for Charlie. He was a man of eager temperament, not the sort to have a thing like that hanging over him for months, and he had the illusion, common to eager men, that all he had to do to speed it up was to call regularly on Cronin whose office was in a little lane off Dame Street, a sunless hole where Charlie could not imagine any prosperous professional man choosing to work. Usually he had to wait for half an hour in the outer office with secretaries as unattractive as the room, and passed the time in trying to sell them his version of the accident. When finally he was admitted and learned that nothing had happened, he burst into a long tirade to which Cronin listened, sitting back in his chair balancing a pencil and looking bored and depressed. Charlie could not stop trying to sell you things, and again he tried to sell Cronin the scandalous story of the drunken jarvey, and the idea that he should bring a counter-suit against the jarvey, but he was beginning to see that you couldn't sell a lawyer a safety-pin even if his braces had burst.

'You don't understand these things, Charlie,' Cronin said wearily, leaning farther back in his chair and playing patiently with his pencil. 'Linnane isn't going to do anything like that. This is a jury case, and juries are trickier than judges and judges are trickier than the devil. You're a fine-looking, well-dressed man, and by your own account this jarvey is a shrimp. Now, what happens if you get a jury of shrimps is that they'll decide the poor shrimp in the box is entitled to compensation for life from the insurance company. They can damn well afford it. If you were a shrimp you'd feel the same. Forget about the booze!'

By the time the case came up for hearing, Charlie was feeling a wreck. For two nights he hadn't slept, going carefully over all the points on which the other side might try to trap him, and all the sins of his past life that they might resurrect against him. Counsel for the jarvey was an old acquaintance of Celia's called Michael Dunn, and Charlie hoped that on this account he might show some consideration. On the other hand, if he decided not to do so, he would know more about Charlie than was desirable. It was a bad business. He went to court with Celia, feeling like death, and saying in a dull voice that he didn't know if he'd ever be able to drive again. It would hang over him for the rest of his days, and it was blackmail, and everyone knew it was blackmail, but the State permitted it and the lawyers encouraged it. Celia said nothing at all. She thought it would have been cheaper to buy off the jarvey for a few pounds. She was going to a dance that night with another man. She had asked Charlie to bring her but he had refused. He even thought it heartless of her, considering that he was a man with no future. And there, at the other end of the seat from him was the jarvey who had blasted his career, looking sick and resigned, his bowler hat on the seat beside him.

Charlie leant forward over the seat ahead of him as he concentrated on the first case, and his depression grew because he didn't understand a word of it. The judge was an oldish man with pink cheeks and white hair. He seemed to be deaf and irritated by everybody. Then the jarvey's case was called and Michael Dunn rose. He was a tall, ascetic-looking man with a neat black moustache and big, dark glasses. To his alarm, Charlie noticed that no considerations of friendship seemed to restrain him in the remarks he made.

The jarvey himself was called and went slowly up the court-room, looking as though he might drop dead at any moment. He answered questions in an ailing voice that was barely audible from the jury-box. He had the jarvey's technique of plausibility, and treated the court as if it were a party of American tourists he was taking on a conducted tour of the Lakes of Killarney. He pointed to the places where he felt the pains as though they were of historic importance. As for reward, he indicated that he was an unworldly little man with no notion of the value of money, and he left it entirely to the natural generosity of his fares. Charlie began to realize that Cronin and Linnane had known what they were about. He knew the technique and despised it. It was the technique of the poor mouth.

Fortunately, it became obvious after a quarter of an hour that the judge thought he was trying another case and was confusing the jarvey with a truck driver who had been hit by a railway wagon. Michael Dunn in his attempt at getting his Lordship on to the right track went into convulsions of deference, almost suggesting that there wasn't really much difference between a jaunting car and a truck, but the judge wasn't having any. He had been insulted and he was going to take it out on somebody. He got down behind his bench as though he were taking up a firing position from which to decimate the court.

'I'd be very pleased if Counsel would realize that I still have my wits about me,' he snapped.

'I beg your Lordship's pardon,' said Dunn. 'I wasn't suggesting for an instant – '

'And though I may not be quite as young as Counsel, I still know the difference between a truck and a jaunting car,' said the judge, and he continued to make comments which ignored witness and counsel till the poor jarvey's pose was completely broken down and he was yelling. The atmosphere of the conducted tour had been completely dissipated.

That did the trick. Charlie had been growing more and more disgusted, more and more terrified, as his own turn drew nearer. Then as he strolled slowly up the court-room to the witness stand he had a sudden moment of revelation and joy. He recited the oath in a thrilling voice that made it perfectly clear that here at least was a man who knew the meaning of words. The judge glanced at him with the air of a child who sees a new toy. Charlie bowed very low to the judge, who was so astonished that he bowed back, then he bowed – not quite so low – to the jury, gave them a winning smile, and sat down, crossing his legs. In that moment of revelation he had seen that the wretched occupants of the court were distracted with boredom, and he knew that the only cure for boredom was to buy something. The whole country was mad with boredom because it had been brought up to count every penny. To express your faith in life it was necessary to buy a stake in the future.

So Charlie proceeded to sell the jury the story which no lawyer would buy. He took Linnane's questions for what they should have been rather than what they were, and disposed of them as though they were no more than the promptings of a good listener. He demonstrated exactly how the supposed accident had occurred, using his hands, his feet, and his magnificent voice till even the judge turned into a possible customer. He threw in amusing little side-swipes at the County Council and the condition of the roads, at the habits of Irish motorists, and – completely ignoring Cronin's warning – at the jarvey's drunkenness as well. Dunn was on his feet at once, protesting, but the judge had still not forgiven him his unmannerly correction and snubbed him. He said that Charlie struck him as an honest and observant witness who told his story in a straightforward and, above all, audible way.

Even when Dunn got up to cross-examine, Charlie did not feel in the least rattled. On the contrary. He no longer saw Dunn as an inquisitor with subtle devices for forcing him to reveal the secrets of his past life, but as a wrecker, a man without confidence, the sort of small-town expert who sneers at even the finest office furniture. Charlie put on the air of melancholy suitable to such a mean-spirited wretch. Dunn, who had a trick of looking away as though in search of inspiration, tried to suggest to Charlie that he was speaking from depths of meditation that no one had ever reached.

'Mr Ford,' he said, looking at Charlie contemptuously over the big horn-rimmed spectacles, 'you ventured to suggest that my client was under the influence of liquor on the night in question. Now, before we go any further, perhaps you wouldn't mind enlightening the court as to where you and your lady friend were coming from?'

'Not in the least,' Charlie replied sweetly. 'We were coming from the Red Cow.'

'The Red Cow?' repeated Dunn, who was under the illusion that to look at the ceiling and repeat a name as though he had never heard it before was a good way of making it seem significant. 'Would I be correct in assuming that the Red Cow is a hostelry?'

'You'd hardly be correct in assuming it, Mr Dunn,' Charlie replied with quiet amusement. 'Assumptions are made about things of which we have no direct knowledge.'

There was a chuckle from the jury-box at this, and Dunn grew red and went on in a hurry.

'And did you have some – um – refreshment there?'

'Yes, sir,' Charlie said meekly. 'That is generally my purpose in going to a bar.'

Dunn pointed at the judge.

'Tell my lord and the jury how many drinks you had.'

'Three,' Charlie said steadily. 'You see, Mr Dunn, it was a very hot night, and I'd been driving for a good part of the day, so I was rather thirsty.'

'And you ask the court to believe that after three drinks – on a very hot night – when you'd been driving for a good part of the day, as you've admitted – you were still capable of driving a car properly?'

'I ask the court to believe that if I wasn't capable of driving properly I wouldn't be driving at all,' said Charlie sternly.

'The guards made no test to ascertain if you were capable of driving?'

'I presume the guards are aware that there is no test known to science that will prove the existence of lemonade in the system,' replied Charlie.

Of course, Charlie didn't know whether there was or not, nor was there much danger of his being examined about it if there was. For several of the jurymen laughed outright and even the judge gave a smile of glee. His own style of wit was rather like that.

'You mean you drink nothing but lemonade?' asked Dunn, who was beginning to lose his temper and with good reason, for it was not often that he had a witness like Charlie to deal with. But Charlie was beginning to get tired of him; he knew that if he was to complete his sale he must crush this knowing customer, so he paused a moment before replying.

'I mean nothing of the sort, Mr Dunn,' he said gravely. 'I mean that a man who drinks anything stronger when he's in charge of a car is a dangerous lunatic.'

'An exceedingly proper remark,' said the judge, nodding four times and knocking his bench in approval. Nothing goes down so well in a court of law as a well-aimed platitude.

Dunn had given up hope of shaking this unruly man, and contented himself with a few perfunctory questions intended to suggest that Charlie and Celia had been too busy in the car to pay attention to the road.

'This young lady and you are friends?' asked Dunn.

'No, Mr Dunn,' Charlie said gently. 'Just engaged.'

'And you hadn't your arm about her shoulder?'

'Ah, no, Mr Dunn,' Charlie said wearily. 'You and I ought to be beyond the adolescent stage.'

This produced a real roar and after a few further efforts Dunn sat down and pretended to be absorbed in his papers. Charlie bowed again to the judge and jury and returned to his seat with the transfigured air of a man who has been to the altar. Cronin winked at him, but Charlie failed to return the wink. Instead he smiled wanly, and closing his eyes, covered them with his fat hand. Charlie of course knew as well as Cronin did that the case was in the bag. Charlie, the universal salesman, had sold his story to the jury and nothing short of an earthquake would break the spell he had woven about them.

But then it was Celia's turn, and Charlie's heart sank when he saw that she had learned nothing from his example. Instead of taking the oath as though she had been waiting months for it, she had it extracted from her word by word like teeth. She looked beautiful and angry, and what was worse, alarmed, and Charlie knew within a few moments that ner unhappiness was spreading to the court-room. She replied to Linnane's friendly questions as though he were cross-examining her, and when Dunn rose she gave him a positive scowl. Charlie hoped that as an old friend of the family he might show some sense of decency, but he was still smarting under Charlie's thrusts.

'And were you also drinking lemonade, Miss Halligan?' he asked with his shoulders hunched while he jingled the coins in his trousers pockets.

'Ah, I was not,' she snapped with a shrug. 'I wouldn't touch the blooming stuff.'

Charlie had noticed the impressive effect of a platitude; now he noticed the effect of a simple statement of prejudice. A shudder seemed to go through the court.

'Tell the court what you were drinking.'

'I was drinking whisky, of course,' she replied in a shrill, shocked tone. 'What do you think?'

Dunn bent forward and looked at her satanically over his glasses.

'I have no opinion, Miss Halligan,' he said reprovingly. 'I

merely wish to find out if at the time of this accident you weren't a little – elevated, shall we say?'

'Is it after three small ones?' she asked incredulously. 'What do you take me for?'

At this point Linnane tried to go to Celia's rescue, but the judge had taken an instant dislike to her. The judge lived in hope that one of these days he would find one of those modern girls before him so that he could say what he really thought about them. He knew it would make headlines, and like most judges he longed for headlines. He had a strong suspicion that Celia was a modern young woman. He told her that this was a court of law, and he would not permit her to reply to counsel in that impudent fashion, at which Celia, who had no intention of being impudent, looked mutinous as well as angry. He held the case up for several minutes to glower at her, waiting for a back-answer that would give the opportunity he wanted. Dunn knew that the signals were set at clear for him, and though Linnane again intervened, the judge snorted that the witness appeared to be one of those modern young women, so she probably expected to be dealt with in a modern way.

Charlie covered his face entirely. To give him his due, he went through agonies. As Dunn framed each question, he answered it in his own mind, tossing off the awkward ones with light feminine banter, lingering gravely over those that raised moral issues; smiling, frowning, and even prepared to shed a tear behind his hands. And on top of the ideal reply came the real one, all in one tone, bewildered and maddened and sounding as though it came from the lips of some international courtesan. Dunn made her admit that she was often at the Red Cow, that she had gone there for years with different men; that she had been kissing Charlie in the car before they started, and almost trapped her into saying that she was in no state to describe what had happened. 'Salesmanship!' Charlie thought despairingly. 'That's what the girl lacks. Salesmanship!'

She came down off the stand, sulky and furious. Charlie rose and stepped out into the passageway with an angelic, welcoming smile to let her into the seat beside him, and tried to put his hand comfortingly on hers, but she pushed past him as though he were to blame for everything and stalked out of the court. He had to wait for the verdict, and though it represented victory for him, it brought him no satisfaction. It even left him wondering why he had gone to all that trouble instead of allowing the insurance company to buy off the jarvey.

Next morning in town he ran into a gossipy woman who had heard all about the case and wanted to talk of it.

'And I saw Celia at the dance last night,' she went on joyously. 'And I'll give you three guesses who she was dancing with.'

'Who, Babe?' asked Charlie, kidding her on.

'Michael Dunn!'

'Dunn?' Charlie asked incredulously. 'Are you sure, Babe?'

'Sure, I saw her, I tell you. He went up and talked to her, and they were laughing and joking, and the next thing was I saw them dancing. Now, what do you make of that?'

'I don't know what to make of it, Babe,' Charlie said, shaking his head gravely. 'I'd hardly have expected it of her.'

But Celia gave him no satisfaction at all. She seemed surprised and irritated by his attitude.

'But why wouldn't I dance with him?' she asked. 'Sure, he only did what he was paid for, the same as anyone else. He'd do the same thing to his own mother. Did you ever know a lawyer that wouldn't?'

But reasonable as she made it sound, it carried no conviction to Charlie. Reason had never yet made a woman friendly to a man she had cause to dislike. Could it be that she hadn't really resented Dunn's tone? That she might even have enjoyed it?

He was still more upset when she returned the ring and told him she was marrying Dunn. Charlie was a rational man, and like all rational men took the irrational hard. It wasn't only the loss of Celia that hurt him, though that was bad enough; it wasn't even the unfairness of her going to the Red Cow with Dunn, as he saw her do with his own eyes. It was the unreasonableness of it all. He took to the drink, and for months it looked as if he would never be himself again. Woebegone and haggard, he went over every detail of it with his friends a hundred times. But gradually as he repeated it, he began to realize that it was an excellent story, a story you could sell to prospective customers. 'Did I ever tell you,' he would ask with a wistful smile, 'how I won the case and lost the girl?'

Suddenly, Charlie was himself again. Art had triumphed over Nature. It was the old story – 'Out of my great sorrows I made little songs.'

In the Train

I

'THERE!' said the sergeant's wife. 'You would hurry me.'

'I always like being in time for a train,' replied the sergeant, with the equability of one who has many times before explained the guiding principle of his existence.

'I'd have had heaps of time to buy the hat,' added his wife.

The sergeant sighed and opened his evening paper. His wife looked out on the dark platform, pitted with pale lights under which faces and faces passed, lit up and dimmed again. A uniformed lad strode up and down with a tray of periodicals and chocolates. Farther up the platform a drunken man was being seen off by his friends.

'I'm very fond of Michael O'Leary,' he shouted. 'He is the most sincere man I know.'

'I have no life,' sighed the sergeant's wife. 'No life at all. There isn't a soul to speak to; nothing to look at all day but bogs and mountains and rain – always rain! And the people! Well, we've had a fine sample of them, haven't we?'

The sergeant continued to read.

'Just for the few days it's been like heaven. Such interesting people! Oh, I thought Mr Boyle had a glorious face! And his voice – it went through me.'

The sergeant lowered his paper, took off his peaked cap, laid it on the seat beside him, and lit his pipe. He lit it in the old-fashioned way, ceremoniously, his eyes blinking pleasurably like a sleepy cat's in the match-flare. His wife scrutinized each face that passed and it was plain that for her life meant faces and people and things and nothing more.

'Oh, dear!' she said again. 'I simply have no existence. I was educated in a convent and play the piano; my father was a literary man, and yet I am compelled to associate with the lowest types of humanity. If it was even a decent town, but a village!'

'Ah,' said the sergeant, gapping his reply with anxious puffs, 'maybe with God's help we'll get a shift one of these days.' But he said it without conviction, and it was also plain that he was well-pleased with himself, with the prospect of returning home with his pipe and his paper.

'Here are Magner and the others,' said his wife as four other policemen passed the barrier. 'I hope they'll have sense enough to let us alone. . . . How do you do? How do you do? Had a nice time, boys?' she called with sudden animation, and her pale, sullen face became warm and vivacious. The policemen smiled and touched their caps but did not halt.

'They might have stopped to say good evening,' she added sharply, and her face sank into its old expression of boredom and dissatisfaction. 'I don't think I'll ask Delancey to tea again. The others make an attempt but, really, Delancey is hopeless. When I smile and say: "Guard Delancey, wouldn't you like to use the butter-knife?" he just scowls at me from under his shaggy brows and says without a moment's hesitation: "I would not."'

'Ah, Delancey is a poor slob,' the sergeant said affectionately.

'Oh, yes, but that's not enough, Jonathan. Slob or no slob, he should make an attempt. He's a young man; he should have a dinner jacket at least. What sort of wife will he get if he won't even wear a dinner jacket?'

'He's easy, I'd say. He's after a farm in Waterford.'

'Oh, a farm! A farm! The wife is only an incidental, I suppose?'

'Well, now, from all I hear she's a damn nice little incidental.'

'Yes, I suppose many a nice little incidental came from a farm,' answered his wife, raising her pale brows. But the irony was lost on him.

'Indeed yes, indeed yes,' he said fervently.

'And here,' she added in biting tones, 'come our charming neighbours.'

Into the pale lamplight stepped a group of peasants. Not such as one sees near a capital but in the mountains and along the coasts. Gnarled, wild, with turbulent faces, their ill-cut clothes full of character, the women in pale brown shawls, the men wearing black sombreros and carrying big sticks, they swept in, ill at ease, laughing and shouting defiantly. And so much part of their natural environment were they that for a moment they seemed to create about themselves rocks and bushes, tarns, turf-ricks, and sea.

With a prim smile the sergeant's wife bowed to them through the open window.

'How do you do? How do you do?' she called. 'Had a nice time?'

At the same moment the train gave a jolt and there was a rush in which the excited peasants were carried away. Some minutes passed; the influx of passengers almost ceased, and a porter began to slam the doors. The drunken man's voice rose in a cry of exultation.

'You can't possibly beat O'Leary,' he declared. 'I'd lay down my life for Michael O'Leary.'

Then, just as the train was about to start, a young woman in a brown shawl rushed through the barrier. The shawl, which came low enough to hide her eyes, she held firmly across her mouth, leaving visible only a long thin nose with a hint of pale flesh at either side. Beneath the shawl she was carrying a large parcel.

She looked hastily around; a porter shouted to her and pushed her towards the nearest compartment, which happened to be that occupied by the sergeant and his wife. He had actually seized the handle of the door when the sergeant's wife sat up and screamed.

'Quick! Quick!' she cried. 'Look who it is! She's coming in. Jonathan! Jonathan!'

The sergeant rose with a look of alarm on his broad red face. The porter threw open the door, with his free hand grasping the woman's elbow. But when she laid eyes on the sergeant's startled face she stepped back, tore herself free, and ran crazily up the platform. The engine shrieked; the porter slammed the door with a curse; somewhere another door opened and shut, and the row of watchers, frozen into effigies of farewell, now dark now bright, began to glide gently past the window, and the stale, smoky air was charged with the breath of open fields.

2

The four policemen spread themselves out in a separate compartment and lit cigarettes.

'Poor old Delancey!' Magner said with his reckless laugh. 'He's cracked on her all right.'

'Cracked on her,' agreed Fox. 'Did ye see the eye he gave her?'

Delancey smiled sheepishly. He was a tall, handsome, black-haired young man with the thick eyebrows described by the sergeant's wife. He was new to the force and suffered from a mixture of natural gentleness and country awkwardness.

'I am,' he said in his husky voice. 'The devil admire me, I never hated anyone yet, but I think I hate the living sight of her.'

'Oh now, oh now!' protested Magner.

'I do. I think the Almighty God must have put that one into the world with the one main object of persecuting me.'

'Well indeed,' said Foley, ''tis a mystery to me how the sergeant puts up with her. If any woman up and called me by an outlandish name like Jonathan when everyone knew my name was plain John I'd do fourteen days for her – by God, I would, and a calendar month.'

The four men were now launched on a favourite topic that held them for more than a hour. None of them liked the sergeant's wife and all had stories to tell against her. From these there emerged the fact that she was an incurable scandalmonger and mischiefmaker who couldn't keep quiet about her own business, much less about that of her neighbours. And while they talked the train dragged across a dark plain, the heart of Ireland, and in the moonless night tiny cottage-windows blew past like sparks from a fire, and a pale simulacrum of the lighted carriages leaped and frolicked over hedges and fields. Magner shut the window and the compartment began to fill with smoke.

'She'll never rest till she's out of Farranchreesht,' he said.

'That she mightn't!' groaned Delancey.

'How would you like the city yourself, Dan?' asked Magner.

'Man dear,' exclaimed Delancey with sudden brightness, 'I'd like it fine. There's great life in a city.'

'You're welcome to it,' said Foley, folding his hands across his paunch.

'Why so? What's wrong with it?'

'I'm better off where I am.'

'But the life!'

'Life be damned! What sort of life is it when you're always under someone's eye? Look at the poor devils in court.'

'True enough, true enough,' agreed Fox.

'Ah, yes, yes,' said Delancey, 'but the adventures they have!'

'What adventures?'

'There was a sergeant in court only yesterday telling me one thing that happened himself. 'Twas an old maid without a soul in the world that died in an old loft on the quays. The sergeant put a new man on duty outside the door while he went back to report, and all he had to do was kick the door and frighten off the rats.'

'That's enough, that's enough!' cried Foley.

'Yes, yes, but listen now, listen can't you?' cried Delancey. 'He was there ten minutes with a bit of candle when the door at the foot of the stairs began to open. "Who's there?" says he, getting a bit nervous. "Who's there I say?" No answer, and still the door kept opening. Then he gave a laugh. What was it only an old cat? "Puss, puss," says he, "come on up, puss." Then he gave another look and the hair stood up on his head. There was another bloody cat coming in. "Get out!" says he to scare them, and then another cat came in and then another, and in his fright he dropped the candle. The cats began to hiss and bawl and that robbed him of the last stitch of sense. He made down the stairs, and if he did he trod on a cat, and went down head over heels, and when he tried to grip something 'twas a cat he gripped, and he felt the claws tearing his face. He was out for three weeks after.'

'That's a bloody fine adventure,' said Foley with bitter restraint.

'Isn't it though?' Delancey said eagerly. 'You'd be a long time in Farranchreesht before anything like that would happen you.'

'That's the thing about Farranchreesht, lad,' said Magner.

''Tis a great ease to be able to put on your cap and go for a drink any hour of the day or night.'

'Yes,' added Foley, 'and to know the worst case you're likely to have in ten years is a bit of a scrap about politics.'

'I don't know,' Delancey sighed dreamily. 'Chrisht, there's great charm about the Criminal Courts.'

'Damn the much they had for you when you were in the box,' growled Foley.

'I know, sure, I know,' admitted Delancey crestfallen. 'I was sweating.'

'Shutting your eyes you were,' said Magner, 'like a kid afraid he was going to get a box on the ear.'

'Still,' said Delancey, 'this sergeant I'm talking about, he said after a while you wouldn't mind that no more than if 'twas a card party. He said you'd talk back to the judge as man to man.'

'I dare say that's true,' agreed Magner.

There was silence in the smoky compartment that jolted and rocked on its way across Ireland, and the four occupants, each touched with that morning wit which afflicts no one so much as state witnesses, thought of how they'd speak to the judge now if only they had him before them as man to man. They looked up to see a fat red face behind the door, and a moment later it was dragged back.

'Is this my carriage, gentlemen?' asked a meek and boozy voice.

'No, 'tisn't. Go on with you!' snapped Magner.

'I had as nice a carriage as ever was put on a railway train,' said the drunk, leaning in, 'a handsome carriage, and 'tis lost.'

'Try farther on,' suggested Delancey.

'Ye'll excuse me interrupting yeer conversation, gentlemen.'

'That's all right, that's all right.'

'I'm very melancholic. My best friend, I parted him this very night, and 'tis unknown to anyone, only the Almighty and Merciful God [here the drunk reverently raised his bowler hat and let it slide down the back of his neck to the floor] if I'll ever lay eyes on him again in this world. Good night, gentlemen, and thanks, thanks for all yeer kindness.'

As the drunk slithered away up the corridor Delancey laughed. Fox, who had remained thoughtful, resumed the conversation where it had left off.

'Delancey wasn't the only one that was sweating,' he said.

'He was not,' agreed Foley. 'Even the sergeant was a bit shook.'

'He was very shook. When he caught up the poison mug to identify it he was shaking, and before he could put it down it danced a jig on the table.'

'Ah, dear God, dear God,' sighed Delancey, 'what killed me most entirely was the bloody old model of the house. I didn't mind anything else only the house. There it was, a living likeness, with the bit of grass in front and the shutter hanging loose, and every time I looked at it I was in the back lane in Farranchreesht, and then I'd look up and see the lean fellow in the wig pointing his finger at me.'

'Well, thank God,' said Foley with simple devotion, 'this time tomorrow I'll be in Ned Ivers's back with a pint in my fist.'

Delancey shook his head, a dreamy smile playing upon his dark face.

'I don't know,' he said. ''Tis a small place, Farranchreesht; a small, mangy old place with no interest or advancement in it.' His face lit up as the sergeant appeared in the corridor.

'Here's the sergeant now,' he said.

'He wasn't long getting tired of Julietta,' whispered Magner maliciously.

The door was pushed back and the sergeant entered, loosening the collar of his tunic. He fell into a corner seat, crossed his legs, and accepted the cigarette which Delancey proffered.

'Well, lads,' he exclaimed. 'What about a jorum?'

'Isn't it remarkable?' said Foley. 'I was only just talking about it.'

'I have noted before now, Peter,' said the sergeant, 'that you and me have what might be called a simultaneous thirst.'

3

The country folk were silent and exhausted. Kendillon

drowsed now and then, but he suffered from blood-pressure,
and after a while his breathing grew thicker and stronger till
at last it exploded in a snort and he started up, broad awake
and angry. In the silence rain spluttered and tapped along the
roof and the dark windowpanes streamed with shining runnels
of water that trickled to the floor. Moll Mhor scowled, her
lower lip thrust out. She was a great flop of a woman with a big,
coarse, powerful face. The other two women whose eyes were
closed had their brown shawls drawn tight about their heads,
but Moll's was round her shoulders and the gap above her
breasts was filled with a blaze of scarlet.

'Aren't we home yet?' Kendillon asked crossly, starting
awake after one of his drowsing fits.

Moll glowered at him.

'No, nor won't be. What scour is on you?'

'My little house,' moaned Kendillon.

'My little house,' mimicked Moll. ''Twasn't enough for you
to board the windows and put barbed wire on the gate.'

''Tis all very well for you that have someone to mind yours
for you,' he snarled.

One of the women laughed softly and turned a haggard
virginal face within the cowl of her shawl.

''Tis that have me laughing,' she explained apologetically.
'Tim Dwyer this week past at the stirabout pot.'

'And making the beds,' chimed in the third woman.

'And washing the children's faces! Glory be to God, he'll be
mad.'

'Ay,' said Moll, 'and his chickens running off with Thade
Kendillon's roof.'

'My roof is it?' he asked.

'Yes.'

''Tis a good roof,' he said roughly. ''Tis a better roof than
ever was seen over your head since the day you married.'

'Oh, Mary my mother!' sighed Moll, ''tis a great pity of me
this three hours and I looking at the likes of you instead of my
own fine bouncing man.'

''Tis a new thing to hear you praising Sean then,' said a
woman.

'I wronged him,' Moll said contritely. 'I did so. I wronged him before God and the world.'

At this moment the drunken man pulled back the door of the compartment and looked from face to face with an expression of deepening melancholy.

'She's not here,' he said in disappointment.

'Who's not here, mister?' asked Moll with a wink at the others.

'I'm looking for my own carriage, ma'am,' said the drunk with melancholy dignity, 'and whatever the bloody hell they done with it, 'tis lost. The railways in this country are gone to hell.'

'Wisha, if that's all that's worrying you, wouldn't you sit here with me?' asked Moll. 'I'm here so long I'm forgetting what a real man looks like.'

'I would with great pleasure,' replied the drunk politely, 'but 'tisn't only the carriage. 'Tis my travelling-companion. I'm a lonely man; I parted my best friend this very night; I found one to console me, and then when I turned my back – God took her!'

And with a dramatic gesture he closed the door and continued on his way. The country folk sat up, blinking. The smoke of the men's pipes filled the compartment and the heavy air was laden with the smell of homespun and turf-smoke, the sweet pungent odour of which had penetrated every fibre of their clothes.

'Listen to the rain!' said one of the women. 'We'll have a wet walk home.'

''Twill be midnight before we're in,' said another.

'Ah, what matter sure when the whole country will be up? There'll be a lot of talking done in Farranchreesht tonight.'

'A lot of talking and no sleep.'

'Oh, Farranchreesht! Farranchreesht!' cried the young woman with the haggard face, the ravaged lineaments of which were suddenly transfigured. 'Farranchreesht and the sky over you, I wouldn't change places with the Queen of England tonight!'

And suddenly Farranchreesht, the bare bogland with the

hump-backed mountain behind, the little white houses and the dark fortifications of turf that made it seem like the flame-blackened ruin of some mighty city, all was lit up in their minds. An old man sitting in a corner, smoking a broken clay pipe, thumped his stick on the floor.

'Well now,' said Kendillon darkly, 'wasn't it great impudence in her to come back?'

'Wasn't it indeed?' echoed one of the women.

'I'd say she won't be there long,' he went on knowingly.

'You'll give her the hunt, I suppose?' asked Moll politely, too politely.

'If no one else do, I'll give her the hunt myself. What right have she in a decent place?'

'Oh, the hunt, the hunt,' agreed a woman. 'Sure, no one could ever darken her door again.'

'And what the hell did we tell all the lies for?' asked Moll with her teeth on edge to be at Kendillon. 'Thade Kendillon there swore black was white.'

'What else would I do, woman? There was never an informer in my family.'

'I'm surprised to hear it,' said Moll vindictively, but the old man thumped his stick three or four times for silence.

'We all told our story,' he said, 'and we told it well. And no one told it better than Moll. You'd think to hear her she believed it herself.'

'I declare to God I very nearly did,' she said with a wild laugh.

'I seen great changes in my time, great changes,' the old man said, shaking his head, 'and now I see a greater change still.'

A silence followed his words. There was profound respect in all their eyes. The old man coughed and spat.

'What change is that, Colm?' asked Moll.

'Did any of ye ever think the day would come when a woman in our parish would do the like of that?'

'Never, never.'

'But she might do it for land?'

'She might.'

'Or for money?'

'She might so.'

'She might indeed. When the hunger is money people kill for the money; when the hunger is land people kill for the land. But what are they killing for now? I tell ye, there's a great change coming. In the ease of the world people are asking more. When I was a boy in the barony if you killed a beast you made six pieces of it, one for yourself and the rest for the neighbours. The same if you made a catch of fish. And that's how it was with us from the beginning of time. But now look at the change! The people aren't as poor or as good or as generous or as strong.'

'Or as wild,' added Moll with a vicious glance at Kendillon. ''Tis in the men you'd mostly notice the change.'

The door opened and Magner, Delancey, and the sergeant entered. Magner was already drunk.

'I was lonely without you, Moll,' he said. 'You're the biggest and brazenest and cleverest liar of the lot and you lost me my sergeant's stripes, but I'll forgive you everything if you'll give us one bar of the "Colleen Dhas Roo".'

4

'I'm a lonely man,' said the drunk. 'And I'm going back to a lonely habitation.'

'My best friend,' he continued, 'I left behind me – Michael O'Leary, the most sincere man I know. 'Tis a great pity you don't know Michael and a great pity Michael don't know you. But look at the misfortunate way things happen! I was looking for someone to console me, and the moment I turned my back you were gone.'

He placed his hand solemnly under the woman's chin and raised her face to the light. With the other hand he stroked her cheeks.

'You have a beautiful face,' he said reverently, 'a beautiful face. But what's more important, you have a beautiful soul. I look into your eyes and I see the beauty of your nature. Allow me one favour. Only one favour before we part.'

He bent and kissed her. Then he picked up his bowler which

had fallen once more, put it on back to front, took his dispatch case, and got out.

The woman sat on alone. Her shawl was thrown open and beneath it she wore a bright blue blouse. The carriage was cold, the night outside black and cheerless, and within her something had begun to contract that threatened to crush the very spark of life in her. She could no longer fight it off even when for the hundredth time she went over the scenes of the previous day; the endless hours in the dock, the wearisome questions and speeches she could not understand, and the long wait in the cells till the jury returned. She felt again the shiver of mortal anguish that went through her when the chief warder beckoned angrily from the stairs and the wardress, glancing hastily in a hand-mirror, pushed her forward. She saw the jury with their expressionless faces. She was standing there alone, in nervous twitches jerking back the shawl from her face to give herself air. She was trying to say a prayer but the words were being drowned in her mind by the thunder of nerves, crashing and bursting. She could feel one which had escaped dancing madly at the side of her mouth, but was powerless to recapture it.

'The verdict of the jury is that Helena Maguire is not guilty.' Which was it? Death or life? She could not say. 'Silence! Silence!' shouted the usher though no one had tried to say anything. 'Any other charge?' asked a weary voice. 'Release the prisoner.' 'Silence!' shouted the usher again. The chief warder opened the door of the dock and she began to run. When she reached the steps she stopped and looked back to see if she was being followed. A policeman held open a door and she found herself in an ill-lit, draughty stone corridor. She stood there, the old shawl about her face. The crowd began to emerge. The first was a tall girl with a rapt expression as though she were walking on air. When she saw the woman she halted, her hands went up in an instinctive gesture, as though to feel her, to caress her. It was that look of hers, that gait as of a sleepwalker that brought the woman to her senses. . . .

But now the memory had no warmth in her mind, and the something within her continued to contract, smothering her with loneliness, shame, and fear. She began to mutter crazily to herself. The train, now almost empty, was stopping at every little wayside station. Now and again a blast from the Atlantic pushed at it as though trying to capsize it.

She looked up as the door slammed open and Moll came in, swinging her shawl behind her.

'They're all up the train. Wouldn't you come?'

'No, no, I couldn't.'

'Why couldn't you? Who are you minding? Is it Thade Kendillon?'

'No, no, I'll stop as I am.'

'Here, take a sup of this.' Moll fumbled in her shawl and produced a bottle of liquor as pale as water. 'Wait till I tell you what Magner said! That fellow is a limb of the devil. "Have you e'er a drop, Moll?" says he. "Maybe I have," says I. "What is it?" says he. "For God's sake, baptize it quick and call it whisky."'

The woman took the bottle and put it to her lips. She shivered as she drank.

'"Tis a good drop,' said Moll approvingly.

Next moment there were loud voices in the corridor. Moll grabbed the bottle and hid it under her shawl. But it was only Magner, the sergeant, and Delancey. After them came the two countrywomen, giggling. Magner held out his hand.

'Helena,' he said, 'accept my congratulations.'

She took his hand, smiling awkwardly.

'We'll get you the next time though,' he added.

'Musha, what are you saying, mister?'

'Not a word. You're a clever woman, a remarkable woman, and I give you full credit for it. You threw dust in all our eyes.'

'Poison is supposed to be an easy thing to trace but it beat me to trace it,' said the sergeant, barely concealing his curiosity.

'Well, well, there's things they're saying about me!' she said with a nervous laugh.

'Tell him,' advised Magner. 'There's nothing he can do to you now. You're as safe as the judge himself. Last night when the jury came in with the verdict you could have stood there in the dock and said: "Ye're wrong. I did it. I got the stuff in such and such a place. I gave it to him because he was old and dirty and cantankerous and a miser. I did it and I'm proud of it.' You could have said every word of that and they couldn't have laid a finger on you.'

'Indeed, what a thing I'd say!'

'Well, you could.'

'The law is truly a remarkable phenomenon,' said the sergeant, who was also rather squiffy. 'Here you are, sitting at your ease at the expense of the state, and for one simple word of a couple of letters you could be up in Mountjoy, waiting for the rope and the morning jaunt.'

The woman shuddered. The young woman with the ravaged face looked up.

''Twas the holy will of God,' she said.

''Twas all the bloody lies Moll Mhor told,' replied Magner.

''Twas the will of God.'

'There was many hanged in the wrong,' said the sergeant.

'Even so, even so, 'twas God's will.'

'You have a new blouse, Helena,' said the other woman in an envious tone.

'I seen it last night in a shop on the quays.'

'How much was it?'

'Honour of God!' exclaimed Magner, looking at the woman in stupefaction. 'Is that all you had to think of? You should have been on your bended knees before the altar.'

'And sure I was,' she answered indignantly.

'Women!' exclaimed Magner with a gesture of despair. He winked at Moll and they retired to the next compartment. But the interior was reflected clearly in the corridor window, and the others could see the pale quivering image of the policeman lift the bottle to his lips and blow a long silent blast on it. The young woman who had spoken of the blouse laughed.

'There'll be one good day's work done on the head of the trial,' she said.

'How so?' asked the sergeant.

'Dan Canty will make a great brew of poteen while he have all yeer backs turned.'

'I'll get Dan Canty yet,' replied the sergeant stiffly.

'You will, the way you got Helena.'

'I'll get him yet,' he said as he consulted his watch. 'We'll be in in another quarter of an hour. 'Tis time we were all getting back to our respective compartments.'

Magner entered and the other policemen rose. The sergeant fastened his collar and buckled his belt. Magner swayed, holding the doorframe, a mawkish smile on his thin, handsome, dissipated face.

'Well, good night to you now, ma'am,' said the sergeant primly. 'I'm as glad for all our sakes things ended as they did.'

'Good night, Helena,' said Magner, bowing low and promptly tottering. 'There'll be one happy man in Farran-chreesht tonight.'

'Come on, Joe,' protested the sergeant.

'One happy man,' Magner repeated obstinately. ''Tis his turn now.'

'You're drunk, man,' said Delancey.

'You wanted him,' Magner said heavily. 'Your people wouldn't let you have him but you have him now in spite of them all.'

'Do you mean Cady Driscoll?' hissed the woman with sudden anger, leaning towards Magner, the shawl tight about her head.

'Never mind who I mean. You have him.'

'He's no more to me now than the salt sea.'

The policemen went out first, the women followed, Moll Mhor laughing boisterously. The woman was left alone. Through the window she could see little cottages stepping down over wet and naked rocks to the water's edge. The flame of life had narrowed in her to a pinpoint, and she could only wonder at the force that had caught her up, mastered her and then thrown her aside.

'No more to me,' she repeated dully to her own image in the glass, 'no more to me than the salt sea.'

Pity

DENIS's school was in the heart of the country, miles from anywhere, and this gave the teachers an initial advantage, because before a boy even got to the railway station he had the prefects on his track. Two fellows Denis knew once got as far as Mellin, a town ten miles off, intending to join the British Army, but like fools the first thing they did in Mellin was to go to a hotel, so they were caught in bed in the middle of the night by prefects and brought back. It was reported that they had been flogged on their knees in front of the picture of the Crucifixion in the hall, but no one was ever able to find out the truth about that. Denis thought they must have been inspired by the legend of two fellows who did once actually get on a boat for England and were never heard of afterwards, but that was before his time, and in those days escapes were probably easier. By the time he got there it was said there was a telescope mounted on the tower and that the prefects took turns at watching for fellows trying to get away.

You could understand that, of course, for the fellows were all rough, the sons of small farmers who smoked and gambled and took a drink whenever they got a chance of one. As his mother said, it wasn't a good school, but what could she do, and the small allowance she got from his father? By this time she and his father were living apart.

But one day a new boy came up and spoke to Denis. His name was Francis Cummins and he came from Dunmore where Denis's mother was now living. He wasn't in the least like the other fellows. He was a funny, solemn kid with a head that was too big for his body and a great flow of talk. It seemed that his people intended him for the priesthood, and you could see that he'd make a good sort of priest for he never wanted to do anything wrong, like breaking out, or smoking, or playing cards, and he was a marvel at music. You had only to whistle a tune to him and he could play it after on the piano.

Even the toughs in school let Francis alone. He was a fellow

you couldn't get into a wax, no matter how you tried. He took
every insult with a smile as if he couldn't believe you were
serious, so that there was no satisfaction in trying to make him
mad. And from the first day he almost pursued Denis. The
other fellows in Denis's gang did not like it because if he saw
them doing anything they shouldn't be doing he started at
once to lecture them, exactly like a prefect, but somehow Denis
found it almost impossible to quarrel with him. It was funny
the way you felt to a fellow from your own place in a school
like that, far from everywhere. And they did not know the
feeling that came over Denis at times when he thought of
Dunmore and his home and Martha, for all that he was for
ever fighting with her. Sometimes he would dream of it at
night, and wake up thinking of it, and all that day it would
haunt him in snatches till he felt like throwing himself on his
bed and bawling. And that wasn't possible either, with forty
kids to a room and the beds packed tight in four rows.

There was also another reason for his toleration of a cissy
like Cummins. Every week of Cummins's life he got a parcel
from home, and it was always an astonishment to Denis, for
his parents sent him tinned meat, tinned fruit, sardines, and
everything. Now, Denis was always hungry. The school food
wasn't much at the best of times, and because his mother
couldn't afford the extras, he never got rashers for breakfast
as most of the others did. His father visited him regularly and
kept on inquiring in a worried way if he was all right, but
Denis had been warned not to complain to him, and the pound
or two he gave Denis never lasted more than a couple of days.
When he was not dreaming of home he dreamt of food. Cummins always shared his parcels with him, and when Denis
grew ashamed of the way he cadged from Cummins, it was a
sop to his conscience that Cummins seemed to enjoy it as much
as he did. Cummins lectured him like an old schoolmistress,
and measured it all out, down to that last candy.

'I'll give you one slice of cake now,' he would say in his
cheerful argumentative way.

'Ah, come on!' Denis would growl, eyeing it hungrily. 'You
won't take it with you.'

'But if I give it to you now you'll only eat it all,' Cummins would cry. 'Look, if I give you one slice now, and another slice tomorrow, and another on Sunday, you'll have cake three days instead of one.'

'But what good will that be if I'm still hungry?' Denis would shout.

'But you'll only be hungrier tomorrow night,' Cummins would say in desperation at his greed. 'You're a queer fellow, Denis,' he would chatter on. 'You're always the same. 'Tis always a feast or a famine with you. If you had your own way you'd never have anything at all. You see I'm only speaking for your good, don't you?'

Denis had no objection to Cummins's speaking for his good so long as he got the cake, as he usually did. You could see from the way Cummins was always thinking of your good that he was bound to be a priest. Sometimes it went too far even for Denis, like the day the two of them were passing the priests' orchard and he suddenly saw that for once there wasn't a soul in sight. At the same moment he felt the hunger-pain sweep over him like a fever.

'Keep nix now, Cummins,' he said, beginning to shin up the wall.

'What are you going to do, Denis?' Cummins asked after him in a frenzy of anxiety.

'I only want a couple of apples,' Denis said, jumping from the top of the wall and running towards the trees. He heard a long, loud wail from the other side of the wall.

'Denis, you're not going to STEAL them. Don't steal them, Denis, please don't steal them!'

But by this time Denis was up in the fork of the tree where the biggest, reddest apples grew. He heard his name called again, and saw that Cummins had scrambled up on to the wall as well, and was sitting astride it with real tears in his eyes.

'Denis,' he bawled, 'what'll I say if I'm caught?'

'Shut up, you fool, or you will get us caught,' Denis snarled back at him.

'But Denis, Denis, it's a sin.'

'It's a what?'

'It's a sin, Denis. I know it's only a venial sin, but venial sins lead to mortal ones. Denis, I'll give you the rest of my cake if you come away. Honest, I will.'

Denis didn't bother to reply, but he was raging. He finished packing apples wherever he had room for them in his clothes, and then climbed slowly back over the wall.

'Cummins,' he said fiercely, 'if you do that again I'm going to kill you.'

'But it's true, Denis,' Cummins said wringing his hands distractedly. ''Tis a sin, and you know 'tis a sin, and you'll have to tell it in Confession.'

'I will not tell it in Confession,' said Denis, 'and if I find out that you did, I'll kill you. I mean it.'

And he did, at the time. It upset him so much that he got almost no pleasure from the apples, but he and Cummins still continued to be friends and to share the parcels of food that Cummins got. These were a complete mystery to Denis. None of the other fellows he knew got a parcel oftener than once a month, and Denis himself hardly got one a term. Of course, Cummins's parents kept a little shop so that it wouldn't be so much trouble to them, making up a parcel, and anyway they would get the things at cost price, but even allowing for all this, it was still remarkable. If they cared all that much for Cummins, why didn't they keep him at home? It wasn't even as if he had another brother or sister. Himself, for instance, a wild kid who was always quarrelling with his sister and whose mother was so often away from home, he could see why he had to be sent away, but what had Cummins done to deserve it? There was a mystery here, and when he got home, Denis was determined to investigate it.

He had his first opportunity at the end of term when Cummins's father and mother came for him in a car and brought Denis back as well. Old Cummins was a small man with glasses and a little greying moustache, and his wife was a roly-poly of a woman with a great flow of talk. Denis noticed the way Cummins's father would wait for minutes on end to ask a question of his own. Cummins's manner to them was affectionate enough. He seemed to have no self-consciousness, and would turn round with one leg on the front seat to hold his mother's hand while he answered her questions about the priests.

A week later, Martha and Denis went up to the Cumminses' for tea. Mr Cummins was behind the counter of the shop with his hat on his head, and he called his wife from the foot of the stairs. She brought them upstairs in her excitable, chattering way to a big front room over the street. Denis and Cummins went out to the back garden with a pistol that Cummins had got at Christmas. It was a wonderful air-pistol that Denis knew must have cost pounds. All Cummins's things were like that. He had also been given a piano accordion. Denis did not envy him the accordion, but he did passionately want the pistol.

'Lend it to us anyway, for the holidays,' he begged.

'But, sure, when I want to practise with it myself!' Cummins protested in that babyish way of his.

'What do you want to practise with it for?' asked Denis. 'When you're a priest, you won't be able to shoot.'

'How do you know?' asked Cummins.

'Because priests aren't let shoot anybody,' said Denis.

'I'll tell you what I'll do with you,' Cummins said in his usual cheese-paring way, 'I'll keep it on weekdays and you can have it on Saturday and Sunday.'

Denis didn't want it for Saturday and Sunday; he wanted it for keeps; and it struck him as very queer in a cissy like Cummins, being so attached to a gun that he'd be scared to use.

Mrs Cummins and the three children had tea in the front room. Then Cummins and Martha played the piano while Mrs Cummins talked to Denis about school.

'Wisha, Denis,' she said, 'isn't it wonderful for ye to be going to a beautiful school like that?'

Denis thought she was joking and began to smile.

'And the grounds so lovely and the house so lovely inside. Don't you love the stained-glass window in the hall?'

Denis had never particularly noticed the stained glass, but he vaguely remembered it as she spoke and agreed.

'Ah, sure 'tis lovely, with the chapel there, to go to whenever you like. And Francis says ye have the grandest films.'

'Oh, yes,' said Denis, thinking he would prefer threepence-worth at the local cinema any day of the week.

'And 'tis so nice having priests for teachers in place of the rough, coarse country fellows you have around here. Oh, Denis, I'm crazy about Father Murphy. Do you know, I'm sure that man is a saint.'

'He's very holy,' said Denis, wondering whether Mrs Cummins would think Murphy such a saint if she saw him with a cane in his hand and his face the colour of blood, hissing and snarling as he chased some fellow round the classroom, flogging him on the bare legs.

'Oh, to be sure he is,' Mrs Cummins rattled on. 'And 'tisn't that at all, Denis boy, but the nice, gentlemanly friends you can make there instead of the savages there are in this town. Look, 'tisn't wishing to me to have Francis out of my sight with those brutes around the streets.'

That finished Denis. A fellow would be a long time in Dunmore before he met savages like the two Corbetts from Cork or Barrett from Clare. But he saw that the woman was in earnest. When he returned home, he told his mother everything about their visit, and her amusement convinced him of what he had already suspected – that Mrs Cummins didn't know any better. She and her husband, small shopkeepers who were accustomed only to a little house in a terrace, nearly died with the grandeur when they saw the grounds and the lake and the tennis courts, just like the gentlemen's residences they had seen before that only from the roadway. Of course, they thought it was Heaven. And it explained the mystery about Francis, because, in place of wanting to get rid of him as his mother had to get rid of Denis, they were probably breaking their hearts at having to part with him at all, and doing it only because they felt they were giving him all the advantages that had been denied to themselves. Despite his mother's mockery he felt rather sorry for them, being taken in like that by appearances.

At the same time it left unexplained something about Francis himself. Denis knew that if he was an only child with a mother and father like that, he would not allow them to remain in ignorance for long. He would soon get away from the filthy dormitory and the brutal society. At first he thought that Francis probably thought it a fine place too, and in a frenzy of altruism decided that it was his duty to talk to Mrs Cummins and tell her the whole truth about it, but then he realized that Francis could not possibly have been taken in in the same way as his parents. He was a weakling and a prig, but he had a sort of country cuteness which enabled him to see through fellows. No, Francis was probably putting up with it because he felt it was his duty, or for the sake of his vocation, because he thought that life was like that, a vale of tears, and whenever he was homesick or when fellows jeered at him, he probably went to the chapel and offered it up. It seemed very queer to Denis because when he was homesick or mad he waited till lights were out and then started to bawl in complete silence for fear his neighbours would hear.

He made a point of impressing on his mother the lavishness of the Cumminses, and told her all about the accordion and the pistol and the weekly parcels with a vague hope of creating larger standards of generosity in her, but she only said that Irish shopkeepers were rotten with money and didn't know how to spend it, and that if only Denis's father would give her what she was entitled to he might go to the best college in Ireland where he would meet only the children of professional people.

All the same when he went back to school, there was a change. A parcel arrived for him, and when he opened it there were all the things he had mentioned to her. For a while he felt a little ashamed. It was probably true that his father did not give her all the money she needed, and that she could only send him parcels by stinting herself; but still, it was a relief to be able to show off in front of the others whose parents were less generous.

That evening he ran into Cummins who smiled at him in his pudding-faced way.

'Do you want anything, Denis?' he asked. 'I have a parcel if you do.'

'I have a parcel of my own today,' Denis said cockily. 'Would you like peaches? I have peaches.'

'Don't be eating it all now,' Cummins said with a comic wail. 'You won't have anything left tomorrow if you do.'

'Ah, what difference does it make?' said Denis with a shrug, and with reckless abandonment he rewarded his friends and conciliated his foes with the contents of his parcel. Next evening he was almost as bad as ever.

'Jay, Denis,' Cummins said with amused resignation, 'you're a blooming fright. I told you what was going to happen. How are you going to live when you grow up if you can never keep anything?'

'Ah, boy,' Denis said, in his embarrassment doing the big shot, 'you wait till I am grown up and you'll see.'

'I know what I'll see all right,' Cummins said, shaking his head sadly. 'Better men than you went to the wall. 'Tis the habits we learn at this age that decide what we're going to be later on. And anyway, how are you going to get a job? Sure, you won't learn anything. If you'd even learn the piano I could teach you.'

Cummins was a born preacher, and Denis saw that there was something in what he said, but no amount of preaching could change him. That was the sort he was. Come day, go day, God send Sunday – and anyway it didn't really make much difference because Cummins with his thrifty habits usually had enough to keep him going till the next parcel came.

Then, about a month later as Denis was opening his weekly parcel under the eyes of his gang, Anthony Harty stood by, gaping with the rest. Harty was a mean, miserable creature from Clare who never got anything, and was consumed with jealousy of everyone who did.

'How well you didn't get any parcels last year, and now you're getting them all the time, Halligan,' he said suspiciously.

'That's only because my mother didn't know about the grub in this place,' Denis declared confidently.

'A wonder she wouldn't address them herself, so,' sneered Harty.

'What do you mean, Harty?' Denis asked, going up to him with his fists clenched. 'Are you looking for a puck in the gob?'

'I'm only saying that's not the writing on your letters,' replied Harty, pointing at the label.

'And why would it be?' shouted Denis. 'I suppose it could be the shopkeepers'.'

'That looks to me like the same writing as on Cummins's parcels,' said Harty.

'And what's wrong with that?' Denis asked, feeling a pang of terror. 'I suppose she could order them there, couldn't she?'

'I'm not saying she couldn't,' said Harty in his sulky, sneering tone. 'I'm only telling you what I think.'

Denis could not believe it, but at the same time he could get no further pleasure from the parcel. He put it back in his locker and went out by himself and skulked away among the trees. It was a dull, misty February day. He took out his wallet in which there was a picture of his mother and Martha, and two letters he had received from his mother. He read the letters through, but there was no reference to any parcel that she was sending. He still could not believe but that there was some simple explanation, and that she had intended the parcels as a surprise, but the very thought of the alternative made his heart turn over. It was something he could talk to nobody about, and after lights out, he twisted and turned madly, groaning at the violence of his own restlessness, and the more he turned, the clearer he saw that the parcels had come from the Cumminses and not from his mother.

He had never before felt so humiliated. Though he had not realized it he had been buoyed up less by the parcels than by the thought that his mother cared so much for him; he had been filled with a new love of her, and now all the love was turning back on him and he realized that he hated her. But he hated the Cumminses worse. He saw that he had pitied and patronized Francis Cummins because he was weak and priggish and because his parents were only poor, ignorant country shopkeepers who did not know a good school from a bad one, while they all the time had been pitying him because he had no one to care for him as the Cumminses cared for Francis. He could clearly imagine the three Cumminses discussing him, his mother and his father exactly as his mother and he had discussed them. The only difference was that however ignorant they might be they had been right. It was he and not Francis who deserved pity.

'What ails you, Halligan?' the chap in the next bed asked – the beds were ranked so close together that one couldn't even sob in peace.

'Nothing ails me,' Denis said between his teeth.

Next day he bundled up what remained of the parcel and took it to Cummins's dormitory. He had intended just to leave it and walk out but Cummins was there himself, sitting on his bed with a book, and Denis had to say something.

'That's yours, Cummins,' he said. 'And if you ever do a thing like that again, I'll kill you.'

'What did I do, Denis?' Cummins wailed, getting up from his bed.

'You got your mother to send me that parcel.'

'I didn't. She did it herself.'

'But you told her to. Who asked you to interfere in my business, you dirty spy?'

'I'm not a spy,' Cummins said, growing agitated. 'You needed it and I didn't – what harm is there in that?'

'There is harm. Pretending my mother isn't as good as yours – a dirty old shopkeeper.'

'I wasn't, Denis,' Cummins said excitedly. 'Honest, I wasn't. I never said a word against your mother.'

'What did he do to you, Halligan?' one of the fellows asked, affecting to take Cummins's part.

'He got his people to send me parcels, as if I couldn't get them myself if I wanted them,' Denis shouted, losing control of himself. 'I don't want his old parcels.'

'Well, that's nothing to cry about.'

'Who's crying?' shouted Denis. 'I'm not crying. I'll fight him and you and the best man in the dormitory.'

He waited a moment for someone to take up his challenge, but they only looked at him curiously, and he rushed out because he knew that in spite of himself he was crying. He went straight to the lavatory and had his cry out there on the seat. It was the only place they had to cry, the only one where there was some sort of privacy. He cried because he had thought he was keeping his secret so well and that no one but himself knew how little toughness and insubordination there was in him till Cummins had come and pried it out.

After that he could never be friendly with Cummins again. It wasn't as Cummins thought that he bore a grudge. It was merely that for him it would have been like living naked.

The Majesty of the Law

OLD Dan Bride was breaking brosna for the fire when he heard a step on the path. He paused, a bundle of saplings on his knee.

Dan had looked after his mother while the life was in her, and after her death no other woman had crossed his threshold. Signs on it, his house had that look. Almost everything in it he had made with his own hands in his own way. The seats of the chairs were only slices of log, rough and round and thick as the saw had left them, and with the rings still plainly visible through the grime and polish that coarse trouser-bottoms had in the course of long years imparted. Into these Dan had rammed stout knotted ash-boughs that served alike for legs and back. The deal table, bought in a shop, was an inheritance from his mother and a great pride and joy to him though it rocked whenever he touched it. On the wall, unglazed and fly-spotted, hung in mysterious isolation a Marcus Stone print, and beside the door was a calendar with a picture of a racehorse. Over the door hung a gun, old but good, and in excellent condition, and before the fire was stretched an old setter who raised his head expectantly whenever Dan rose or even stirred.

He raised it now as the steps came nearer and when Dan, laying down the bundle of saplings, cleaned his hands thoughtfully on the seat of his trousers, he gave a loud bark, but this expressed no more than a desire to show off his own watchfulness. He was half human and knew people thought he was old and past his prime.

A man's shadow fell across the oblong of dusty light thrown over the half-door before Dan looked round.

'Are you alone, Dan?' asked an apologetic voice.

'Oh, come in, come in, sergeant, come in and welcome,' exclaimed the old man, hurrying on rather uncertain feet to the door which the tall policeman opened and pushed in. He stood there, half in sunlight, half in shadow, and seeing him so, you would have realized how dark the interior of the house really was. One side of his red face was turned so as to catch the light, and behind it an ash tree raised its boughs of airy green against the sky. Green fields, broken here and there by clumps of red-brown rock, flowed downhill, and beyond them, stretched all across the horizon, was the sea, flooded and almost transparent with light. The sergeant's face was fat and fresh, the old man's face, emerging from the twilight of the kitchen, had the colour of wind and sun, while the features had been so shaped by the struggle with time and the elements that they might as easily have been found impressed upon the surface of a rock.

'Begor, Dan,' said the sergeant, ''tis younger you're getting.'

'Middling I am, sergeant, middling,' agreed the old man in a voice which seemed to accept the remark as a compliment of which politeness would not allow him to take too much advantage. 'No complaints.'

'Begor, 'tis as well because no one would believe them. And the old dog doesn't look a day older.'

The dog gave a low growl as though to show the sergeant that he would remember this unmannerly reference to his age, but indeed he growled every time he was mentioned, under the impression that people had nothing but ill to say of him.

'And how's yourself, sergeant?'

'Well, now, like the most of us, Dan, neither too good nor too bad. We have our own little worries, but, thanks be to God, we have our compensations.'

'And the wife and family?'

'Good, praise be to God, good. They were away from me for a month, the lot of them, at the mother-in-law's place in Clare.'

'In Clare, do you tell me?'

'In Clare. I had a fine quiet time.'

The old man looked about him and then retired to the bedroom, from which he returned a moment later with an old shirt. With this he solemnly wiped the seat and back of the log-chair nearest the fire.

'Sit down now, sergeant. You must be tired after the journey. 'Tis a long old road. How did you come?'

'Teigue Leary gave me the lift. Wisha now, Dan, don't be putting yourself out. I won't be stopping. I promised them I'd be back inside an hour.'

'What hurry is on you?' asked Dan. 'Look, your foot was only on the path when I made up the fire.'

'Arrah, Dan, you're not making tea for me?'

'I am not making it for you, indeed; I'm making it for myself, and I'll take it very bad of you if you won't have a cup.'

'Dan, Dan, that I mightn't stir, but 'tisn't an hour since I had it at the barracks!'

'Ah, whisht, now, whisht! Whisht, will you! I have something here to give you an appetite.'

The old man swung the heavy kettle on to the chain over the open fire, and the dog sat up, shaking his ears with an expression of the deepest interest. The policeman unbuttoned his tunic, opened his belt, took a pipe and a plug of tobacco from his breast pocket, and, crossing his legs in an easy posture, began to cut the tobacco slowly and carefully with his pocket knife. The old man went to the dresser and took down two handsomely decorated cups, the only cups he had, which, though chipped and handleless, were used at all only on very rare occasions; for himself he preferred his tea from a basin. Happening to glance into them, he noticed that they bore signs of disuse and had collected a lot of the fine white turf-dust that always circulated in the little smoky cottage. Again he thought of the shirt, and, rolling up his sleeves with a stately gesture, he wiped them inside and out till they shone. Then he bent and opened the cupboard. Inside was a quart bottle of pale liquid, obviously untouched. He removed the cork and smelt the contents, pausing for a moment in the act as though to recollect where exactly he had noticed that particular smoky smell before. Then, reassured, he stood up and poured out with a liberal hand.

'Try that now, sergeant,' he said with quiet pride.

The sergeant, concealing whatever qualms he might have felt at the idea of drinking illegal whisky, looked carefully into the cup, sniffed, and glanced up at old Dan.

'It looks good,' he commented.

'It should be good,' replied Dan with no mock modesty.

'It tastes good too,' said the sergeant.

'Ah, sha,' said Dan, not wishing to praise his own hospitality in his own house, ''tis of no great excellence.'

'You'd be a good judge, I'd say,' said the sergeant without irony.

'Ever since things became what they are,' said Dan, carefully guarding himself against a too-direct reference to the peculiarities of the law administered by his guest, 'liquor isn't what it used to be.'

'I've heard that remark made before now, Dan,' said the sergeant thoughtfully. 'I've heard it said by men of wide experience that it used to be better in the old days.'

'Liquor,' said the old man, 'is a thing that takes time. There was never a good job done in a hurry.'

''Tis an art in itself.'

'Just so.'

'And an art takes time.'

'And knowledge,' added Dan with emphasis. 'Every art has its secrets, and the secrets of distilling are being lost the way the old songs were lost. When I was a boy there wasn't a man in the barony but had a hundred songs in his head, but with people running here, there, and everywhere, the songs were lost. . . . Ever since things became what they are,' he repeated on the same guarded note, 'there's so much running about the secrets are lost.'

'There must have been a power of them.'

'There was. Ask any man today that makes whisky do he know how to make it out of heather.'

'And was it made of heather?' asked the policeman.

'It was.'

'You never drank it yourself?'

'I didn't, but I knew old men that did, and they told me that no whisky that's made nowadays could compare with it.'

'Musha, Dan, I think sometimes 'twas a great mistake of the law to set its hand against it.'

Dan shook his head. His eyes answered for him, but it was not in nature for a man to criticize the occupation of a guest in his own home.

'Maybe so, maybe not,' he said noncommittally.

'But sure, what else have the poor people?'

'Them that makes the laws have their own good reasons.'

'All the same, Dan, all the same, 'tis a hard law.'

The sergeant would not be outdone in generosity. Politeness required him not to yield to the old man's defence of his superiors and their mysterious ways.

'It is the secrets I'd be sorry for,' said Dan, summing up. 'Men die and men are born, and where one man drained another will plough, but a secret lost is lost forever.'

'True,' said the sergeant mournfully. 'Lost forever.'

Dan took his cup, rinsed it in a bucket of clear water by the door and cleaned it again with the shirt. Then he placed it carefully at the sergeant's elbow. From the dresser he took a jug of milk and a blue bag containing sugar; this he followed up with a slab of country butter and – a sure sign that he had been expecting a visitor – a round cake of home-made bread, fresh and uncut. The kettle sang and spat and the dog, shaking his ears, barked at it angrily.

'Go away, you brute!' growled Dan, kicking him out of his way.

He made the tea and filled the two cups. The sergeant cut himself a large slice of bread and buttered it thickly.

'It is just like medicines,' said the old man, resuming his theme with the imperturbability of age. 'Every secret there was is lost. And leave no one tell me that a doctor is as good a man as one that had the secrets of old times.'

'How could he be?' asked the sergeant with his mouth full.

'The proof of that was seen when there were doctors and wise people there together.'

'It wasn't to the doctors the people went, I'll engage?'

'It was not. And why?' With a sweeping gesture the old man took in the whole world outside his cabin. 'Out there on the hillsides is the sure cure for every disease. Because it is written' – he tapped the table with his thumb – 'it is written by the poets "wherever you find the disease you will find the cure". But people walk up the hills and down the hills and all they see is flowers. Flowers! As if God Almighty – honour and praise

to Him! – had nothing better to do with His time than be to
making old flowers!'

'Things no doctor could cure the wise people cured,' agreed
the sergeant.

'Ah, musha, 'tis I know it,' said Dan bitterly. 'I know it, not
in my mind but in my own four bones.'

'Have you the rheumatics at you still?' the sergeant asked
in a shocked tone.

'I have. Ah, if you were alive, Kitty O'Hara, or you, Nora
Malley of the Glen, 'tisn't I'd be dreading the mountain wind
or the sea wind; 'tisn't I'd be creeping down with my misfortunate red ticket for the blue and pink and yellow dribble-
drabble of their ignorant dispensary.'

'Why then indeed,' said the sergeant, 'I'll get you a bottle
for that.'

'Ah, there's no bottle ever made will cure it.'

'That's where you're wrong, Dan. Don't talk now till you try
it. It cured my own uncle when he was that bad he was shouting
for the carpenter to cut the two legs off him with a handsaw.'

'I'd give fifty pounds to get rid of it,' said Dan magnilo-
quently. 'I would and five hundred.'

The sergeant finished his tea in a gulp, blessed himself, and
struck a match which he then allowed to go out as he answered
some question of the old man. He did the same with a second
and third, as though titillating his appetite with delay. Finally
he succeeded in getting his pipe alight and the two men pulled
round their chairs, placed their toes side by side in the ashes,
and in deep puffs, lively bursts of conversation, and long, long
silences enjoyed their smoke.

'I hope I'm not keeping you?' said the sergeant, as though
struck by the length of his visit.

'Ah, what would you keep me from?'

'Tell me if I am. The last thing I'd like to do is waste another
man's time.'

'Begor, you wouldn't waste my time if you stopped all night.'

'I like a little chat myself,' confessed the policeman.

And again they became lost in conversation. The light grew
thick and coloured and, wheeling about the kitchen before it

disappeared, became tinged with gold; the kitchen itself sank into cool greyness with cold light on the cups and basins and plates of the dresser. From the ash tree a thrush began to sing. The open hearth gathered brightness till its light was a warm, even splash of crimson in the twilight.

Twilight was also descending outside when the sergeant rose to go. He fastened his belt and tunic and carefully brushed his clothes. Then he put on his cap, tilted a little to side and back.

'Well, that was a great talk,' he said.

''Tis a pleasure,' said Dan, 'a real pleasure.'

'And I won't forget the bottle for you.'

'Heavy handling from God to you!'

'Good-bye now, Dan.'

'Good-bye, sergeant, and good luck.'

Dan didn't offer to accompany the sergeant beyond the door. He sat in his old place by the fire, took out his pipe once more, blew through it thoughtfully, and just as he leaned forward for a twig to kindle it, heard the steps returning. It was the sergeant. He put his head a little way over the half-door.

'Oh, Dan!' he called softly.

'Ay, sergeant?' replied Dan, looking round, but with one hand still reaching for the twig. He couldn't see the sergeant's face, only hear his voice.

'I suppose you're not thinking of paying that little fine, Dan?'

There was a brief silence. Dan pulled out the lighted twig, rose slowly, and shambled towards the door, stuffing it down in the almost empty bowl of the pipe. He leaned over the half-door while the sergeant with hands in the pockets of his trousers gazed rather in the direction of the laneway, yet taking in a considerable portion of the sea line.

'The way it is with me, sergeant,' replied Dan unemotionally, 'I am not.'

'I was thinking that, Dan; I was thinking you wouldn't.'

There was a long silence during which the voice of the thrush grew shriller and merrier. The sunken sun lit up rafts of purple cloud moored high above the wind.

'In a way,' said the sergeant, 'that was what brought me.'

'I was just thinking so, sergeant, it only struck me and you going out the door.'

'If 'twas only the money, Dan, I'm sure there's many would be glad to oblige you.'

'I know that, sergeant. No, 'tisn't the money so much as giving that fellow the satisfaction of paying. Because he angered me, sergeant.'

The sergeant made no comment on this and another long silence ensued.

'They gave me the warrant,' the sergeant said at last, in a tone which dissociated him from all connexion with such an unneighbourly document.

'Did they so?' exclaimed Dan, as if he was shocked by the thoughtlessness of the authorities.

'So whenever 'twould be convenient for you –'

'Well, now you mention it,' said Dan, by way of throwing out a suggestion for debate, 'I could go with you now.'

'Ah, sha, what do you want going at this hour for?' protested the sergeant with a wave of his hand, dismissing the notion as the tone required.

'Or I could go tomorrow,' added Dan, warming to the issue.

'Would it be suitable for you now?' asked the sergeant, scaling up his voice accordingly.

'But, as a matter of fact,' said the old man emphatically, 'the day that would be most convenient to me would be Friday after dinner, because I have some messages to do in town, and I wouldn't have the journey for nothing.'

'Friday will do grand,' said the sergeant with relief that this delicate matter was now practically disposed of. 'If it doesn't they can damn well wait. You could walk in there yourself when it suits you and tell them I sent you.'

'I'd rather have yourself there, sergeant, if it would be no inconvenience. As it is, I'd feel a bit shy.'

'Why then, you needn't feel shy at all. There's a man from my own parish there, a warder; one Whelan. Ask for him; I'll tell him you're coming, and I'll guarantee when he knows you're a friend of mine he'll make you as comfortable as if you were at home.'

'I'd like that fine,' Dan said with profound satisfaction. 'I'd like to be with friends, sergeant.'

'You will be, never fear. Good-bye again now, Dan. I'll have to hurry.'

'Wait now, wait till I see you to the road.'

Together the two men strolled down the laneway while Dan explained how it was that he, a respectable old man, had had the grave misfortune to open the head of another old man in such a way as to require his removal to hospital, and why it was that he couldn't give the old man in question the satisfaction of paying in cash for an injury brought about through the victim's own unmannerly method of argument.

'You see, sergeant,' Dan said, looking at another little cottage up the hill, 'the way it is, he's there now, and he's looking at us as sure as there's a glimmer of sight in his weak, wandering, watery eyes, and nothing would give him more gratification than for me to pay. But I'll punish him. I'll lie on bare boards for him. I'll suffer for him, sergeant, so that neither he nor any of his children after him will be able to raise their heads for the shame of it.'

On the following Friday he made ready his donkey and butt and set out. On his way he collected a number of neighbours who wished to bid him farewell. At the top of the hill he stopped to send them back. An old man, sitting in the sunlight, hastily made his way indoors, and a moment later the door of his cottage was quietly closed.

Having shaken all his friends by the hand, Dan lashed the old donkey, shouted: 'Hup there!' and set out alone along the road to prison.

The Paragon

JIMMY GARVIN lived with his mother in a little house in what we called the Square, though there wasn't much of a square about it. He was roughly my own age, but he behaved as if he were five years older. He was a real mother's darling, with pale hair and eyes, a round, soft, innocent face that seemed to become rounder and softer and more innocent from the time he began to wear spectacles, and one of those astonishingly clear complexions that keep their owners looking years younger than their real age. He talked slowly and carefully in a precise, old-fashioned way and hardly mixed at all with the other kids.

His mother was a pretty, excitable woman with fair hair like Jimmy's, a long, thin face and a great flow of nervous chatter. She had been separated for years from her husband who was supposed to be in England somewhere. She had been a waitress in a club on the South Mall, and he was reputed to be of a rather better class, as class is understood in Cork, which is none too well. His family made her a small allowance, but it was not enough to support herself and Jimmy, and she eked it out with housework. It was characteristic of our poverty-stricken locality that the little allowance made her an object of great envy and that people did not like her and called her 'Lady Garvin'.

Each afternoon after school you would see Jimmy making for one of the fashionable districts where his mother worked, raising his cap and greeting any woman he knew in his polite, old-fashioned way. His mother brought him into the kitchen and gave him whatever had been left over from lunch, and he read there till it was time for them to go home. He was no trouble; all he ever needed to make him happy was a book – any book – from the shelves or the lumber room, and he read with his head resting on his hands which formed a screen between him and the domestic world.

'Mum,' he would say, beaming, 'this book is about a very interesting play they have every year in a place called Ober-ammergau. Oberammergau is in Germany. In Germany the language they speak is German. Don't you think I should learn German?'

'Should you, Jimmy?' she would ask tenderly. 'Don't you think you're learning enough as it is?'

'But if we go to Germany,' he exclaimed with his triumphant smile, 'one of us has to know German. If we don't know how to ask our way to the right platform, how will we know we're on the right train? Perhaps they'll take us to Russia.'

'Oh, dear,' she would say, 'that would be dreadful.'

At the same time she was, of course, terribly proud of him, particularly if the maid was there to hear him. For as Jimmy told the story, his mother was always the heroine and he Prince Charming. In a year or two he would begin to earn a lot of money, and then they would have a big house on the river, exactly like the one they were in, with a maid to wait on them who would be paid more than any maid in the neighbourhood, and they would spend their holidays in France and Italy. If his mother was friendly with the maid she was working with, he even offered the position to her. There was nothing like having the whole thing arranged.

This was how he liked to pass the time while his mother worked, reading, or – if she had the house to herself – wander-ing gravely from room to room and imagining himself already the owner, looking at himself in the dressing-table mirrors as he poured bay rum on his hair and brushed it with the silver brushes, speaking to himself in a lingo he took to be German, touching the keys of the piano lightly, or watching from the tall windows as people hurried by along the river-bank in the rainy dusk. Late in the evening they would go home together, holding hands, while he still chattered on in his grave, ancient, innocent way; the way of a child on whom Life has laid too heavy a burden.

But as time went on things grew easier. The monks saw that Jimmy was out on his own as a student. Finally, Mrs Garvin gave up the housework and took in boarders. She rented a big house on the road near the tram-stop and accepted only lodgers of the best class. There at last Jimmy could have a piano of his own, though the instrument he did take up was the violin.

2

By the time he was ready for the university he had developed into a tall, gangling, good-looking boy, though his years of study had left their mark on him. He had a pleasant tenor voice and sang in one of the city choirs. He had got the highest mark in Ireland in the Intermediate exams, and his picture had appeared in the *Examiner*, with his right arm resting on a pedestal and his left hand supporting it to keep it from shaking.

And this, of course, was where the trouble really began, for his father's family saw the picture and read the story and realized that they – poor, innocent, good-natured, country folk – were being done out of something by the city slickers. The Garvins were a family you couldn't do out of much, and they coveted their share of Jimmy's glory, all the more because they saw that he had got it all from the Garvins who had always been intellectual – witness Great Uncle Harvey who had been the greatest scholar in the town of Macroom, consulted even by the parish priest. Some sort of reconciliation was necessary; Mrs Garvin's allowance was increased, and she was almost silly with happiness since it seemed so much like a foretaste of all the things Jimmy had promised to do for her.

At the same time she feared the Garvins, a feeling in which Jimmy could not sympathize because he had no experience of his father's family. He was mildly curious, that was all. To him they were just another audience for whom he could perform on the violin or to whom he could explain the facts of the international situation. At her request he called on his Aunt Mary who lived in a new red-brick house a stone's throw from the College. Aunt Mary had been involved in a peculiar marriage with a middle-aged engineer who had left her some money but no children. She was a shrewd, coaxing, old West Cork woman with a face that must once have been good-looking. No sooner did she realize that Jimmy was presentable as well as 'smart' than she saw that it was the will of God that she should annex him. She was the family genealogist, and while she fed him excellently on tea, home-made scones and cakes, she filled in for him in a modest and deprecating way the family background he had missed.

It never occurred to her that this might come as an anti-climax to Jimmy. He listened to her with a vacant smile and even made fun of Great Uncle Harvey to her face, a thing no one had ever presumed to do before, and when he left her she sat, looking out of the window after his tall, swinging figure, and wondered if it was really worth her while to pay the call she had promised.

Mrs Garvin had even worse misgivings.

'I don't want that woman in the house, Jimmy,' she said, clasping her hands feverishly. 'She's the one I really blame for the trouble with your father.'

'Well, she's hardly going to make trouble between you and me,' said Jimmy, who had privately decided that his aunt was a fool.

'That's all you know,' his mother said bitterly.

In this she was right, but even she did not realize the full extent of the trouble Aunt Mary was preparing for them when she called. From Jimmy's point of view there was nothing wrong. Aunt Mary cluck-clucked with astonishment when he played the violin for her, when he sang, and when he explained what was really happening in Europe.

'Oh, Jimmy,' she said, 'I'd love your father to hear you sing. You have his voice. I can hear him in you.'

'Oh, no, I don't think so, Mrs Healy,' his mother said hastily. 'Jimmy has far too much to do.'

'Ah, I was only thinking of a week or ten days.' Aunt Mary said. ''Twould be a change for him.'

'I think he's much too young to travel alone,' Mrs Garvin said, quivering. 'In a year or two perhaps.'

'Oh, really, Mum!' exclaimed Jimmy, cast down from the heights of abstract discussion. 'I think I'm able to travel alone by now.'

Aunt Mary had engaged his interest, and well she knew it.

He had always been curious in a human way about the father he did not remember, and, being a born learner, was even more curious about England, a country he was always reading about and hearing of but had never seen. He had more than his share of boyish vanity, and he knew that English contacts would assure him prestige among his fellow-students.

For twelve months, off and on, he argued with his mother about it, but each time it alarmed her again. When she finally did consent it was only because she felt that it might be unfair to deprive him of a chance of widening his knowledge of the world.

So at least she said. But whatever she might say, and for all her fears, she was flattered, and with every bit of feminine vanity in her she desired the opportunity of showing off to her husband and his family the child they had abandoned and whom she had made into a paragon.

3

Jimmy's first sight of his father in Paddington Station came as a considerable shock to him. Somehow, whenever he had imagined his father it had been as a heavy man with a big, red face and a grey moustache, slow-spoken and portentous; but the man who met him in a bowler hat and a pale grey tie was tall and stringy with a neat dark moustache and an irritable, worried air. His speech was pleasant and well-bred; his manner was unaffected without being demonstrative, and he had a sense of quiet fun that put Jimmy at his ease. But he didn't like to see such a distinguished-looking man carrying his cheap suitcase for him.

'Do let me carry that!' he said anxiously.

'Oh, that's all right, son,' his father said lightly. 'By the way,' he added smoothly, 'you'll find I talk an awful lot, but you don't have to pay any attention. If you talk too we'll get on fine. That's a hell of a heavy bag. We'd better get a taxi.'

It was another surprise to Jimmy when, instead of taking him to some boarding-house in the suburbs, his father took him on an electric train to a station twenty-odd miles from

London. To Jimmy it seemed that this must be the heart of the country, but the big houses and the tall, red buses he saw did not seem countrified. There was a car waiting outside the station, and his father drove him over high, hilly country full of woods and streams down into a little red-brick market town with a market house on stilts in the middle of the street, and up the hills again. To Jimmy it was all new and exciting, and he kept looking out and asking intelligent questions to which he rarely got satisfactory answers.

'Oh, this damn country!' his father said testily. 'You have to drive five miles out of your way to avoid a hole in the road that's preserved because Alfred the Great fell into it. For God's sake, look at this for a main road!'

While Jimmy was still wondering how you would preserve a hole in the road they reached a village on top of the hills, a long, low street open on to a wide common, with a school, a church, a row of low cottages, and a public house with a brightly painted inn-sign and with green chairs and tables ranged in front of it. They stopped a little up the road outside a cottage with high pilastered chimneys and diamond-shaped windows, and a row of tall elms behind.

'You'd want to mind your head in this damn hole,' his father said as he pushed in the door. 'It may have been all right for Queen Elizabeth but it's not all right for me.'

Jimmy found himself in a combination living- and dining-room with a huge stone fireplace and low oak beams. A door on the right led into a modern kitchen and another at the end of the room seemed to lead on to a stairway of sorts. A woman and a little girl of four or five came slowly through this door, the woman lowering her head.

'This is Martha, Jim,' his father tossed off lightly as he kissed her. 'Any time you want her, just let me know. She's on the youthful side for me. Gussie, you old humbug,' he added to the little girl, 'this is your big brother. If you're nice to him he might give you five bob.'

Jimmy was stunned and his face showed it. This was something he had never anticipated and did not know how to deal with. He was too innocent to know even if it was right or wrong. Of course, things might be different in England. But, whatever he believed, his behaviour had been conditioned by years of deference, and he smiled shyly and shook hands with Martha, a heavy, good-looking woman who smiled back without warmth. As for Gussie, she stood in a corner with her legs splayed and a finger in her mouth.

'Sherry for you, son,' his father called from the farther room. 'I have to take this damn whisky for my health.'

'Before you take it I'd better show you your room;' said Martha, picking up his case. 'You'll need to mind your head.'

'Oh, please, Martha!' he said anxiously, but she preceded him with the bag, through the farther room where his father was measuring whisky in a glass against the light and up a staircase similar to that in the dining-room. In spite of the warning, Jimmy bumped his head badly, and looked in good-humoured disgust at the low doorway. The stairs opened on to an attic room with high beams, a floor that sloped under the grey rug as though the house were on the point of collapse, and a low window that overlooked the garden, the roadway and the common beyond, a cold blue-green compared with the golden green of home. Beyond the common was a row of distant hills.

When he went downstairs again they all sat in the big room under his and he took the sherry his father offered him. He was too shy to say he didn't drink. It was a nice room, not too heavily furnished, with diamond-paned windows looking on to the gardens at the front and back, and with a small piano beside the latter. It gave Jimmy the opening he needed. It seemed that Martha played the piano. In spite of their common interest he found her very disconcerting. She was polite, and her accent was pleasant, but there seemed to him to be no warmth in her. He had trained himself to present a good impression without wasting time; he knew that he was polite, that he was intelligent and that he had a fine voice; and it was a new experience for him to find his friendliness coming back to him like a voice in an empty house. It made him raise his voice and enlarge his gestures until he felt that he was even creating a disturbance. His father seemed to enjoy his loud-voiced caricature of Aunt Mary extolling the scholarship of Great Uncle Harvey, a character who struck Jimmy as being pure farce, but a moment later, having passed from amusement to indignation, he was irritably denouncing Great Uncle Harvey as the biggest bloody old humbug that had ever come out of Macroom. He was a man who seemed to move easily from mood to mood, and Jimmy whose own moods were static and monumental, found himself laughing outright at the sheer unexpectedness of his remarks.

After supper, when Martha had gone to put Gussie to bed, he stood with his hands behind his back before the big stone fireplace (which according to him had already asphyxiated three historical personages and would soon do for him). He was developing a stomach and a double chin, and Jimmy noticed a fundamental restlessness about him as when he failed to find some letter he was searching for and called petulantly for Martha. She came in with an expressionless air, found the letter, and went out again. He was a man of many enthusiasms. At one moment he was emotional about Cork and its fine schools, so different from English ones where children never learned anything but insolence, but a few minutes later, almost without a change of tone, he seemed to be advising Jimmy to get out as quick as he could before the damn place smothered him. When Jimmy, accustomed to an adoring feminine audience, gave him the benefit of his views on the Irish educational system, its merits and drawbacks, he sat with crossed legs looking away and smiling as though to himself while he twirled the glass in his long, sensitive fingers. He was something of a puzzle to Jimmy.

'I suppose you must think me a bit of a blackguard,' he said gruffly, rising again to give the fire a kick. 'The truth is, I hadn't the faintest idea what was happening to you. Your mother wouldn't write – not that I'm criticizing her, mind you. We didn't get on, and she deserves every credit for you, whatever your aunt or anyone else may say. I'd be proud of her if she was my mother.'

'So I am,' said Jimmy with a beaming smile.

'All I mean is that she put herself to a lot of unnecessary trouble, not letting me help you. I can easily see you through college if that's all you want.'

'Thanks,' Jimmy replied with the same air of triumph. 'But I think I can manage pretty well on scholarships.'

'All the better. Anyway, you can have the money. It's an investment. It always pays to have one member of the family with brains: you never know when you'll need them. I'm doing fairly well,' he added complacently. 'Not that you can be sure of anything. Half the people in a place like this are getting by on credit.'

It was all very strange to Jimmy. He bumped his head again going up to bed and chuckled to himself. From far away he heard the whistle of a train, probably going north on its way up the valley towards Ireland, and for a long time he lay in bed, his hands joined on his stomach, wondering what it all meant and what he should do about it. It became plainer when he contemplated it like this. He would just ask his father as man to man whether or not he and Martha were married, and if the answer were unsatisfactory he would pack his bag and go, money or no money. No doubt his father would make a scene and it would all be very unpleasant, but later on, he would realize that Jimmy was right. Jimmy would explain this to him, and make it clear that anything he did was done as much in his father's interests as his own; that nothing was to be gained by defying the laws of morality and the church. Jimmy knew he had this power of dominating people; he had seen old women's eyes fill with tears when he had sung 'I'll Take You Home, Again, Kathleen', and though he rejoiced in the feeling of confidence it gave him, he took care never to abuse it, never to try and convince unless he was first convinced himself. He fell asleep in a haze of self-righteousness.

Next morning, after his father had driven him to Mass in the gymnasium of the local club, it did not seem quite so easy. His father seemed a more formidable character than any he had yet met. But Jimmy had resolution and obstinacy. He summed it all up and asked in a casual sort of way: 'Was it there you were married?'

His father's face grew stern, but he answered urbanely enough.

'No. Why?'

'Nothing,' Jimmy said weakly. 'I just wondered.'

'Whether a marriage in a gymnasium would be binding? I was wondering the same thing myself.'

And, as he got into the car, Jimmy realized that this was as far as ever he would get with his big scene. Whatever the reason was, he was overawed by his father. He put it down partly to the difference in age, and partly to the inflexibility of his own reactions. His father's moods moved too fast for him; beside him he felt like a knight in heavy armour trying to chase a fleet-footed mountainy man. He resolved to wait for a more suitable opportunity. They drove on, and his father stopped the car near the top of the hill where there was a view of the valley up which the railway passed. Grey trees squiggled across it in elaborate patterns, and grey church towers and red-tiled roofs showed between them in the sunlight that overflowed into it from heavy, grey and white clouds.

'Lovely, isn't it?' his father said quietly.

Then he smiled, and suddenly his face became extraordinarily young and innocent. There was a sort of sweetness in it that for a moment took Jimmy's breath away.

'You see, son,' he said, 'when I was sixteen my father should have taken me aside and told me something about women. But he was a shy man, and my mother wouldn't have liked it, so you see, I'm in a bit of a mess. I'd have done the same for you, but I never got the chance, and I dare say when you're a bit older you'll find yourself in a thundering big mess too. I wouldn't worry too much about it if I were you. Time enough for that when it happens.'

Then he drove on to the pub, apparently under the impression that he had now explained everything. It suddenly struck Jimmy that perhaps he would never reach the point of asking his father for an explanation.

His father had changed again and become swaggering and insolent. He made Jimmy play a game of darts with him, flirted with the woman of the house, and made cutting remarks to her husband about the local cricket team which her husband seemed to enjoy. Jimmy had the impression that for some reason they all liked his father.

'Silly, bloody game anyway,' he added with a snort. 'More like a serial story than a game. Give me a good rousing game of hurling where somebody's head gets split.'

'God, this is a beautiful country,' he muttered to Jimmy, standing at the door with one hand in his trousers pocket, the other holding his pint while he smiled across the sunlit common, and again his face had the strange sweetness that Jimmy had noticed on it before. 'You'd be a long time at home before you could go into a country pub on Sunday and meet a crowd like this.'

There was a sort of consistency about his father's inconsistencies that reminded Jimmy of the sky with its pennants of blue and cascades of silver, but he found he did not like him any the less for these. He did not feel quite so comfortable on the train back to Ireland, wondering what he should tell his mother, feeling that he should tell her nothing and knowing at the same time that this was something he was almost incapable of doing.

Naturally, he told her everything in the first half hour, and when she grew disgusted and bitter, felt he had betrayed a confidence.

'What did I say about your aunt?' she exclaimed. 'All the time she was pressing you to go there, she knew what it was like.'

'I'm not so sure that she did know,' Jimmy said doubtfully. 'I don't think Father tells her much.'

'Oh, Jimmy, you're too innocent to know what liars and cheats they all are, all the Garvins.'

. 'I didn't think there was much of the cheat about Father,' Jimmy protested. 'He was honest enough about it with me.'

'He was brazen about it,' his mother said contemptuously. 'Like all liars. 'Tisn't alike.'

'I'm not sure that he was brazen,' Jimmy protested weakly, trying in vain to assert himself again in his old authoritative way. 'It's just that he's not a good liar. And besides,' he added knowingly, folding his hands on his lap and looking at her owlishly over his spectacles, 'we don't know the sort of temptations people have in a place like England.'

'Temptations aren't confined to England,' she said with a flash of temper.

By this time she was regretting bitterly her own folly in allowing him to visit his father. She resented, too, his father's having brought him to a public house even though Jimmy explained that he had only drunk cider, and that public houses there were different. But her full bitterness about this was reserved till later, when Jimmy started going to public houses on his own. He now had a small allowance from his father, and proceeded to indulge his mother and himself. He had made friends with a group that centred on the college; a couple of instructors, some teachers, some Civil Servants – the usual run of small-town intellectuals. Up to now, Jimmy had been a young fellow with no particular friends, partly because he had had no time for them, partly because like most kids who have no time for friends, he was scared of them when they made advances.

It was about this time too that he acknowledged my existence, and the pair of us went for occasional walks together. I admired him almost extravagantly. Whatever he did, from the way he chose his ties to the way he greeted a woman on the road or the way he climbed a fence, was done with an air, while I stumbled over all of them. It was the same with ideas; by the time I had picked myself up after making a point, Jimmy would be crossing the next obstacle, looking back at me and laughing triumphantly. He had a disciplined personality and a trained mind, and though he was sometimes impressed by my odd bits of knowledge, he was puzzled by my casual, impractical interests and desultory reading. He was a born teacher, so he lent me some elementary books and then started to take me through them, step by step but without much effect. I had not even the groundwork of knowledge while he was a real examination-passer with a power of concentration that I lacked completely.

At the same time I was put off by his other friends. They argued as people do who spend too much of their time in public houses – for effect. They were witty and clever and said wounding things. In spite of my shortcomings, I had a sort of snobbery all my own. I felt they were failures, and I had the feeling that Jimmy only liked them for that very reason. His great weakness was showing-off. I sat with them one evening, watching Jimmy lower his beer and listening to him defend orthodoxy against a couple of the others who favoured various forms of agnosticism. He argued well enough in the stubborn manner of a first year philosophy student. Then he sang for us, a little too well for the occasion. I did not like it; the picture of the fellow I had known as a slim-faced, spectacled schoolboy, laying down the law and singing in a pub. He was idling; he was drinking – though not anything like as much as his mother believed – and he had even picked up a girl, a schoolteacher called Anne Reidy with whom he went to Crosshaven on week-ends. In fact, for the first time in his life Jimmy was enjoying himself, and like all those who have not enjoyed themselves in childhood, he was enjoying himself rather too much.

At first his mother was bewildered; then she became censorious and bitter. Naturally she blamed his father for it all. She even told Jimmy that his father had deliberately set out to corrupt him just to destroy whatever she had been able to do for him, which wasn't exactly tactful as Jimmy felt most of the credit was due to himself. And then she, who for all those years had managed to keep her mind to herself, started to complain to Jimmy about her marriage, and the drinking, cheating, and general light-mindedness of his father, exactly as though it had all just newly happened. Jimmy listened politely but with a wooden face, which would have revealed to anyone but her that he thought she was obsessed by the subject.

She was a pathetic figure because though she was proud and sensitive beyond any woman I knew – the sort who would not call at all unless she brought some little gift and who took flight if you put on the kettle or looked at the clock – she haunted our house. She was, I think, secretly convinced that I had influence over Jimmy. It made me uncomfortable because not only did I realize how much it cost her to plead for her paragon with a nonentity like myself, but I knew I had no influence over him. He was far too clever to be influenced by anyone like me. He was also, though I do not mean it in a derogatory way, too conceited. Once when I did try in a clumsy way to advise him he laughed uproariously.

'Listen to him!' he said. 'Listen to the steady man! Why, you slug, you never in your whole life put in one week's connected work at anything.'

'That may be true enough, Jimmy,' I said without rancour, 'but all the same you should watch out. You could lose that scholarship.'

'Oh, I don't think so,' he said with a smile which expressed his enormous self-confidence. 'But at any rate, even if I did, the old man has plenty.'

But though his mother continued to appeal to me silently, in conversation she developed a sort of facile pessimism that I found it harder to understand. It was a kind of cynicism which failed to come off.

'Oh, I know what will happen,' she said with a shrug. 'I've seen it happen before. His father will get tired of him as he gets tired of everybody, and then he'll find himself with nothing.'

4

That was not quite how it happened. One month Jimmy's allowance failed to arrive, and when he wrote his father a bantering letter, threatening to refer the matter to his lawyers, it was Martha who replied. There was no banter about her. His father had been arrested for embezzlement, and house, furniture, and business had all been swallowed up. Martha wrote as though she blamed his father for everything.

'I suppose God's vengeance catches up on them all sooner or later,' Mrs Garvin said bitterly.

'Something caught up on him,' Jimmy said with a stunned air. 'The poor devil must have been half out of his mind for years.'

'And now it's the turn of the widows and orphans he robbed,' said his mother.

'Oh, he didn't rob anybody,' Jimmy said.

'You should tell the police that.'

'I'm sure the police know it already,' said Jimmy. 'People like Father don't steal. They find themselves saddled with an expensive wife or family, and they borrow, intending to put it back. Everybody does it one way or another, but some people don't know where to stop. Then they get caught up in their own mistakes. I wish to God I'd known when I was there. I might have been able to help him.'

'You'll have enough to do to help yourself,' she said sharply.

'Oh, I'll manage somehow,' he said doubtfully. 'I dare say I can get a job.'

'As a labourer?' she asked mockingly.

'Not necessarily,' he said steadily, looking at her with some surprise. 'I can probably get an office job.'

'Yes,' she said bitterly, 'as a clerk. And all your years of study to go for nothing.'

That was something she scarcely needed to remind him of, though when he tried to get help he was reminded even more forcefully of the fact that most paragons learn sooner or later; that a cracked paragon is harder to dispose of than plain delft. He had made too much of a fool of himself. The County Council scholarship would not be renewed and the college would promise nothing.

Even his mother had lost confidence in him, and as time went on his relations with her became more strained. She could not resist throwing the blame for everything on his father, and here she found herself up against a wall of obstinacy in him. He had already silently separated himself from his Aunt Mary who had thrown herself on him in tears, and told him his father had dragged the good name of the Garvins in the gutter. Jimmy didn't know about the good name of the Garvins, but somewhere in the back of his mind was a picture of his father facing a police officer alone with that weak, innocent smile on his face, and whenever he thought of it a cloud came over his mind. He even wrote affectionately to his father in prison – something his mother found it hard to forgive. Her taunts had become almost a neurosis because she could not stop them, and when she began nothing was too extravagant for her. Not only had his father deliberately corrupted Jimmy, but it would almost seem as if he had got himself gaoled with no other object than that of disgracing him.

'Oh, give it a rest, Mum,' Jimmy said, glowering at her from over his book. 'I made a bit of a fool of myself but Father had nothing to do with that.'

'Don't tell me it wasn't his fault, Jimmy,' she said cuttingly. 'Is it you who never touched drink till you set foot in his house? You who never looked at the side of the road a girl walked at till you stayed with that – *filthy* thing?'

'All right, all right,' he said angrily. 'Maybe I am a black-guard, but if I am, that's my fault, not his. He only did what he thought was the best thing for me. Why do you always assume that everybody but yourself is acting with bad motives?'

'That's what the police seem to think too,' she said.

Jimmy suddenly lost all control of himself. Like all who have missed the safety valves of childhood he had an almost insane temper. He flung his book to a corner of the room and went to the door, white and shaking.

'Damn you!' he said in a low, bitter voice. 'I think you're almost glad to see that poor, unfortunate devil ruined.'

It scared her, because for the first time she saw that her son, the boy for whom she had slaved her life away, was no better than a stranger. But it scared Jimmy even more. He had become so accustomed to obedience, gentleness, and industry that he could not even imagine how he had come to speak to his mother in such a tone. He, too, was a stranger to himself, a stranger who seemed to have nothing whatever to do with the Jimmy Garvin who had worked so happily every evening at home, and all he could do was to get away from it all with a couple of cronies and drink and argue till he was himself again.

What neither of them saw was that the real cause of the breach was that his mother wanted him back, wanted him all to herself as in the old days, forgetting that he had ever met or liked his foolish, wayward father, and that this was something he could not forget, even for her.

The situation could not last, of course. One evening he came in, looking distressed and pale.

'Mum,' he said with a guilty air, 'I have the offer of a room with a couple of students in Sheares' Street. I can help them with their work, and I'll have a place to myself to do my own. I think it's a good idea, don't you?'

She sat in the dusk, looking into the fire with a strained air, but when she spoke her voice was even enough.

'Oh, is that so, Jimmy?' she said. 'I suppose this house isn't good enough for you any longer?'

'Now, you know it's not that, Mum,' he replied. 'It's just that I have to work, and I can't while you and I are sparring. This is only for the time being, and anyway, I can always spend the week-ends here.'

'Very well, Jimmy,' she said coldly. 'If the house is here you'll be welcome. Now, I'd better go and pack your things.'

By the time he left he was in tears, but she was like a woman of ice. Afterwards she came to our house and sat over the fire in the kitchen. She tried to speak with calm, but she was shivering all over.

'Wisha, child, what ails you?' Mother asked in alarm.

'Nothing, only Jimmy's left me,' Mrs Garvin answered in a thin, piping voice while she tried to smile.

'Who?' Mother asked in horror, clasping her hands. 'Jimmy?'

'Packed and left an hour ago. He's taken a room with some students in town . . . I suppose it was the best thing. He said he couldn't stand living in the same house with me.'

'Ah, for goodness' sake!' wailed Mother.

'That's what he said, Mrs Delaney.'

'And who cares what he said?' Mother cried in a blaze of anger. 'How can you be bothered with what people say? Half their time they don't know what they're saying. Twenty-five years I'm living in the one house with Mick Delaney, and where would I be if I listened to what he says? . . . 'Tis for the best, girl,' she added gently, resting her hand on Mrs Garvin's knee. ''Tisn't for want of love only that ye were hurting one another. Jimmy is a fine boy, and he'll be a fine man yet.'

Almost immediately Jimmy got himself a small job in the Court-house with the taxation people. In the evenings he worked and over the week-ends he came home. There was no trouble about this. He enjoyed his good meals and his soft bed, and in the evenings you could hear him bellowing happily away at the piano. His mother and he were better friends than they had been for a long time, but something seemed to have broken in her. Nothing, I believe, could now have roused her to any fresh effort. At the best of times she would have taken her son's liberation hard, but now the facile pessimism that had only been a crust over her real feelings seemed to have become part of her. It wasn't obtrusive or offensive; when we met she still approached me with the same eagerness, but suddenly she would give a bitter little smile and shrug and say: 'It's well to be you, Larry. You still have your dreams.' She seemed to me to spend more of her time in the church.

The rooms in Sheares' Street were not all they might have been and Jimmy finally married Anne Reidy, the girl he had been walking out with. Anne had always struck me as a fine, jolly, bouncing girl. They lived in rooms on the Dyke Parade with the gas-stove in the hall and the bathroom up the stairs, and even for these small comforts Anne had to hold down a job and dodge an early pregnancy, which according to her was 'a career in itself'. Jimmy was studying for a degree from London University, and doing the work by post. They were two hot-blooded people and accustomed to comfort, and the rows between them were shattering. Later, they reported them in detail to me almost as though they enjoyed them, which perhaps they did. Sometimes I met them up the tree-shadowed walk late at night, and went back for an hour to drink tea with them. Jimmy was thin, and there was a translucency about his skin that I didn't like. I guessed they were pretty close to starvation, yet in their queer way they seemed to be enjoying that too.

By this time Jimmy could have had a permanent job in the County Council – people like him have the knack of making themselves indispensable – but he turned it down – foolishly, I thought. He wanted a degree, though he seemed to me to have no clear notion of what use it was going to be to him when he got it. He talked of Anne and himself getting jobs together in England, but that struck me as no more than old talk. It was only later that I understood it. He wanted a degree because it was the only pattern of achievement he understood, and the only one that could re-establish him in his own esteem. This was where he had failed, and this was where he must succeed. And this was what they were really fighting for, living on scraps, quarrelling like hell, dressing in old clothes, and cracking jokes about their poverty till they had the bailiffs in, and Anne's career of childlessness had broken down with a bang.

Then one night I found them at supper in a little restaurant in a lane off Patrick Street. Jimmy was drunk and excited, and when he saw me he came up to me demonstratively and embraced me.

'Ah, the stout man!' he shouted with his eyes burning. 'The steady Delaney! Look at him! Thirty if he's a day, and not a letter to his name!'

'He's celebrating,' Anne said rather unnecessarily, laughing at me with her mouth full. 'He's got his old degree. Isn't it a blessing? This is our first steak in six months.'

'And what are you going to do now?' I asked.

'Tomorrow,' said Jimmy, 'we're going on our honeymoon.'

'Baby and all!' Anne said, and exploded in laughter. 'Now tell him where!'

'Why wouldn't I tell him where?' shouted Jimmy. 'Why wouldn't I tell everybody? What's wrong with going to see the old man in gaol before they let him out? Nobody else did, even that bitch of a woman. Never went to see him and never sent the kid.'

'That's right,' Anne said almost hysterically. 'Now tell him about baby sister, Gussie. That's the bit my mother is dying to hear.'

'You know what your mother can do,' Jimmy said exultantly. 'Where's that waitress?' he called, his long, pale face shining. 'Delaney needs drink.'

'Garvin has too much drink,' said Anne. 'And I'll be up all night putting wet cloths on his head. ... You should see him when he's sick,' she said indignantly. '"Oh, I'm finished! Oh, I'm going to die!" That's what his mother did for him!'

That may have been what his mother had done for him; I didn't know, but what interested me was what his father had done for him. All that evening while they chattered and laughed in a sort of frenzy of relief, I was thinking of the troubles that Jimmy's discovery of his father had brought into his life, but I was thinking too of the strength it had given him to handle them. Now, whatever he had inherited from his parents, he had combined it into something that belonged to neither of them, that was his only, and a very fine thing it seemed to me.

Song Without Words

EVEN if there were only two men left in the world and both of them saints they wouldn't be happy. One of them would be bound to try and improve the other. That is the nature of things.

I am not, of course, suggesting that either Brother Arnold or Brother Michael was a saint. In private life Brother Arnold was a postman, but as he had a great name as a cattle doctor they had put him in charge of the monastery cows. He had the sort of face you would expect to see advertising somebody's tobacco; a big, innocent, contented face with a pair of blue eyes that were always twinkling. According to the rule he was supposed to look sedate and go about in a composed and measured way, but he could not keep his eyes downcast for any length of time and wherever his eyes glanced they twinkled, and his hands slipped out of his long white sleeves and dropped some remark in sign language. Most of the monks were good at the deaf and dumb language; it was their way of getting round the rule of silence, and it was remarkable how much information they managed to pick up and pass on.

Now, one day it happened that Brother Arnold was looking for a bottle of castor oil and he remembered that he had lent it to Brother Michael, who was in charge of the stables. Brother Michael was a man he did not get on too well with; a dour, dull sort of man who kept to himself. He was a man of no great appearance, with a mournful wizened little face and a pair of weak red-rimmed eyes – for all the world the sort of man who, if you shaved off his beard, clapped a bowler hat on his head and a cigarette in his mouth, would need no other reference to get a job in a stable.

There was no sign of him about the stable yard, but this was only natural because he would not be wanted till the other monks returned from the fields, so Brother Arnold pushed in the stable door to look for the bottle himself. He did not see the bottle, but he saw something which made him wish he had not come. Brother Michael was hiding in one of the horse-boxes; standing against the partition with something hidden behind his back and wearing the look of a little boy who has been caught at the jam. Something told Brother Arnold that at that moment he was the most unwelcome man in the world. He grew red, waved his hand to indicate that he did not wish to be involved, and returned to his own quarters.

It came as a shock to him. It was plain enough that Brother Michael was up to some shady business, and Brother Arnold could not help wondering what it was. It was funny, he had noticed the same thing when he was in the world; it was always the quiet, sneaky fellows who were up to mischief. In chapel he looked at Brother Michael and got the impression that Brother Michael was looking at him, a furtive look to make sure he would not be noticed. Next day when they met in the yard he caught Brother Michael glancing at him and gave back a cold look and a nod.

The following day Brother Michael beckoned him to come over to the stables as though one of the horses was sick. Brother Arnold knew it wasn't that; he knew he was about to be given some sort of explanation and was curious to know what it would be. He was an inquisitive man; he knew it, and blamed himself a lot for it.

Brother Michael closed the door carefully after him and then leaned back against the jamb of the door with his legs crossed and his hands behind his back, a foxy pose. Then he nodded in the direction of the horse-box where Brother Arnold had almost caught him in the act, and raised his brows inquiringly. Brother Arnold nodded gravely. It was not an occasion he was likely to forget. Then Brother Michael put his hand up his sleeve and held out a folded newspaper. Brother Arnold shrugged his shoulders as though to say the matter had nothing to do with him, but the other man nodded and continued to press the newspaper on him.

He opened it without any great curiosity, thinking it might be some local paper Brother Michael smuggled in for the sake of the news from home and was now offering as the explanation of his own furtive behaviour. He glanced at the name and then a great light broke on him. His whole face lit up as though an electric torch had been switched on behind, and finally he burst out laughing. He couldn't help himself. Brother Michael did not laugh but gave a dry little cackle which was as near as he ever got to laughing. The name of the paper was the *Irish Racing News*.

Now that the worst was over Brother Michael grew more relaxed. He pointed to a heading about the Curragh and then at himself. Brother Arnold shook his head, glancing at him expectantly as though he were hoping for another laugh. Brother Michael scratched his head for some indication of what he meant. He was a slow-witted man and had never been good at the sign talk. Then he picked up the sweeping brush and straddled it. He pulled up his skirts, stretched out his left hand holding the handle of the brush, and with his right began flogging the air behind him, a grim look on his leathery little face. Inquiringly he looked again and Brother Arnold nodded excitedly and put his thumbs up to show he understood. He saw now that the real reason Brother Michael had behaved so queerly was that he read racing papers on the sly and he did so because in private life he had been a jockey on the Curragh.

He was still laughing like mad, his blue eyes dancing, wishing only for an audience to tell it to, and then he suddenly remembered all the things he had thought about Brother Michael and bowed his head and beat his breast by way of asking pardon. Then he glanced at the paper again. A mischievous twinkle came into his eyes and he pointed the paper at himself. Brother Michael pointed back, a bit puzzled. Brother Arnold chuckled and stowed the paper up his sleeve. Then Brother Michael winked and gave the thumbs-up sign. In that slow cautious way of his he went down the stable and reached to the top of the wall where the roof sloped down on it. This, it seemed, was his hiding-hole. He took down several more papers and gave them to Brother Arnold.

For the rest of the day Brother Arnold was in the highest spirits. He winked and smiled at everyone till they all wondered what the joke was. He still pined for an audience. All that evening and long after he had retired to his cubicle he rubbed his hands and giggled with delight whenever he thought of it; it was like a window let into his loneliness; it gave him a warm, mellow feeling, as though his heart had expanded to embrace all humanity.

It was not until the following day that he had a chance of looking at the papers himself. He spread them on a rough desk under a feeble electric-light bulb high in the roof. It was four years since he had seen a paper of any sort, and then it was only a scrap of local newspaper which one of the carters had brought wrapped about a bit of bread and butter. But Brother Arnold had palmed it, hidden it in his desk, and studied it as if it were a bit of a lost Greek play. He had never known until then the modern appetite for words – printed words, regardless of their meaning. This was merely a County Council wrangle about the appointment of seven warble-fly inspectors, but by the time he was done with it he knew it by heart.

So he did not just glance at the racing papers as a man would in the train to pass the time. He nearly ate them. Blessed words like fragments of tunes coming to him out of a past life; paddocks and point-to-points and two-year-olds, and again he was in the middle of a racecourse crowd on a spring day with silver streamers of light floating down the sky like heavenly bunting. He had only to close his eyes and he could see the refreshment tent again with the golden light leaking like spilt honey through the rents in the canvas, and the girl he had been in love with sitting on an upturned lemonade box. 'Ah, Paddy,' she had said, 'sure there's bound to be racing in heaven!' She was fast, too fast for Brother Arnold, who was a steady-going fellow and had never got over the shock of discovering that all the time she had been running another man. But now all he could remember of her was her smile and the tone of her voice as she spoke the words which kept running through his head, and afterwards whenever his eyes met Brother Michael's he longed to give him a hearty slap on the back and say: 'Michael, boy, there's bound to be racing in heaven.' Then he grinned and Brother Michael, though he didn't hear the words or the tone of voice, without once losing his casual melancholy air, replied with a wall-faced flicker of the horny eyelid, a tick-tack man's

signal, a real, expressionless, horsy look of complete understanding.

One day Brother Michael brought in a few papers. On one
he pointed to the horses he had marked, on the other to the
horses who had won. He showed no signs of his jubilation. He
just winked, a leathery sort of wink, and Brother Arnold gaped
as he saw the list of winners. It filled him with wonder and
pride to think that when so many rich and clever people had
lost, a simple little monk living hundreds of miles away could
work it all out. The more he thought of it the more excited he
grew. For one wild moment he felt it might be his duty to tell
the Abbot, so that the monastery could have the full advantage
of Brother Michael's intellect, but he realized that it wouldn't
do. Even if Brother Michael could restore the whole abbey from
top to bottom with his winnings, the ecclesiastical authorities
would disapprove of it. But more than ever he felt the need of
an audience.

He went to the door, reached up his long arm, and took down
a loose stone from the wall above it. Brother Michael shook his
head several times to indicate how impressed he was by Brother
Arnold's ingenuity. Brother Arnold grinned. Then he took
down a bottle and handed it to Brother Michael. The ex-jockey
gave him a questioning look as though he were wondering if
this wasn't cattle-medicine; his face did not change but he
took out the cork and sniffed. Still his face did not change. All
at once he went to the door, gave a quick glance up and a
quick glance down and then raised the bottle to his lips. He
reddened and coughed; it was good beer and he wasn't used to
it. A shudder as of delight went through him and his little eyes
grew moist as he watched Brother Arnold's throttle working on
well-oiled hinges. The big man put the bottle back in its
hiding-place and indicated by signs that Brother Michael
could go there himself whenever he wanted a drink. Brother
Michael shook his head doubtfully, but Brother Arnold nodded
earnestly. His fingers moved like lightning while he explained
how a farmer whose cow he had cured had it left in for him
every week.

The two men were now fast friends. They no longer had any

secrets from one another. Each knew the full extent of the other's little weakness and liked him the more for it. Though they couldn't speak to one another they sought out one another's company and whenever other things failed they merely smiled. Brother Arnold felt happier than he had felt for years. Brother Michael's successes made him want to try his hand, and whenever Brother Michael gave him a racing paper with his own selections marked, Brother Arnold gave it back with his, and they waited impatiently till the results turned up three or four days late. It was also a new lease of life to Brother Michael, for what comfort is it to a man if he has all the winners when not a soul in the world can ever know whether he has or not. He felt now that if only he could have a bob each way on a horse he would ask no more of life.

It was Brother Arnold, the more resourceful of the pair, who solved that difficulty. He made out dockets, each valued for so many Hail Marys, and the loser had to pay up in prayers for the other man's intention. It was an ingenious scheme and it worked admirably. At first Brother Arnold had a run of luck. But it wasn't for nothing that Brother Michael had had the experience; he was too tough to make a fool of himself even over a few Hail Marys, and everything he did was carefully planned. Brother Arnold began by imitating him, but the moment he struck it lucky he began to gamble wildly. Brother Michael had often seen it happen on the Curragh and remembered the fate of those it had happened to. Men he had known with big houses and cars were now cadging drinks in the streets of Dublin. It struck him that God had been very good to Brother Arnold in calling him to a monastic life where he could do no harm to himself or to his family.

And this, by the way, was quite uncalled for, because in the world Brother Arnold's only weakness had been for a bottle of stout and the only trouble he had ever caused his family was the discomfort of having to live with a man so good and gentle, but Brother Michael was rather given to a distrust of human nature, the sort of man who goes looking for a moral in everything even when there is no moral in it. He tried to make Brother Arnold take an interest in the scientific side of betting but the man seemed to treat it all as a great joke. A flighty sort of fellow! He bet more and more wildly with that foolish good-natured grin on his face, and after a while Brother Michael found himself being owed a deuce of a lot of prayers, which his literal mind insisted on translating into big houses and cars. He didn't like that either. It gave him scruples of conscience and finally turned him against betting altogether. He tried to get Brother Arnold to drop it, but as became an inventor, Brother Arnold only looked hurt and indignant, like a child who has been told to stop his play. Brother Michael had that weakness on his conscience too. It suggested that he was getting far too attached to Brother Arnold, as in fact he was. It would have been very difficult not to. There was something warm and friendly about the man which you couldn't help liking.

Then one day he went in to Brother Arnold and found him with a pack of cards in his hand. They were a very old pack which had more than served their time in some farmhouse, but Brother Arnold was looking at them in rapture. The very sight of them gave Brother Michael a turn. Brother Arnold made the gesture of dealing, half playfully, and the other shook his head sternly. Brother Arnold blushed and bit his lip but he persisted, seriously enough now. All the doubts Brother Michael had been having for weeks turned to conviction. This was the primrose path with a vengeance, one thing leading to another. Brother Arnold grinned and shuffled the deck; Brother Michael, biding his time, cut for deal and Brother Arnold won. He dealt two hands of five and showed the five of hearts as trump. He wanted to play twenty-five. Still waiting for a sign, Brother Michael looked at his own hand. His face grew grimmer. It was not the sort of sign he had expected but it was a sign all the same; four hearts in a bunch; the ace, jack, two other trumps, and the three of spades. An unbeatable hand. Was that luck? Was that coincidence, or was it the Adversary himself, taking a hand and trying to draw him deeper in the mire.

He liked to find a moral in things, and the moral in this was plain, though it went to his heart to admit it. He was a lonesome, melancholy man and the horses had meant a lot to him in his bad spells. At times it had seemed as if they were the only thing that kept him sane. How could he face twenty, perhaps thirty, years more of life, never knowing what horses were running or what jockeys were up – Derby Day, Punchestown, Leopardstown, and the Curragh all going by while he knew no more of them than if he were already dead?

'O Lord,' he thought bitterly, 'a man gives up the whole world for You, his chance of a wife and kids, his home and his family, his friends and his job, and goes off to a bare mountain where he can't even tell his troubles to the man alongside him; and still he keeps something back, some little thing to remind him of what he gave up. With me 'twas the horses and with this man 'twas the sup of beer, and I dare say there are fellows inside who have a bit of a girl's hair hidden somewhere they can go and look at it now and again. I suppose we all have our little hiding-hole if the truth was known, but as small as it is, the whole world is in it, and bit by bit it grows on us again till the day You find us out.'

Brother Arnold was waiting for him to play. He sighed and put his hand on the desk. Brother Arnold looked at it and at him. Brother Michael idly took away the spade and added the heart and still Brother Arnold couldn't see. Then Brother Michael shook his head and pointed to the floor. Brother Arnold bit his lip again as though he were on the point of crying, then threw down his own hand and walked to the other end of the cow-house. Brother Michael left him so for a few moments. He could see the struggle going on in the man, could almost hear the Devil whisper in his ear that he (Brother Michael) was only an old woman – Brother Michael had heard that before; that life was long and a man might as well be dead and buried as not have some little innocent amusement – the sort of plausible whisper that put many a man on the gridiron. He knew, however hard it was now, that Brother Arnold would be grateful to him in the other world. 'Brother Michael,' he would say, 'I don't know what I'd ever have done without your example.'

Then Brother Michael went up and touched him gently on the shoulder. He pointed to the bottle, the racing paper, and the cards. Brother Arnold fluttered his hands despairingly but he nodded. They gathered them up between them, the cards, the bottle, and the papers, hid them under their habits to avoid all occasion of scandal, and went off to confess their guilt to the Prior.

Uprooted

SPRING had only come and already he was tired to death; tired of the city, tired of his job. He had come up from the country intending to do wonders, but he was as far as ever from that. He would be lucky if he could carry on, be at school each morning at half past nine and satisfy his half-witted principal.

He lodged in a small red-brick house in Rathmines that was kept by a middle-aged brother and sister who had been left a bit of money and thought they would end their days enjoyably in a city. They did not enjoy themselves, regretted their little farm in Kerry, and were glad of Ned Keating because he could talk to them about all the things they remembered and loved.

Keating was a slow, cumbrous young man with dark eyes and a dark cow's-lick that kept tumbling into them. He had a slight stammer and ran his hand through his long limp hair from pure nervousness. He had always been dreamy and serious. Sometimes on market days you saw him standing for an hour in Nolan's shop, turning the pages of a schoolbook. When he could not afford it he put it back with a sigh and went off to find his father in a pub, just raising his eyes to smile at Jack Nolan. After his elder brother Tom had gone for the church he and his father had constant rows. Nothing would do Ned now but to be a teacher. Hadn't he all he wanted now? his father asked. Hadn't he the place to himself? What did he want going teaching? But Ned was stubborn. With an obstinate, almost despairing determination he had fought his way through the training college into a city job. The city was what he had always wanted. And now the city had failed him. In the evenings you could still see him poking round the second-hand bookshops on the quays, but his eyes were already beginning to lose their eagerness.

It had all seemed so clear. But then he had not counted on

his own temper. He was popular because of his gentleness, but how many concessions that involved! He was hesitating, good-natured, slow to see guile, slow to contradict. He felt he was constantly underestimating his own powers. He even felt he lacked spontaneity. He did not drink, smoked little, and saw dangers and losses everywhere. He blamed himself for avarice and cowardice. The story he liked best was about the country boy and the letter box. 'Indeed, what a fool you think I am! Put me letther in a pump!'

He was in no danger of putting his letter in a pump or anywhere else for the matter of that. He had only one friend, a nurse in Vincent's Hospital, a wild, light-hearted, light-headed girl. He was very fond of her and supposed that some day when he had money enough he would ask her to marry him; but not yet: and at the same time something that was both shyness and caution kept him from committing himself too far. Sometimes he planned excursions beside the usual weekly walk or visit to the pictures but somehow they seldom came to anything.

He no longer knew why he had come to the city, but it was not for the sake of the bed-sitting room in Rathmines, the oblong of dusty garden outside the window, the trams clanging up and down, the shelf full of second-hand books, or the occasional visit to the pictures. Half humorously, half despairingly, he would sometimes clutch his head in his hands and admit to himself that he had no notion of what he wanted. He would have liked to leave it all and go to Glasgow or New York as a labourer, not because he was romantic, but because he felt that only when he had to work with his hands for a living and was no longer sure of his bed would he find out what all his ideals and emotions meant and where he could fit them into the scheme of his life.

But no sooner did he set out for school next morning, striding slowly along the edge of the canal, watching the trees become green again and the tall claret-coloured houses painted on the quiet surface of the water, than all his fancies took flight. Put his letter in a pump indeed! He would continue to be submissive and draw his salary and wonder how much he could save and when he would be able to buy a little house to bring his girl into; a nice thing to think of on a spring morning: a house of his own and a wife in the bed beside him. And his nature would continue to contract about him, every ideal, every generous impulse another mesh to draw his head down tighter to his knees till in ten years' time it would tie him hand and foot.

2

Tom who was a curate in Wicklow wrote and suggested that they might go home together for the long week-end, and on Saturday morning they set out in Tom's old Ford. It was Easter weather, pearly and cold. They stopped at several pubs on the way and Tom ordered whiskies. Ned was feeling expansive and joined him. He had never quite grown used to his brother, partly because of old days when he felt that Tom was getting the education he should have got, partly because his ordination seemed to have shut him off from the rest of the family, and now it was as though he were trying to surmount it by his boisterous manner and affected *bonhomie*. He was like a man shouting to his comrades across a great distance. He was different from Ned; lighter in colour of hair and skin; fatheaded, fresh-complexioned, deep-voiced, and autocratic; an irascible, humorous, friendly man who was well-liked by those he worked for. Ned, who was shy and all tied up within himself, envied him his way with men in garages and barmaids in hotels.

It was nightfall when they reached home. Their father was in his shirt-sleeves at the gate waiting to greet them, and immediately their mother rushed out as well. The lamp was standing in the window and threw its light as far as the whitewashed gate-posts. Little Brigid, the girl from up the hill who helped their mother now she was growing old, stood in the doorway in half-silhouette. When her eyes caught theirs she bent her head in confusion.

Nothing was changed in the tall, bare, whitewashed kitchen. The harness hung in the same place on the wall, the rosary on the same nail in the fireplace, by the stool where their mother usually sat; table under the window, churn against the back door, stair without banisters mounting straight to the attic door that yawned in the wall – all seemed as unchanging as the sea outside. Their mother sat on the stool, her hands on her knees, a coloured shawl tied tightly about her head, like a gipsy woman with her battered yellow face and loud voice. Their father, fresh-complexioned like Tom, stocky and broken bottomed, gazed out the front door, leaning with one hand on the dresser in the pose of an orator while Brigid wet the tea.

'I said ye'd be late,' their father proclaimed triumphantly, twisting his moustache. 'Didn't I, woman? Didn't I say they'd be late?'

'He did, he did,' their mother assured them. ''Tis true for him.'

'Ah, I knew ye'd be making halts. But damn it, if I wasn't put astray by Thade Lahy's car going east!'

'And was that Thade Lahy's car?' their mother asked in a shocked tone.

'I told ye 'twas Thade Lahy's,' piped Brigid, plopping about in her long frieze gown and bare feet.

'Sure I should know it, woman,' old Tomas said with chagrin. 'He must have gone into town without us noticing him.'

'Oye, and how did he do that?' asked their mother.

'Leave me alone now,' Tomas said despairingly. 'I couldn't tell you, I could not tell you.'

'My goodness, I was sure that was the Master's car,' their mother said wonderingly, pulling distractedly at the tassels of her shawl.

'I'd know the rattle of Thade Lahy's car anywhere,' little Brigid said very proudly and quite unregarded.

It seemed to Ned that he was interrupting a conversation that had been going on since his last visit, and that the road outside and the sea beyond it, and every living thing that passed before them, formed a pantomime that was watched endlessly and passionately from the darkness of the little cottage.

'Wisha, I never asked if ye'd like a drop of something,' their father said with sudden vexation.

'Is it whisky?' boomed Tom.

'Why? Would you sooner whisky?'

'Can't you pour it out first and ask us after?' growled Tom.

'The whisky, is it?'

''Tis not. I didn't come all the ways to this place for what I can get better at home. You'd better have a bottle ready for me to take back.'

'Coleen will have it. Damn it, wasn't it only last night I said to Coleen that you'd likely want a bottle? Some way it struck me you would. Oh, he'll have it, he'll have it.'

'Didn't they catch that string of misery yet?' asked Tom with the cup to his lips.

'Ah, man alive, you'd want to be a greyhound to catch him. God Almighty, hadn't they fifty police after him last November, scouring the mountains from one end to the other and all they caught was a glimpse of the white of his ass. Ah, but the priest preached a terrible sermon against him – by name, Tom, by name!'

'Is old Murphy blowing about it still?' growled Tom.

'Oh, let me alone now!' Tomas threw his hands to heaven and strode to and fro in his excitement, his bucket-bottom wagging. Ned knew to his sorrow that his father could be prudent, silent, and calculating; he knew only too well the cock of the head, the narrowing of the eyes, but, like a child, the old man loved innocent excitement and revelled in scenes of the wildest passion, all about nothing. Like an old actor he turned everything to drama. 'The like of it for abuse was never heard, never heard, never heard! How Coleen could ever raise his head again after it! And where the man got the words from! Tom, my treasure, my son, you'll never have the like.'

'I'd spare my breath to cool my porridge,' Tom replied scornfully. 'I dare say you gave up your own still so?'

'I didn't, Tom, I didn't. The drop I make, 'twould harm no one. Only a drop for Christmas and Easter.'

The lamp was in its own place on the rear wall, and made a circle of brightness on the fresh lime-wash. Their mother was leaning over the fire with joined hands, lost in thought. The front door was open and night thickening outside, the coloured

night of the west; and as they ate their father walked to and fro
in long ungainly strides, pausing each time at the door to give
a glance up and down the road and at the fire to hoist his broken
bottom to warm. Ned heard steps come up the road from the
west. His father heard them too. He returned to the door and
glued his hand to the jamb. Ned covered his eyes with his
hands and felt that everything was as it had always been. He
could hear the noise of the strand as a background to the voices.

'God be with you, Tomas,' the voice said.

'God and Mary be with you, Teig.' (In Irish they were speaking.) 'What way are you?'

'Well, honour and praise be to God. 'Tis a fine night.'

''Tis, 'tis, 'tis so indeed. A grand night, praise be to God.'

'Musha, who is it?' their mother asked, looking round.

''Tis young Teig,' their father replied, looking after him.

'Shemus's young Teig?'

''Tis, 'tis, 'tis.'

'But where would Shemus's young Teig be going at this
hour of night? 'Tisn't to the shop?'

'No, woman, no, no, no. Up to the uncle's I suppose.'

'Is it Ned Willie's?'

'He's sleeping at Ned Willie's,' Brigid chimed in in her high-
pitched voice, timid but triumphant. ''Tis since the young
teacher came to them.'

There was no more to be said. Everything was explained and
Ned smiled. The only unfamiliar voice, little Brigid's, seemed
the most familiar of all.

3

Tom said first Mass next morning and the household, all but
Brigid, went. They drove, and Tomas in high glee sat in front
with Tom, waving his hand and shouting greetings at all they
met. He was like a boy, so intense was his pleasure. The chapel
was perched high above the road. Outside the morning was
grey and beyond the windy edge of the cliff was the sea. The
wind blew straight in, setting cloaks and petticoats flying.

After dinner as the two boys were returning from a series of
visits to the neighbours' houses their father rushed down the

road to meet them, shaking them passionately by the hand and asking were they well. When they were seated in the kitchen he opened up the subject of his excitement.

'Well,' he said, 'I arranged a grand little outing for ye to-morrow, thanks be to God,' and to identify further the source of his inspiration he searched at the back of his neck for the peak of his cap and raised it solemnly.

'Musha, what outing are you talking about?' their mother asked angrily.

'I arranged for us to go over the bay to your brother's.'

'And can't you leave the poor boys alone?' she bawled. 'Haven't they only the one day? Isn't it for the rest they came?'

'Even so, even so, even so,' Tomas said with mounting passion. 'Aren't their own cousins to lay eyes on them?'

'I was in Carriganassa for a week last summer,' said Tom.

'Yes, but I wasn't, and Ned wasn't. 'Tis only decent.'

''Tisn't decency is worrying you at all but drink,' growled Tom.

'Oh!' gasped his father, fishing for the peak of his cap to swear with, 'that I might be struck dead!'

'Be quiet, you old heathen!' crowed his wife. 'That's the truth, Tom my pulse. Plenty of drink is what he wants where he won't be under my eye. Leave ye stop at home.'

'I can't stop at home, woman,' shouted Tomas. 'Why do you be always picking at me? I must go whether they come or not. I must go, I must go, and that's all there is about it.'

'Why must you?' asked his wife.

'Because I warned Red Pat and Dempsey,' he stormed. 'And the woman from the island is coming as well to see a daughter of hers that's married there. And what's more, I borrowed Cassidy's boat and he lent it at great inconvenience, and 'twould be very bad manners for me to throw his kindness back in his face. I must go.'

'Oh, we may as well all go,' said Tom.

It blew hard all night and Tomas, all anxiety, was out at break of day to watch the whitecaps on the water. While the boys were at breakfast he came in and, leaning his arms on the table with hands joined as though in prayer, he announced in a caressing voice that it was a beautiful day, thank God, a pet day with a moist gentle little bit of a breezheen that would only blow them over. His voice would have put a child to sleep, but his wife continued to nag and scold, and he stumped out again in a fury and sat on the wall with his back to the house and his legs crossed, chewing his pipe. He was dressed in his best clothes, a respectable blue tailcoat and pale frieze trousers with only one patch on the seat. He had turned his cap almost right way round so that the peak covered his right ear.

He was all over the boat like a boy. Dempsey, a haggard, pock-marked, melancholy man with a soprano voice of astounding penetration, took the tiller and Red Patrick the sail. Tomas clambered into the bows and stood there with one knee up, leaning forward like a figurehead. He knew the bay like a book. The island woman was perched on the ballast with her rosary in her hands and her shawl over her eyes to shut out the sight of the waves. The cumbrous old boat took the sail lightly enough and Ned leaned back on his elbows against the side, rejoicing in it all.

'She's laughing,' his father said delightedly when her bows ran white.

'Whose boat is that, Dempsey?' he asked, screwing up his eyes as another brown sail tilted ahead of them.

''Tis the island boat,' shrieked Dempsey.

''Tis not, Dempsey. 'Tis not indeed, my love. That's not the island boat.'

'Whose boat is it then?'

'It must be some boat from Carriganassa, Dempsey.'

''Tis the island boat I tell you.'

'Ah, why will you be contradicting me, Dempsey, my treasure? 'Tis not the island boat. The island boat has a dark-brown sail; 'tis only a month since 'twas tarred, and that's an old tarred sail, and what proves it out and out, Dempsey, the island boat has a patch in the corner.'

He was leaning well over the bows, watching the rocks that fled beneath them, a dark purple. He rested his elbow on his raised knee and looked back at them, his brown face sprinkled with spray and lit from below by the accumulated flickerings of

the water. His flesh seemed to dissolve, to become transparent,
while his blue eyes shone with extraordinary brilliance. Ned
half-closed his eyes and watched sea and sky slowly mount and
sink behind the red-brown, sun-filled sail and the poised and
eager figure.

'Tom!' shouted his father, and the battered old face peered
at them from under the arch of the sail, with which it was
almost one in tone, the silvery light filling it with warmth.

'Well?' Tom's voice was an inexpressive boom.

'You were right last night, Tom, my boy. My treasure, my
son, you were right. 'Twas for the drink I came.'

'Ah, do you tell me so?' Tom asked ironically.

''Twas, 'twas, 'twas,' the old man said regretfully. ''Twas
for the drink. 'Twas so, my darling. They were always decent
people, your mother's people, and 'tis her knowing how decent
they are makes her so suspicious. She's a good woman, a fine
woman, your poor mother, may the Almighty God bless her
and keep her and watch over her.'

'Aaaa-men,' Tom chanted irreverently as his father shook
his old cap piously towards the sky.

'But Tom! Are you listening, Tom?'

'Well, what is it now?'

'I had another reason.'

'Had you indeed?' Tom's tone was not encouraging.

'I had, I had, God's truth, I had. God blast the lie I'm telling
you, Tom, I had.'

''Twas boasting out of the pair of ye,' shrieked Dempsey
from the stern, the wind whipping the shrill notes from his lips
and scattering them wildly like scraps of paper.

''Twas so, Dempsey, 'twas so. You're right, Dempsey.
You're always right. The blessing of God on you, Dempsey,
for you always had the true word.' Tomas's laughing leprechaun countenance gleamed under the bellying, tilting,
chocolate-coloured sail and his powerful voice beat Dempsey's
down. 'And would you blame me?'

'The O'Donnells hadn't the beating of them in their own
hand,' screamed Dempsey.

'Thanks be to God for all His goodness and mercy,' shouted

Tomas, again waving his cap in a gesture of recognition towards the spot where he felt the Almighty might be listening, 'they have not. They have not so, Dempsey. And they have a good hand. The O'Donnells are a good family and an old family and a kind family, but they never had the like of my two sons.'

'And they were stiff enough with you when you came for the daughter,' shrieked Dempsey.

'They were, Dempsey, they were. They were stiff. They were so. You wouldn't blame them, Dempsey. They were an old family and I was nothing only a landless man.' With a fierce gesture the old man pulled his cap still farther over his ear, spat, gave his moustache a tug, and leaned at a still more precarious angle over the bow, his blue eyes dancing with triumph. 'But I had the gumption, Dempsey. I had the gumption, my love.'

The islands slipped past; the gulf of water narrowed and grew calmer, and white cottages could be seen scattered under the tall ungainly church. It was a wild and rugged coast, the tide was full, and they had to pull in as best they could among the rocks. Red Patrick leaped lightly ashore to draw in the boat. The others stepped after him into several inches of water and Red Patrick, himself precariously poised, held them from slipping. Rather shamefastly, Ned and Tom took off their shoes.

'Don't do that!' shrieked their father. 'We'll carry ye up. Mother of God, yeer poor feet!'

'Will you shut your old gob?' Tom said angrily.

They halted for a moment at the stile outside Caheraghs. Old Caheragh had a red beard and a broad, smiling face. Then they went on to O'Donnell's who had two houses, modern and old, separated by a yard. In one lived Uncle Maurice and his family and in the other Maurice's married son, Sean. Ned and Tom remained with Sean and his wife. Tom and he were old friends. When he spoke he rarely looked at Tom, merely giving him a sidelong glance that just reached to his chin and then dropped his eyes with a peculiar timid smile. ''Twas,' Ned heard him say, and then: 'He did,' and after that: 'Hardly.' Shuvaun was tall, nervous and matronly. She clung to their hands with an excess of eagerness as though she couldn't bear to let them go, uttering ejaculations of tenderness, delight, astonishment, pity, and admiration. Her speech was full of diminutives: 'childeen', 'handeen', 'boateen'. Three young children scrambled about the floor with a preoccupation scarcely broken by the strangers. Shuvaun picked her way through them, filling the kettle and cutting the bread, and then, as though afraid of neglecting Tom, she clutched his hand again. Her feverish concentration gave an impression that its very intensity bewildered her and made it impossible for her to understand one word they said. In three days' time it would all begin to drop into place in her mind and then she would begin quoting them.

Young Niall O'Donnell came in with his girl; one of the Deignans from up the hill. She was plump and pert; she had been in service in town. Niall was a well-built boy with a soft, wild-eyed, sensuous face and a deep mellow voice of great power. While they were having a cup of tea in the parlour where the three or four family photos were skyed, Ned saw the two of them again through the back window. They were standing on the high ground behind the house with the spring sky behind them and the light in their faces. Niall was asking her something but she, more interested in the sitting-room window, only shook her head.

'Ye only just missed yeer father,' said their Uncle Maurice when they went across to the other house for dinner. Maurice was a tightlipped little man with a high bald forehead and a snappy voice. 'He went off to Owney Pat's only this minute.'

'The devil!' said Tom. 'I knew he was out to dodge me. Did you give him whisky?'

'What the hell else could I give him?' snapped Maurice. 'Do you think 'twas tea the old coot was looking for?'

Tom took the place of honour at the table. He was the favourite. Through the doorway into the bedroom could be seen a big canopy bed and on the whiteness of a raised pillow a skeleton face in a halo of smoke-blue hair surmounted with what looked suspiciously like a mauve tea-cosy. Sometimes the white head would begin to stir and everyone fell silent while Niall, the old man's pet, translated the scarcely audible whisper. Sometimes Niall would go in with his stiff ungainly swagger and repeat one of Tom's jokes in his drawling, powerful bass. The hens stepped daintily about their feet, poking officious heads between them, and rushing out the door with a wild flutter and shriek when one of the girls hooshed them. Something timeless, patriarchal, and restful about it made Ned notice everything. It was as though he had never seen his mother's house before.

'Tell me,' Tom boomed with mock concern, leaning over confidentially to his uncle and looking under his brows at young Niall, 'speaking as a clergyman and for the good of the family and so on, is that son of yours coorting Delia Deignan?'

'Why? Was the young blackguard along with her again?' snapped Maurice in amusement.

'Of course I might be mistaken,' Tom said doubtfully.

'You wouldn't know a Deignan, to be sure,' Sean said dryly.

'Isn't any of them married yet?' asked Tom.

'No, by damn, no,' said Maurice. 'Isn't it a wonder?'

'Because,' Tom went on in the same solemn voice, 'I want someone to look after this young brother of mine. Dublin is a wild sort of place and full of temptations. Ye wouldn't know a decent little girl I could ask?'

'Cait! Cait!' they all shouted, Niall's deep voice loudest of all.

'Now all the same, Delia looks a smart little piece,' said Tom.

'No, Cait! Cait! Delia isn't the same since she went to town. She has notions of herself. Leave him marry Cait!'

Niall rose gleefully and shambled in to the old man. With a gamesome eye on the company Tom whispered:

'Is she a quiet sort of girl? I wouldn't like Ned to get anyone rough.'

'She is, she is,' they said, 'a grand girl!'

Sean rose quietly and went to the door with his head bowed.

'God knows, if anyone knows he should know and all the times he manhandled her.'

Tom sat bolt upright with mock indignation while the table rocked. Niall shouted the joke into his grandfather's ear. The mauve tea-cosy shook; it was the only indication of the old man's amusement.

4

The Deignans' house was on top of a hill high over the road and commanded a view of the countryside for miles. The two brothers with Sean and the O'Donnell girls reached it by a long winding boreen that threaded its way uncertainly through little grey rocky fields and walls of unmortared stone which rose against the sky along the edges of the hill like lacework. On their way they met another procession coming down the hill. It was headed by their father and the island woman, arm in arm, and behind came two locals with Dempsey and Red Patrick. All the party except the island woman were well advanced in liquor. That was plain when their father rushed forward to shake them all by the hand and ask them how they were. He said that divil such honourable and kindly people as the people of Carriganassa were to be found in the whole world, and of these there was no one a patch on the O'Donnells; kings and sons of kings as you could see from one look at them. He had only one more call to pay and promised to be at Caheraghs within a quarter of an hour.

They looked over the Deignans' half-door. The kitchen was empty. The girls began to titter. They knew the Deignans must have watched them coming from Maurice's door. The kitchen was a beautiful room; woodwork and furniture, homemade and shapely, were painted a bright red-brown and the painted dresser shone with pretty ware. They entered and looked about them. Nothing was to be heard but the tick of the cheap alarm clock on the dresser. One of the girls began to giggle hysterically. Sean raised his voice.

'Are ye in or are ye out, bad cess to ye!'

For a moment there was no reply. Then a quick step sounded in the attic and a girl descended the stairs at a run, drawing a black knitted shawl tighter about her shoulders. She was perhaps twenty-eight or thirty, with a narrow face, sharp like a ferret's, and blue nervous eyes. She entered the kitchen awkwardly sideways, giving the customary greetings but without looking at anyone.

'A hundred welcomes. . . . How are ye? . . . 'Tis a fine day.'

The O'Donnell girls giggled again. Nora Deignan looked at

them in astonishment, biting nervously at the tassel of her shawl. She had tiny sharp white teeth.

'What is it, aru?' she asked.

'Musha, will you stop your old cimeens,' boomed Tom, 'and tell us where's Cait from you? You don't think 'twas to see your ugly puss that we came up here?'

'Cait!' Nora called in a low voice.

'What is it?' another voice replied from upstairs.

'Damn well you know what it is,' bellowed Tom, 'and you cross-eyed expecting us since morning. Will you come down out of that or will I go up and fetch you?'

There was the same hasty step and a second girl descended the stairs. It was only later that Ned was able to realize how beautiful she was. She had the same narrow pointed face as her sister, the same slight features sharpened by a sort of animal instinct, the same blue eyes with their startled brightness; but all seemed to have been differently composed, and her complexion had a transparency as though her whole nature were shining through it. 'Child of Light, thy limbs are burning through the veil which seems to hide them,' Ned found himself murmuring. She came on them in the same hostile way, blushing furiously. Tom's eyes rested on her; soft, bleary, emotional eyes incredibly unlike her own.

'Have you nothing to say to me, Cait?' he boomed, and Ned thought his very voice was soft and clouded.

'Oh, a hundred welcomes.' Her blue eyes rested for a moment on him with what seemed a fierce candour and penetration and went past him to the open door. Outside a soft rain was beginning to fall; heavy clouds crushed down the grey landscape, which grew clearer as it merged into one common plane; the little grey bumpy fields with the walls of grey unmortared stone that drifted hither and over across them like blown sand, the whitewashed farmhouses lost to the sun sinking back into the brown-grey hillsides.

'Nothing else, my child?' he growled, pursing his lips.

'How are you?'

'The politeness is suffocating you. Where's Delia?'

'Here I am,' said Delia from the doorway immediately

behind him. In her furtive way she had slunk round the house. Her bland impertinence raised a laugh.

'The reason we called,' said Tom, clearing his throat, 'is this young brother of mine that's looking for a wife.'

Everyone laughed again. Ned knew the oftener a joke was repeated the better they liked it, but for him this particular joke was beginning to wear thin.

'Leave him take me,' said Delia with an arch look at Ned who smiled and gazed at the floor.

'Be quiet, you slut!' said Tom. 'There are your two sisters before you.'

'Even so, I want to go to Dublin. . . . Would you treat me to lemonade, mister?' she asked Ned with her impudent smile. 'This is a rotten hole. I'd go to America if they left me.'

'America won't be complete without you,' said Tom. 'Now, don't let me hurry ye, ladies, but my old fellow will be waiting for us in Johnny Kit's.'

'We'll go along with you,' said Nora, and the three girls took down three black shawls from inside the door. Some tension seemed to have gone out of the air. They laughed and joked between themselves.

'Ye'll get wet,' said Sean to the two brothers.

'Cait will make room for me under her shawl,' said Tom.

'Indeed I will not,' she cried, starting back with a laugh.

'Very shy you're getting,' said Sean with a good-natured grin.

''Tisn't that at all but she'd sooner the young man,' said Delia.

'What's strange is wonderful,' said Nora.

Biting her lip with her tiny front teeth, Cait looked angrily at her sisters and Sean, and then began to laugh. She glanced at Ned and smilingly held out her shawl in invitation, though at the same moment angry blushes chased one another across her forehead like squalls across the surface of a lake. The rain was a mild, persistent drizzle and a strong wind was blowing. Everything had darkened and grown lonely and, with his head in the blinding folds of the shawl, which reeked of turf-smoke, Ned felt as if he had dropped out of Time's pocket.

They waited in Caheragh's kitchen. The bearded old man sat in one chimney corner and a little bare-legged boy in the other. The dim blue light poured down the wide chimney on their heads in a shower with the delicacy of light on old china, picking out surfaces one rarely saw; and between them the fire burned a bright orange in the great whitewashed hearth with the black, swinging bars and pothook. Outside the rain fell softly, almost soundlessly, beyond the half door. Delia, her black shawl trailing from her shoulders, leaned over it, acting the part of watcher as in a Greek play. Their father's fifteen minutes had strung themselves out to an hour and two little barefooted boys had already been sent to hunt him down.

'Where are they now, Delia?' one of the O'Donnells would ask.

'Crossing the fields from Patsy Kit's.'

'He wasn't there so.'

'He wouldn't be,' the old man said. 'They'll likely go on to Ned Kit's now.'

'That's where they're making for,' said Delia. 'Up the hill at the far side of the fort.'

'They'll find him there,' the old man said confidently.

Ned felt as though he were still blanketed by the folds of the turf-reeking shawl. Something seemed to have descended on him that filled him with passion and loneliness. He could scarcely take his eyes off Cait. She and Nora sat on the form against the back wall, a composition in black and white, the black shawl drawn tight under the chin, the cowl of it breaking the curve of her dark hair, her shadow on the gleaming wall behind. She did not speak except to answer some question of Tom's about her brother, but sometimes Ned caught her looking at him with naked eyes. Then she smiled swiftly and secretly and turned her eyes again to the door, sinking back into pensiveness. Pensiveness or vacancy? he wondered. While he gazed at her face with the animal instinctiveness of its over-delicate features it seemed like a mirror in which he saw again the falling rain, the rocks and hills and angry sea.

The first announced by Delia was Red Patrick. After him

came the island woman. Each had last seen his father in a different place. Ned chuckled at a sudden vision of his father, eager and impassioned and aflame with drink, stumping with his broken bottom across endless fields through pouring rain with a growing procession behind him. Dempsey was the last to come. He doubted if Tomas would be in a condition to take the boat at all.

'What matter, aru?' said Delia across her shoulder. 'We can find room for the young man.'

'And where would we put him?' gaped Nora.

'He can have Cait's bed,' Delia said innocently.

'Oye, and where would Cait sleep?' Nora asked and then skitted and covered her face with her shawl. Delia scoffed. The men laughed and Cait, biting her lip furiously, looked at the floor. Again Ned caught her eyes on him and again she laughed and turned away.

Tomas burst in unexpected on them all like a sea-wind that scattered them before him. He wrung Tom's hand and asked him how he was. He did the same to Ned. Ned replied gravely that he was very well.

'In God's holy name,' cried his father, waving his arms like a windmill, 'what are ye all waiting for?'

The tide had fallen. Tomas grabbed an oar and pushed the boat on to a rock. Then he raised the sail and collapsed under it and had to be extricated from its drenching folds, glauming and swearing at Cassidy's old boat. A little group stood on a naked rock against a grey background of drifting rain. For a long time Ned continued to wave back to the black shawl that was lifted to him. An extraordinary feeling of exultation and loss enveloped him. Huddled up in his overcoat he sat with Dempsey in the stern, not speaking.

'It was a grand day,' his father declared, swinging himself to and fro, tugging at his Viking moustache, dragging the peak of his cap farther over his ear. His gestures betrayed a certain lack of rhythmical cohesion; they began and ended abruptly. 'Dempsey, my darling, wasn't it a grand day?'

''Twas a grand day for you,' shrieked Dempsey as if his throat would burst.

''Twas, my treasure, 'twas a beautiful day. I got an honourable reception and my sons got an honourable reception.'

By this time he was flat on his belly, one leg completely over the edge of the boat. He reached back a clammy hand to his sons.

''Twas the best day I ever had,' he said. 'I got porter and I got whisky and I got poteen. I did so, Tom, my calf. Ned, my brightness, I went to seven houses and in every house I got seven drinks and with every drink I got seven welcomes. And your mother's people are a hand of trumps. It was no slight they put on me at all even if I was nothing but a landless man. No slight, Tom. No slight at all.'

Darkness had fallen, the rain had cleared, the stars came out of a pitch-black sky under which the little tossing, nosing boat seemed lost beyond measure. In all the waste of water nothing could be heard but the splash of the boat's sides and their father's voice raised in tipsy song.

> *The evening was fair and the sunlight was yellow,*
> *I halted, beholding a maiden bright*
> *Coming to me by the edge of the mountain,*
> *Her cheeks had a berry-bright rosy light.*

5

Ned was the first to wake. He struck a match and lit the candle. It was time for them to be stirring. It was just after dawn, and at half past nine he must be in his old place in the schoolroom before the rows of pinched little city-faces. He lit a cigarette and closed his eyes. The lurch of the boat was still in his blood, the face of Cait Deignan in his mind, and as if from far away he heard a line of the wild love-song his father had been singing: 'And we'll drive the geese at the fall of night.'

He heard his brother mumble something and nudged him. Tom looked big and fat and vulnerable with his fair head rolled sideways and his heavy mouth dribbling on to the sleeve of his pyjamas. Ned slipped quietly out of bed, put on his trousers, and went to the window. He drew the curtains and let in the thin cold daylight. The bay was just visible and perfectly still. Tom began to mumble again in a frightened voice and Ned shook him. He started out of his sleep with a cry of fear, grabbing at the bed clothes. He looked first at Ned, then at the candle and drowsily rubbed his eyes.

'Did you hear it too?' he asked.

'Did I hear what?' asked Ned with a smile.

'In the room,' said Tom.

'There was nothing in the room,' replied Ned. 'You were ramaishing so I woke you up.'

'Was I? What was I saying?'

'You were telling no secrets,' said Ned with a quiet laugh.

'Hell!' Tom said in disgust and stretched out his arm for a cigarette. He lit it at the candle flame, his drowsy red face puckered and distraught. 'I slept rotten.'

'Oye!' Ned said quietly, raising his eyebrows. It wasn't often Tom spoke in that tone. He sat on the edge of the bed, joined his hands, and leaned forward, looking at Tom with wide gentle eyes.

'Is there anything wrong?' he asked.

'Plenty.'

'You're not in trouble?' Ned asked without raising his voice.

'Not that sort of trouble. The trouble is in myself.'

Ned gave him a look of intense sympathy and understanding. The soft emotional brown eyes were searching him for a judgement. Ned had never felt less like judging him.

'Ay,' he said gently and vaguely, his eyes wandering to the other side of the room while his voice took on its accustomed stammer, 'the trouble is always in ourselves. If we were contented in ourselves the other things wouldn't matter. I suppose we must only leave it to time. Time settles everything.'

'Time will settle nothing for me,' Tom said despairingly. 'You have something to look forward to. I have nothing. It's the loneliness of my job that kills you. Even to talk about it would be a relief but there's no one you can talk to. People come to you with their troubles but there's no one you can go to with your own.'

Again the challenging glare in the brown eyes and Ned

realized with infinite compassion that for years Tom had been living in the same state of suspicion and fear, a man being hunted down by his own nature; and that for years to come he would continue to live in this way, and perhaps never be caught again as he was now.

'A pity you came down here,' stammered Ned flatly. 'A pity we went to Carriganassa. 'Twould be better for both of us if we went somewhere else.'

'Why don't you marry her, Ned?' Tom asked earnestly.

'Who?' asked Ned.

'Cait.'

'Yesterday,' said Ned with the shy smile he wore when he confessed something, 'I nearly wished I could.'

'But you can, man,' Tom said eagerly, sitting upon his elbow. Like all men with frustration in their hearts he was full of schemes for others. 'You could marry her and get a school down here. That's what I'd do if I was in your place.'

'No,' Ned said gravely. 'We made our choice a long time ago. We can't go back on it now.'

Then with his hands in his trouser pockets and his head bowed he went out to the kitchen. His mother, the coloured shawl about her head, was blowing the fire. The bedroom door was open and he could see his father in shirt-sleeves kneeling beside the bed, his face raised reverently towards a holy picture, his braces hanging down behind. He unbolted the half-door, went through the garden and out on to the road. There was a magical light on every thing. A boy on a horse rose suddenly against the sky, a startling picture. Through the apple-green light over Carriganassa ran long streaks of crimson, so still they might have been enamelled. Magic, magic, magic! He saw it as in a children's picture-book with all its colours intolerably bright; something he had outgrown and could never return to, while the world he aspired to was as remote and intangible as it had seemed even in the despair of youth.

It seemed as if only now for the first time was he leaving home; for the first time and forever saying good-bye to it all.

The Miser

HE used to sit all day, looking out from behind the dirty little window of his dirty little shop in Main Street; a man with a smooth oval pate and bleared, melancholy-looking, unblinking eyes; a hanging lip with a fag dangling from it, and hanging unshaven chins. It was a face you'd remember; swollen, ponderous, crimson, with a frame of jet-black hair plastered down on either side with bear's grease; and though the hair grew grey and the face turned yellow it seemed to make no difference: because he never changed his position you did not notice the change which came over him from within, and saw him at the end as you had seen him at first, planted there like an oak or a rock. He scarcely stirred even when someone pushed in the old glazed door and stumbled down the steps from the street. The effort seemed to be too much for him; the bleary, bloodshot eyes travelled slowly to some shelf, the arm reached lifelessly out; the coins dropped in the till. Then he shrugged himself and gazed out into the street again. Sometimes he spoke, and it always gave you a shock, for it was as if the statue of O'Connell had descended from its pedestal and inquired in a melancholy bass voice and with old-fashioned politeness for some member of your family. It was a thing held greatly in his favour that he never forgot an old neighbour.

Sometimes the children tormented him, looking in and making faces at him through the glass, so that they distracted him from his vigil, and then he roared at them without stirring. Sometimes they went too far and his face swelled and grew purple; he staggered to the door and bellowed after them in a powerful resonant voice that echoed to the other end of the town. But mostly he stayed there silent and undisturbed, and the dirt and disorder round him grew and greased his hair and clothes, while his face and chin with their Buddha-like gravity were shiny with spilt gravy. His only luxury was the Woodbine that went out between his lips. The cigarettes were on the shelf behind him, and all he had to do was to reach out for them; he didn't need to turn his head.

He was the last of a very good family, the Devereuxs, who had once been big merchants in the town. People remembered his old father driving into town in his own carriage; indeed, they remembered Tom Devereux himself as a bit of a masher, smoking a cigar and wearing a new flower in his buttonhole every day. But then he married beneath him and the match turned out badly. There was a daughter called Joan but she turned out badly too, started a child and went away, God knows where, and now he had no one to look after him but an old soldier called Faxy, a tall, stringy, ravaged-looking man, toothless and half mad Faxy had attached himself to Tom years before as a batman. He boiled the kettle and brought the old man a cup of tea in the mornings.

'Orders for the day, general!' he would say then, springing to attention; and Devereux, after a lot of groaning, would fish out sixpence from under his pillow.

'And what the hell do you think I'm going to get for that?' Faxy would snarl, the smile withering from his puss.

'Oh, indeed,' Devereux would bellow complacently, 'you can get a very nice bit of black pudding for that.'

'And is it black pudding you're going to drink instead of tea?'

'But when I haven't it, man?' the old man would shout, turning purple.

'You haven't, I hear!' Faxy would hiss with a wolfish grin, stepping from one foot to the other like a child short-taken. 'Come on now, can't you? I can't be waiting the whole day for it. Baksheesh! Baksheesh for the sahib's tiffin!'

'I tell you to go away and not be annoying me,' Devereux would shout, and that was all the satisfaction Faxy got. It was a nightmare to Faxy, trying to get money or credit.

'But he have it, man, he have it,' he would hiss, leaning over the counters, trying to coax more credit out of the shopkeepers. 'Boxes of it he have, man; nailed down and flowing over. He have two big trunks of it under the bed alone.'

That was the report in town as well; everyone knew that the Devereuxs always had the tin and that old Tom hadn't lessened it much, and at one time or other, every shopkeeper had given him credit, and all ended by refusing it, seeing the old man in the window, day after day, looking as though he were immortal.

2

At long last he did have a stroke and had to take to his bed, upstairs in a stinking room with the sagging windowpanes padded and nailed against draughts from the Main Street, and the flowery wallpaper, layer on layer of it, hanging in bangles from the walls, while Faxy looked after the shop and made hay of the Woodbines and whatever else came handy. Not that there was much, only paraffin oil and candles and maybe a few old things like cards of castor-oil bottles that the commercials left on spec. Whenever a customer went out, bang, bang, bang! old Devereux thumped on the floor for Faxy.

'Who was that went out, Faxy?' he would groan. 'I didn't recognize the voice.'

'That was the Sheehan girl from the lane.'

'Did you ask her how her father was?'

'I did not, indeed, ask how her father was. I have something else to think about.'

'You ought to have asked her all the same,' the old man grumbled. 'What did she want?'

'A couple of candles,' hissed Faxy. 'Is there anything else you'd like to know?'

'It wasn't a couple of candles, Donnell. Don't you try and deceive me. I heard every word of it. I distinctly heard her asking for something else as well.'

'A pity the stroke affected your hearing,' snarled Faxy.

'Don't you try and deceive me, I say,' boomed Devereux. 'I have it all checked, Donnell, every ha'p'orth. Mind now what I'm saying!'

Then one morning while Faxy was smoking a cigarette and studying the racing in the previous day's paper, the shop door opened gently and Father Ring came in. Father Ring was a plausible little Kerryman with a sand-coloured face and a shock of red hair. He was always very deprecating, with an excuse-me air, and came in sideways, on tiptoe, wearing a shocked expression – it is only Kerrymen who can do things like that.

'My poor man,' he whispered, leaning over the counter to Faxy. 'I'm sorry for your trouble. Himself isn't well on you.'

'If he isn't,' snarled Faxy, looking as much like the Stag at Bay as made no difference, 'he's well looked after.'

'I know that, Faxy,' the priest said, nodding. 'I know that well. Still, 'twould be no harm if I had a few words with him. A man like that might go in a flash. . . . Tell me, Faxy,' he whispered with his hand across his lips and his head to one side, 'are his affairs in order?'

'How the hell would I know when the old devil won't even talk about them?' asked Faxy.

'That's bad, Faxy,' said Father Ring gravely. 'That's very bad. That's a great risk you're running, a man like you that must be owed a lot of money. If anything happened him you might be thrown on the road without a ha'penny. Whisper here to me,' he went on, drawing Faxy closer and whispering into his ear the way no one but a Kerryman can do it, without once taking his eyes off Faxy's face. 'If you want to make sure of your rights, you'd better see he has his affairs in order. Leave it to me and I'll do what I can.' Then he nodded and winked, and away with him upstairs, leaving Faxy gaping after him.

He opened the bedroom door a couple of inches, bowed, and smiled in with his best excuse-me-God-help-me expression. The smile was one of the hardest things he had ever had to do, because the smell was something shocking. Then he tiptoed in respectfully, his hand outstretched.

'My poor man!' he whispered. 'My poor fellow! How are you at all? I needn't ask.'

'Poorly, father, poorly,' rumbled Devereux, rolling his lazy bloodshot eyes at him.

'I can see that. I can see you are. Isn't there anything I can do for you?' Father Ring tiptoed back to the door and gave a glance out at the landing. 'I'm surprised that man of yours didn't send for me,' he said reproachfully. 'You don't look very comfortable. Wouldn't you be better off in hospital?'

'I won't tell you a word of a lie, father,' Devereux said candidly. 'I couldn't afford it.'

'No, to be sure, to be sure, 'tis expensive, 'tis, 'tis,' Father Ring agreed feelingly. 'And you have no one to look after you?'

'I have not, father, I'm sorry to say.'

'Oh, my, my, my! At the end of your days! You couldn't get in touch with the daughter, I suppose?'

'No, father, I could not,' Devereux said shortly.

'I'm sorry about that. Wisha, isn't life queer. A great disappointment, that girl, Julia.'

'Joan, father.'

'Joan I mean. To be sure, to be sure, Joan. A great disappointment.'

'She was, father.'

And then, when Devereux had told his little story, Father Ring, bending forward with his hairy hands joined, whispered:

'Tell me, wouldn't it be a good thing if you had a couple of nuns?'

'A couple of what, father?' asked Devereux in astonishment.

'A couple of nuns. From the hospital. They'd look after you properly.'

'Ah, father,' Devereux said indignantly as though the priest had accused him of some nasty mean action, 'sure I have no money for nuns.'

'Well now,' Father Ring said thoughtfully, 'that's a matter you might leave to me. Myself and the nuns are old friends. Sure, that man, that What's-his-name, that fellow you have downstairs – sure, that poor unfortunate could do nothing for you.'

'Only break my heart, father,' Devereux sighed gustily. 'I won't tell you a word of a lie. He have me robbed.'

'Well, leave it to me,' Father Ring said with a wink. 'He might meet his match.'

Downstairs he whispered into Faxy's ear with his hand shading his mouth and his eyes following someone down the street:

'I'd say nothing just at present, Faxy. I'll get a couple of nuns to look after him. You might find him easier to deal with after that.'

3

It wasn't until the following morning that Faxy understood the full implications of that. Then it was too late. The nuns were installed and couldn't be shifted; one old, tough, and hairy, whom Faxy instantly christened 'the sergeant-major', the other young and good-looking.

'Come now,' the sergeant-major said to Faxy. 'Put on this apron and give that floor a good scrubbing.'

'Scrubbing?' bawled Faxy. 'Name of Ja – ' and stopped himself just in time. 'What's wrong with that floor?' he snarled. 'You could eat your dinner off that floor.'

'You'd have the makings of it anyway,' the sergeant-major said dryly, 'only 'twouldn't be very appetizing. I have a bath of water on for you. And mind and put plenty of Jeyes' Fluid.'

'I was discharged from the army with rheumatics,' Faxy said, grabbing his knee illustratively. 'Light duty is all I'm fit for. I have it on my discharge papers. And who's going to look after the shop?'

It was all no use. Down he had to go on his knees like any old washerwoman with a coarse apron round his waist and scrub every inch of the floor with carbolic soap and what he called Jeyes's Fluid. The sergeant-major was at his heels the whole time, telling him to change the water and wash the brush and cracking jokes about his rheumatics till she had him leaping. Then, under the eyes of the whole street, he had to get out on the window-ledge, wash the window, and strip away the comforting felt that had kept out generations of draughts; and afterwards scrape the walls while the young nun went after him with a spray, killing the bugs, she said – as if a couple of bugs ever did anyone any harm!

Faxy muttered rebelliously to himself about people who never saw anything of life only to plank their ass in a feather-bed while poor soldiers had to sleep out with nothing but gravestones for mattresses and corpses all round them and never complained. From his Way of the Cross he glared at Devereux, only asking for one word of an order to mutiny, but the old man only looked away at the farther wall with bleared and frightened eyes. He seemed to imagine that all he had to do was lie doggo to make the sergeant-major think he was dead.

But then his own turn came and Faxy, on face and hands on the landing, looked up through the chink in the door and saw them strip Devereux naked to God and the world and wash him all down the belly. 'Sweet Christ preserve us!' he muttered. It looked to him like the end of the world. Then they turned the old man over and washed him all down the back. He never uttered a groan or a moan, and relaxed like a Christian martyr in the flames, looking away with glassy eyes at floor and ceiling so that he would not embarrass them seeing what they had no right to see.

He contained himself till he couldn't contain himself any longer and then burst into a loud wail for Faxy and the bucket, but Faxy realized to his horror that even this little bit of decency was being denied him and that he was being made to sit up in bed with the young one holding him under the armpits while the sergeant-major planted him on top of some new-fangled yoke she was after ordering up from the chemist's.

It was too much for Faxy. At heart he was a religious man and to see women dressed as nuns behaving with no more modesty than hospital orderlies broke his spirit entirely. He moaned and tore his hair and cursed his God. He didn't wait to see the old man's hair cut, and his mattress and bedclothes that he had lain in so comfortably all the long years taken out to be burned, but prowled from shop to street and street back to shop, looking up at the window or listening at the foot of the stairs, telling his sad tale to all who passed. 'We didn't know how happy we were,' he snarled. 'God pity the poor that fall into their hands! We had a king's life and look at us now, like paupers in the workhouse without a thing we can call our own!'

He was even afraid to go into his own kitchen for fear the sergeant-major would fall on him and strip him as well. The

woman had no notion of modesty. She might even say he was
dirty. A woman who'd say what she had said about the bedroom floor would stop at nothing. It was only when her back
was turned that he crept up the stairs on tiptoe and silently
pushed in the bedroom door. The change from the morning
was terrible. It went to Faxy's heart. He knew now he no longer
had a home to call his own: windows open above and below, a
draught that would skin a brass monkey and flowers in a vase
on a table near the bed. The old man was lying there like a
corpse, clean, comfortable, and collapsed. It was only after a few
moments that he opened his weary bloodshot eyes and gazed
at Faxy with a far-away, heartbroken air. Faxy glared down at
him like a great gaunt bird of prey, clutching his ragged old
shirt back from his chest and shaking his skeleton head.

'Jasus!' he whispered in agony. "'Tis like a second crucifixion.'

'Would you gimme a fag, Faxy, if you please?' pleaded
Devereux in a dying voice.

'Ask your old jenny-asses for one!' hissed Faxy malevolently.

4

Devereux was just beginning to get over the shock when Father
Ring called again. Whatever it might have cost himself and
Faxy, the clean-up was a great ease to Father Ring.

'My poor man!' he said, shaking Devereux's hand and
casting a sly glance round the room, 'how are you today?
You're looking better. Well, now, aren't they great little women?
Tell me, are they feeding you properly?'

'Very nice, father,' Devereux said feebly in a tone of astonishment, as if he thought after the shocking way they had
already behaved to him, starvation was the only thing he could
have expected. 'Very nice indeed. I had a nice little bit of
chicken and a couple of poppies and a bit of cabbage.'

'Sure, you couldn't have nicer,' said Father Ring, smacking
his own lips over it.

'I had, indeed,' Devereux boomed, raising his arm and
looking at the clean hairy skin inside the shirtband as though

he wondered whom it belonged to. 'And I had rice pudding,' he added reflectively, 'and a cup of tea.'

'Ah, man, they'll have you trotting like a circus pony before they're done with you,' said Father Ring.

'I'm afraid it come too late, father,' sighed the old man as if the same notion had crossed his mind. 'I had a lot of hardship.'

'You had, you poor soul, you had,' sighed Father Ring. 'And, of course, when it comes to our turn we must be resigned. I say we must be resigned,' he added firmly. 'It comes to us all, sooner or later, and if our conscience is clear and our – oh, by the way, I nearly forgot it; my head is going – I suppose your own little affairs are in order?'

'What's that you say, father?' Devereux whispered with a timed, trapped air, raising his head from the pillow.

'Your affairs,' murmured Father Ring. 'Are they in order? I mean, have you your will made?'

'I won't tell you a word of a lie, father,' the old man said bashfully. 'I have not.'

'Well, now, listen to me,' Father Ring said persuasively, pulling his chair closer to the bed, 'wouldn't it be a good thing for you to do? 'Tisn't, God knows, for the little that either of us will leave, but for the sake of peace and quietness after we've gone. You saw them as I did myself, fighting over a few sticks.'

'I did, father, I did.'

''Tis the scandal of it,' said Father Ring. 'And God between us and all harm, the hour might come for any of us. It might come for myself and I a younger man than you.'

'Wouldn't I want an attorney, father?' Devereux asked timidly.

'Ah, what attorney?' exclaimed Father Ring. 'Aren't I better than any attorney? 'Pon my soul, I don't know why I didn't go in for the law. As it happens,' he added, scowling and fumbling in his pockets, 'I have some writing paper with me. I hope I didn't leave my specs behind. I did! As sure as you're there, I did. What sort of old head have I? ... No, I declare to my goodness, I brought them for once. Ah, man alive,' he exclaimed, looking at Devereux over the specs, 'I have to do this every month of my life. 'Tis astonishing, the number of people, that put it on the long finger. . . . I may as well get it down as I'm here. I can write the rigmarole in after. . . . What'll we say to begin with? You'd like to leave a couple of pounds for Masses, I suppose?'

'God knows I would, father,' Devereux said devoutly.

'Well, what'll we say? Give me a figure! Ten? Twenty?'

'I suppose so, father,' Devereux replied hesitatingly.

'Well, now, make it whatever you like,' said Father Ring, pointing the fountain pen like a dart at him and giving him a long look through the spectacles, a sort of professional look, quite different from the ones he gave over and round them. 'But, remember, Masses are the only investment you can draw on in the next world. The only friends you can be sure won't forget you. Think again before you say the last word on Masses.'

'How much would you say yourself, father?' asked Devereux, hypnotized by the gleam of the spectacles like a rabbit by the headlights of a car.

'Well, that's a matter for you. You know what you can afford. You might like to make it a hundred. Or even more.'

'We'll say a hundred so,' said Devereux.

'Good man! Good man! I like a man that knows his own mind. You'd be astonished, the people that don't seem to be able to say "yes" or "no". And what'll we do about the –' he nodded towards the door – 'the holy ladies? 'Twould be expected.'

'Would the same thing be enough, father?'

'To tell you the truth, Mr Devereux, I think it would,' said Father Ring, bobbing his head and giving Devereux an unprofessional dart over the top of his spectacles. 'I'll go farther. I'd say 'twould be generous. Women are lick alike. I don't know how it is, Mr Devereux, but a woman crossed in love finds some fatal attraction in building. Building is the ruin of those poor women. A fool and his money – but you know the old proverb.'

'I do, father.'

'And the monks? As we're on the subject of charities, what are we going to do about the monks?'

Devereux gave him an appealing glance. Father Ring rose, pursing his lips and putting his hands behind his back. He stood at the window and gazed down the street, his head on his chest and his eyes strained over his glasses.

'Look at that scut, Foley, sneaking into Johnny Desmond's,' he said as though to himself. 'That fellow will be the death of his poor unfortunate wife. . . . I think so, Mr Devereux,' he added in a loud voice, turning on his heel and raising his head like a man who has received a sudden illumination. 'I think so. Religious orders! 'Tisn't for me to be criticizing them, God knows, but they'd surprise you. 'Pon my soul, they'd surprise you! The jealousy between them over a miserable couple of hundred pounds! Those poor fellows would be fretting over a slight like that for years to come.'

''Twouldn't be wishing to me,' said Devereux, shaking his head regretfully.

''Twouldn't, man, 'twouldn't, 'twouldn't,' cried Father Ring as if astonished at Devereux's perspicacity, and implying by his tone that if the bad wishes of the monks didn't actually follow the old man to the next world they'd make very heavy weather for any prayers which did. 'You're right, Mr Devereux, it would not be wishing to you. . . . Now, coming nearer home,' he whispered with a nervous glance over his shoulder, 'what about that man of yours? They'll be expecting you to provide for him.'

'He robbed me, father,' Devereux said sullenly, his heavy face settling into the expression of an obstinate child.

'Ah, let me alone, let me alone!' said Father Ring, waving the paper in his face with exasperation. 'I know all about it. That British Army! 'Tis the ruination of thousands.'

'The couple of cigarettes I'd have,' the old man went on, turning his red eyes on the priest while his deep voice throbbed like a 'cello with the dint of self-pity, 'he'd steal them on me. Often and often – I won't tell you a word of a lie, father – I'd go down to the shop of a morning and I wouldn't have a smoke. Not a smoke!'

'Oh, my, my!' said Father Ring, clucking and nodding over the villainy of man.

'The packets of Lux,' intoned Devereux solemnly, raising his right hand in affirmation, 'that's as true as the Almighty God is looking down on me this moment, father, he'd take them and sell them from door to door, a half dozen for the price of a medium. And I sitting here, gasping for a cigarette!'

'Well, well!' sighed the priest. 'But still, Mr Devereux, you know you're after forgiving him all that.'

'Forgiving him is one thing,' the old man said stubbornly, 'but leaving him a legacy is another thing entirely, father. Oh, no.'

'But as a sign you forgive him!' the priest said coaxingly. 'A – what'll I call it? – a token! Some little thing.'

'Not a ha'penny, father,' said Devereux in the voice of a judge with the black cap on. 'Not one solitary ha'penny.'

'Well, now, Mr Devereux,' Father Ring pleaded, 'fifty pounds. What is it? 'Tis neither here nor there and 'twould mean a lot to that poor wretch.'

Suddenly the door burst open and Faxy, who had been listening at the keyhole, charged in on them, a great, gaunt skeleton of a man with mad eyes and clenched fists.

'Fifty pounds?' he shouted. 'Fifty pounds? Is it mad ye are, the pair of ye?'

Old Devereux began to struggle frantically up in the bed, throwing off the clothes with his swollen old hands and gasping for breath so that he could tell Faxy what he thought of him.

'You robber!' he croaked away back in his throat. 'If I done you justice I'd have you up in the body of the jail.'

'Come now, Mr Devereux, come, come!' cried Father Ring, alarmed that the old man might drop dead on him before the will was even sketched. 'Compose yourself,' he said, putting down his papers and trying to get Devereux to lie back.

'I won't give him a ha'penny,' roared Devereux in a voice that could be heard at the opposite side of the street. 'Not one ha'penny! Leave him support himself out of all he stole from the till!'

'And a hell of a lot there ever was to steal!' hissed Faxy with his gaunt head bowed, grinning back at him.

'Not a ha'penny!' repeated the old man frantically, pummeling his knees with his fists and blowing himself up like a balloon till he turned all colours.

'Two hundred and fifty pounds,' snarled Faxy with his toothless gums, pointing at the palm of his left hand as if he had it all noted there. 'That's what I'm owed. I have it all down in black and white. Back wages. The War Office won't see me wronged.'

'You robber!' panted Devereux.

'Sister!' cried Father Ring, throwing the door open. 'Sister Whatever-your-name is, send for the police! Tell them I want this fellow locked up.'

'Leave that one out of it!' hissed Faxy, dragging Father Ring back from the door. Faxy wasn't afraid of the police, but he was scared out of his wits by the sergeant-major of the nuns. 'We want no women in it. Play fair and fight like a man. Fair play is all I ask. I done for him what no one else would do.'

'Mr Devereux,' Father Ring said earnestly, 'he's right. The man is right. He's entitled to something. He could upset the will.'

'God knows, father, that's not what I want,' said Faxy. He sat on the edge of the bed, began to sob, and brushed away the tears with his hand. 'I deserved better after my years of hardship. No one knows what I went through with him.'

'You sweet God, listen to him!' croaked Devereux despairingly. 'Black puddings and old sausages. Not one decent bite of food crossed my lips, father, all the long years he's with me. Not till the blessed nuns came.'

'Because they can get the credit,' snarled Faxy, shaking his fist at his boss while his tears dried as though by magic. 'If you handed me out the money instead of locking it up, you could have bacon and cabbage every day of the week. I was batman to better men than you. You were too near, you old bugger, you, and now 'tis going on you whether you like it or not on medicines and Jeyes's Fluid and chamberpots. That's all you have out of it at the end of your days.'

'Be quiet now, be quiet!' said Father Ring. 'You'll get something, even though you don't deserve it. I'll take it on

myself to put him down for another hundred, Mr Devereux.
You won't deny me that?'

'A hundred strokes of the cat-and-nine-tails,' grumbled the
old man. 'But I won't deny you, father. I'll offer it up. . . . That
it might choke you!' he added charitably to Faxy.

'And now, Mr D., I won't keep you much longer. There's
just Julia.'

'Joan, father.'

'Joan I mean. To be sure, Joan. Or the little – you know who
I'm talking of. Was it a little boy? 'Pon my soul, my memory
is gone.'

'Nothing, father,' Devereux said firmly, settling himself
back in his pillows and gazing out the window.

'What's that?' Faxy shouted, scandalized. 'Your daughter!'

'This have nothing to do with you, Donnell,' said Devereux.
'It have nothing to do with anyone.'

'Now, you're wrong there, Mr Devereux,' Father Ring said
with a quelling professional glance. 'I say you're wrong there.
Whatever little disagreement ye might have or whatever upset
she might cause you, this is no time to remember it.'

'I won't leave her a ha'penny, father,' Devereux said
firmly.
''Tis no use to be at me. Anything that's over can go to the
Church.'

'Christ look down on the poor!' cried Faxy, raising his arms
to heaven. 'Stick and stone instead of flesh and bone.'

'Will you be quiet?' snapped Father Ring. 'Now, Mr
Devereux, I understand your feelings; I understand them
perfectly, but 'tisn't right. Do you know what they'd say? Have
you any notion of the wickedness of people in this town?
They'd say there was undue influence, Mr Devereux. You
might have the whole will upset on you for the sake of – what'll
I say? A hundred? Two hundred? A trifle anyway.'

'This is my will, father, not yours,' Devereux said with
sudden, surprising dignity. 'I'm after telling you my wishes,
and Donnell here is a witness. Everything else is to go to the
Church, barring a few pounds to keep the family vault in
order. The Devereuxs are an old family, father,' he added with

calm pride. 'They were a great family in their day, and I'd like the grave to be respected when I'm gone.'

That night the will was signed and the substance of it was the talk of the town. Many blamed old Devereux for being hard and unnatural; more blamed Father Ring for being so grasping. Faxy got credit on the strength of it and came home fighting drunk, under the impression that the old man was already dead and that the priest had cheated him out of his inheritance; but the nuns locked him out and he slept in the straw in Kearney's yard, waking in the middle of the night and howling like a dog for his lost master.

But Devereux had no intention of dying. He began to improve visibly under the nuns' care. He had a little handbell on the table by his bed, and whenever he felt bored he rang for the sergeant-major to keep him company. He had taken a great fancy to her, and he just rang whenever he remembered anything more about the history of the Devereuxs. When he tired of this he held her hand while she read him a chapter from *The Imitation of Christ* or *The Lives of the Saints*.

'That's beautiful reading, Sister,' he said, stroking her hand.

'Sure, there's nothing like it,' said the sergeant-major.

'Beautiful reading,' sighed Devereux with a far-away air. 'Don't we miss a lot in life, sister?'

'Ah, musha, we all miss a lot, but God will make it up to us, we hope. Sunshine in this life, shadow in the next.'

'I'd like a bit of sunshine too, sister,' he said. 'Ye're very good to me and I didn't forget ye in my will.'

He talked a lot about his will and even said he was thinking of changing it in favour of the nuns. The only trouble was that Father Ring wouldn't approve, being a strong-minded man himself, and Devereux could never warm to solicitors from the time they started sending him letters. The rudeness of some of those solicitors' letters was still on his mind. He got really lively at times and even suggested that the sergeant-major might read him some novels by Mrs Braddon. He was very fond of the works of Mrs Braddon, he said.

'I suppose you'll be renewing that bottle for me, sister?' he said on one occasion. 'I wonder would you get me something else at the same time?'

'I will to be sure, Mr Devereux. What is it?'

'Well,' he said bashfully, 'I'd like a little drop of hair-oil, if you please. My hair doesn't lie down well without it. The scented kind is the kind I like.'

She got him the hair-oil and did his hair for him while he looked at her fondly and commented on her hands. Beautiful, gentle hands she had, he said. Then she gave him the mirror to see himself, and he was so shocked that tears came to his eyes.

'Now,' she said briskly, 'there's a fine handsome man for you!'

'I was very handsome once, sister,' he said mournfully. 'The handsomest man in the town, I was supposed to be. People used to stop and look after me in the street. Dandy Devereux they used to call me.'

Then he asked for the scissors to clip his moustache.

He made a most beautiful and edifying death, with the nuns at either side of him saying the prayers for the dying, and when they had laid him out the sergeant-major went down to the kitchen and had a good cry to herself.

''Tis a hard old life,' she said to the young nun. 'You're left with them long enough to get fond of them, and then either they get better or they die on you, and you never see them again. If 'twas only an old dog you'd be sorry for him, and he was a fine gentlemanly old man, God rest him.'

Then, having tidied away her pots and pans and had a last look at old Tom Devereux, the man who had stroked her hands and praised them as no one else had done since she was a girl, she washed her eyes and went back to her convent.

After Requiem High Mass next day Devereux went to join the rest of his family within the ruined walls of the abbey they had founded in the fifteenth century, and by the time Father Ring got back from the funeral Faxy had already started prying. The great iron-bound chests were in the centre of the floor and Faxy had borrowed a set of tools. They opened the chests between them but there was nothing inside only old screws, bolts, washers, bits of broken vases and an enormous selection of pipe-bowls and stems. Father Ring was so incredulous that he put on his glasses to examine them better. By that time he was ready to believe they were pieces of eight in disguise.

'I made a great mistake,' he said, sitting back on the floor beside the chest. 'I should have asked him where he had it.'

He still had not even faced the possibility that Devereux. hadn't it. They stayed on till midnight, searching. Next day they had two men from the builders in. Every floor was ripped up, every chimney searched, every hollow bit of wall burst in. Faxy was first everywhere with a lighted candle, and Father Ring followed, stroking his chin. A crowd had gathered in the street, and at intervals the priest stood at the window and surveyed them moodily over his glasses. He had a nasty feeling that the crowd would be well pleased if he failed.

Eddie Murphy, the undertaker, came up the stairs looking anxious. Eddie was owed thirty quid so he had good cause for anxiety.

'Did ye find it, father?' he asked.

'I'm afraid, Eddie,' Father Ring said, looking round his glasses, 'we were had. We were had, boy, all of us. 'Tis a great disappointment, a great disappointment, Eddie, but 'pon my soul, he was a remarkable man.'

Then he took his shabby old soft hat and went home.

The Cheapjack

I

EVERYONE was sorry after Sam Higgins, the headmaster. Sam was a right good skin, one of the decentest men in Ireland, but too honest.

He was a small fat man with a round, rosy, good-natured face, a high bald brow, and specs. He wore a bowler hat and a stiff collar the hottest day God sent, because no matter how sociable he might be, he never entirely forgot his dignity. He lived with his sister, Delia, in a house by the station and suffered a good deal from nerves and dyspepsia. The doctors tried to make out that they were one and the same thing but they weren't; they worked on entirely different circuits. When it was the nerves were bad Sam went on a skite. The skite, of course, was good for the nerves but bad for the dyspepsia, and for months afterwards he'd be on a diet and doing walks in the country. The walks, on the other hand, were good for the dyspepsia but played hell with the nerves, so Sam had to try and take the harm out of them by dropping into Johnny Desmond's on the way home for a pint. Johnny had a sort of respect for him as an educated man, which Johnny wasn't, and a sort of contempt for him as a man who, for all his education, couldn't keep his mind to himself – an art Johnny was past master of.

One day they happened to be discussing the Delea case, which Johnny, a cautious, religious man, affected to find peculiar. There was nothing peculiar about it. Father Ring had landed another big fish; that was all. Old Jeremiah Delea had died and left everything to the Church, nothing to his wife and family. There was to be law about that, according to what Johnny had heard – ah, a sad business, a peculiar business! But Sam, who hated Father Ring with a hate you might describe as truly religious, rejoiced.

'Fifteen thousand, I hear,' he said with an ingenuous smile.

'So I believe,' said Johnny with a scowl. 'A man that couldn't write his own name for you! Now what do you say to the education?'

'Oh, what I always said,' replied Sam with his usual straight-forwardness. ''Tis nothing only a hindrance.'

'Ah, I wouldn't go so far as that,' said Johnny, who, though he tended to share this view, was too decent to criticize any man's job to his face, and anyway had a secret admiration for the polish which a good education can give. 'If he might have held on to the wireless shares he'd be good for another five thousand. I suppose that's where the education comes in.'

Having put in a good word for culture, Johnny now felt it was up to him to say something in the interests of religion. There was talk about Father Ring and Johnny didn't like it. He didn't think it was lucky. Years of observation of anti-clericals in his pub had convinced Johnny that none of them ever got anywhere.

'Of course, old Jerry was always a very good-living man,' he added doubtfully.

'He was,' Sam said dryly. 'Very fond of the Children of Mary.'

'That so?' said Johnny, as if he didn't know what a Child of Mary would be.

'Young and old,' Sam said enthusiastically. 'They were the poor man's great hobbies.'

That was Sam all out; too outspoken, too independent! No one like that ever got anywhere. Johnny went to the shop door and looked after him as he slouched up Main Street with his sailor's roll and his bowler hat and wondered to himself that an educated man wouldn't have more sense.

2

Delia and Mrs MacCann, the new teacher in the girls' school, were sitting on deck-chairs in the garden when Sam got back. It did more than the pint to rouse his spirits after that lone-some rural promenade. Mrs MacCann was small, gay, and go-as-you-please. Sam thought her the pleasantest woman he had ever met and would have told her as much only that she was barely out of mourning for her first husband. He felt it was no time to approach any woman with proposals of marriage, which showed how little Sam knew of women.

'How're ye, Nancy?' he cried heartily, holding out a fat paw.

'Grand, Sam,' she replied, sparkling with pleasure. 'How's the body?'

'So-so,' said Sam. He took off his coat and squatted to give the lawnmower a drop of oil. 'As pleasant a bit of news as I heard this long time I'm after hearing today.'

'What's that, Sam?' Delia asked in her high-pitched, fluting voice.

'Chrissie Delea that's going to law with Ring over the legacy.'

'Ah, you're not serious, Sam?' cried Nancy.

'Oh, begod I am,' growled Sam. 'She has Canty the solicitor in Asragh on to it. Now Ring will be having Sister Mary Milkmaid and the the rest of them making novenas to soften Chrissie's hard heart. By God I tell you 'twill take more than novenas to do that.'

'But will she get it, Sam?' asked Nancy.

'Why wouldn't she get it?'

'Anyone that got money out of a priest ought to have a statue put up to her.'

'She'll get it all right,' Sam said confidently. 'After all the other scandals the bishop will never let it go to court. Sure, old Jerry was off his rocker years before he made that will. I'd give evidence myself that I saw him stopping little girls on their way from school to try and look up their clothes.'

'Oh, God, Sam, the waste of it!' said Nancy with a chuckle. 'Anyway, we'll have rare gas with a lawcase and a new teacher.'

'A new what?' asked Sam, stopping dead in his mowing.

'Why? Didn't Ormond tell you he got the shift?' she asked in surprise.

'No, Nancy, he did not,' Sam said gravely.

'But surely, Ormond would never keep a thing like that from you?'

'He wouldn't,' said Sam, 'and I'll swear he knows nothing about it. Where did you hear it?'

'Plain Jane told me.' (She meant Miss Daly, the head.)

'And she got it from Ring, I suppose,' Sam said broodingly. 'And Ring was in Dublin for the last couple of days. Now we know what he was up for. You didn't hear who was coming in Ormond's place?'

'I didn't pay attention, Sam,' Nancy said with a frown. 'But she said he was from Kerry. Isn't that where Father Ring comes from?'

'Oh, a cousin of Ring's for a fortune!' Sam said dolefully, wiping his sweaty brow. He felt suddenly very depressed and very tired. Even the thought of Chrissie Delea's lawcase couldn't cheer him. He felt the threat of Ring now shadowing himself. A bad manager is difficult enough. A bad manager with a spy in the school can destroy a teacher.

He was right about the relationship with Ring. The new teacher arrived in a broken-down two-seater which he seemed to think rather highly of. His name was Carmody. He was tall and thin with a high, bumpy forehead, prominent cheekbones, and a dirty complexion. He held himself stiffly, obviously proud of his figure. He wore a tight-fitting cheap city suit with stripes, and Sam counted two fountain pens and a battery of coloured pencils in his breast pocket. He had a little red diary sticking from the top pocket of his waistcoat, and while Sam was talking he made notes – a business-like young fellow. Then he pushed the pencil behind his ear, stuck his thumbs in the armholes of his vest, and giggled at Sam. Giggled was the only way Sam could describe it. It was almost as though he found Sam funny. Within five minutes he was giving him advice on the way they did things in Kerry. Sam, his hands in his trouser pockets and wearing his most innocent air, looked him up and down and his tone grew dryer.

'You seem to get on very well with your class,' he said later in the day.

'I make a point of it,' Carmody explained pompously.

'Treat them as man to man, like?' Sam said, luring him on.

'That's the modern method, of course,' said Carmody.

'That so?' Sam said dryly, and at the same moment he made a face. It was the first twinge of the dyspepsia.

He and Nancy usually had their lunch together in the open

air, sitting on the low wall between the two schools. They were there a few minutes when Carmody came out. He stood on the steps and sunned himself, thrusting out his chest and drawing in deep gulps of what a Kerryman would call the ozone.

'Fine figure of a man, Sam,' Nancy said, interpreting and puncturing his pose.

As though he had heard her and taken it in earnest Carmody came up to them with an air which he probably thought quizzical.

'That's a fine view you have,' he said jocularly.

'You won't be long getting tired of it,' Sam said coldly.

'I believe 'tis a quiet sort of place,' said Carmody, unaware of any lack of warmth.

'It must be simply shocking after Kerry,' Sam said, giving Nancy a nudge. 'Were you ever in Kerry, Mrs Mac?'

'Never, Mr Higgins,' said Nancy, joining in the sport. 'But I believe 'tis wonderful.'

'Wonderful,' Sam agreed mournfully. 'You'd wonder where the people got the brains till you saw the scenery.'

Carmody, as became a modest man, overlooked the implication that the intellect of a Kerryman might be due to environment rather than heredity; he probably didn't expect better from a native.

'Tell me,' he asked with great concern, 'what *do* you do with yourselves?'

The impudence of this was too much even for Sam. He gaped at Carmody to see was he in earnest. Then he pointed to the town.

'See the bridge?'

'I do.'

'See the abbey tower near it?'

'Yes.'

'When we get tired of life we chuck ourselves off that.'

'I was being serious,' Carmody said icily.

'Oh, begor, so was I,' said Sam. 'That tower is pretty high.'

'I believe you have some sort of dramatic society,' Carmody went on to Nancy as though he couldn't be bothered carrying on conversation at Sam's level.

'We have,' said Nancy brightly. 'Do you act?'

'A certain amount,' said Carmody. 'Of course, in Kerry we go in more for the intellectual drama.'

'Go on!' said Sam. 'That'll be a shock to the dramatic society.'

'It probably needs one,' said Carmody.

'It does,' said Sam blithely, getting down and looking at Carmody with his lower lip hanging and the sunlight dazzling on his spectacles. 'The town needs a bit of attention too. You might notice 'tis on the downgrade. And then you can have the whole country to practise on. It often struck me it needed a bombshell to wake it up. Maybe you're the bombshell.'

It wasn't often that Sam, who was a bit tongue-tied, made a speech as long as that. It should have shut anyone up, but Carmody only stuck his thumbs in his armholes, thrust out his chest, and giggled.

'But of course I'm a bombshell,' he said with a sidelong glance at Nancy. You couldn't pierce Carmody's complacency so easily.

3

A week or two later Sam dropped into Johnny Desmond's for his pint.

'Mrs Mac and the new teacher seem to be getting very great,' Johnny said by way of no harm.

'That so, Johnny?' Sam replied in the same tone.

'I just saw them going off for a spin together,' added Johnny.

'Probably giving her a lift home,' said Sam. 'He does it every day. I hope she's insured.'

'Twasn't that at all,' Johnny said, opening a bottle of boiled sweets and cramming a fistful into his mouth. 'Out Bauravullen way they went. Have a couple of these, Mr Higgins!'

'Thanks, Johnny, I won't,' Sam said sourly, glancing out the door the way Johnny wouldn't notice how he was hit. There was damn little Johnny didn't notice, though. He went to the door and stood there, crunching sweets.

'Widows are the devil,' he said reflectively. 'Anything at all so long as 'tis in trousers. I suppose they can't help it.'

'You seem to know a lot about them,' said Sam.

'My own father died when I was only a boy,' Johnny explained discreetly. 'Clever chap, young Carmody,' he added with his eyes on the ground.

'A human bombshell,' said Sam with heavy irony.

'So I believe, so I believe,' said Johnny, who didn't know what irony was but who was going as far as a man like himself could go towards indicating that there were things about Carmody he didn't approve of. 'A pity he's so quarrelsome in drink,' he said, looking back at Sam.

'Is he so?' said Sam.

'Himself and Donovan of the Exchange were at it here last night. I believe Father Ring is hoping he'll settle down. I dunno will he?'

'God forbid!' said Sam.

He went home but he couldn't read or rest. It was too cold for the garden, too hot for the room. He put on his hat again and went for a walk. At least, he explained it to himself as going for a walk, but it took him past Nancy's bungalow. There was no sign of life in that and Sam didn't know whether this was a good sign or a bad one. He dropped into Johnny's expecting to find the Bombshell there, but there were only a couple of fellows from the County Council inside, and Sam had four drinks which was three more than was good for him. When he came out the moon was up. He returned the same way, and there, sure enough, was a light in Nancy's sitting-room window and the Bombshell's car standing outside.

For two days Sam didn't show his nose in the playground at lunchtime. When he looked out he saw Carmody leaning over the wall, talking to Nancy, and giggling.

On the afternoon of the third day, while Sam was in the garden, Nancy called and Delia opened the door.

'Oh, my!' Delia cried in her laughing, piping voice. 'Such a stranger as you're becoming!'

'You'd never guess what I was up to?' Nancy asked.

'I believe you were motoring,' replied Delia with a laugh.

'Ah, you can't do anything in this old town,' Nancy said with a shrug of disgust. 'Where the blazes is Sam? I didn't see him these ages.'

'He's in the workshop,' said Delia. 'Will I call him in?'

'Time enough,' Nancy said gaily, grabbing her by the arm. 'Come on in till I talk to you.'

'And how's your friend, Mr Carmody?' asked Delia, trying to keep the hurt out of her voice.

'He's all right as long as you don't go out in a motor-car with him,' laughed Nancy, not noticing Delia's edginess. 'Whoever gave him that car was no friend.'

'I'm not in much danger of being asked, dear, am I?' Delia asked, half joking, half wincing. 'And is he still homesick for Kerry? I dare say not.'

'He'll settle down,' said Nancy, blithely unconscious of the volcano of emotion under her feet. 'A poor gom like that, brought up in the wilds, what more could you expect?'

'I dare say,' said Delia. 'He has every inducement.'

Just then Sam came up the garden and in the back door without noticing Nancy's presence. He stood at the door, wiping his boots, his hat shading his eyes, and laughed in an embarrassed way. Even then, if only he could have welcomed her as he longed to do, things might have been all right, but no more than Delia was he able to conceal his feelings.

'Oh, hullo,' he drawled idly. 'How're you?'

'Grand, Sam,' Nancy said, sitting up and flashing him an extra-special look. 'Where were you the last couple of days?'

'Working,' said Sam. 'Or trying to. It's hard to do anything with people pinching your things. Did you take the quarter-inch chisel, Delia?'

'Is that a big chisel, Sam?' she asked innocently.

'No,' he drawled. 'Not much bigger than a quarter of an inch, if you know what that is.'

'I think it might be on top of the press, Sam,' she said guiltily.

'Why the hell women can't put things back where they find them!' he grunted as he got a chair. He pawed about on top of the press till he found the chisel. Then he held it up to the light and closed one eye. 'Holy God!' he moaned. 'Were you using it as a screwdriver or what?'

'I thought it was a screwdriver, Sam,' she replied with a nervous laugh.

'You ought to use it on yourself,' he said with feeling, and went out again.

Nancy frowned. Delia laughed again, even more nervously. She knew what the scene meant, but Nancy was still incredulous.

'He seems very busy,' she said in a hurt tone.

'He's always pulling the house to pieces,' Delia explained apologetically.

'There's nothing wrong with him?' Nancy asked suspiciously.

'No, dear,' Delia said. 'Only his digestion. That's always a trouble to him.'

'I suppose it must be,' said Nancy, growing pale. Only now was she beginning to realize that the Higginses wanted to have no more to do with her. Deeply offended, she began to collect her things.

'You're not going so soon, Nancy?'

'I'd better. I promised Nellie the afternoon off.'

'Oh, dear, Sam will be so disappointed,' sighed Delia.

'He'll get over it,' said Nancy. 'So long, Delia.'

'Good-bye, dear,' said Delia and, after shutting the door, began to cry. In a small town the end of a friendship has something of death about it. Delia had had hopes of something closer than friendship. Nancy had broken down her jealousy of other women; when she came to the house Sam was more cheerful and Delia found herself more cheerful too. She brought youth and gaiety into their lives.

Delia had a good long cry before Sam came in from the back. He said nothing about Nancy but went into the front room and took down a book. After a while Delia washed her eyes and went in. It was dark inside, and when she opened the door he started, always a bad sign.

'You wouldn't like to come for a little walk with me, dear?' Delia asked in a voice that went off into a squeak.

'No, Dee,' he said without looking round. 'I wouldn't be able.'

'I'm sure a little drink in Johnny's would cheer you up,' she persisted.

'No, Dee,' he went on dully. 'I couldn't stand his old guff.'

'Then wouldn't you run up to town and see a doctor, Sam?'

'Ah, what good are doctors?'

'But it must be something, Sam,' she said. She wished he'd say it and be done with it and let her try to comfort him as best she could: the two of them there, growing old, in a lonesome, unfriendly place.

'I know what it is myself,' he said. 'It's that cheapjack, Carmody. Twenty years I'm in that school and I was never laughed at to my face before. Now he's turning the boys against me.'

'I think you only fancy that, dear,' she said timidly. 'I don't believe Mr Carmody could ever turn anybody against you.'

'There's where you're wrong, Dee,' he replied, shaking his head, infallible even in despair. 'That fellow was put there with a purpose. Ring chose his man well. They'll be having a new head one of these days.'

4

School had become a real torture to Sam. Carmody half-suspected his jealousy and played on it. He sent boys to the girls' school with notes and read the replies with a complacent smirk. Sam went about as though he was doped. He couldn't find things he had just left out of his hand, he forgot the names of the boys, and sometimes sat for a quarter of an hour at a time in a desk behind his class, rubbing his eyes and brow in a stupor.

He came to life only when he wrangled with Carmody. There was a window that Sam liked open and Carmody liked shut. That was enough to set the pair of them off. When Carmody sent a boy to shut the window Sam asked the boy who gave him permission. Then Carmody came up, stiff and blustering, and said no one was going to make him work with a draught down the back of his neck and Sam replied that a better man had worked there for ten years without noticing any draught at all.

It was all as silly as that, and Sam knew it was silly, but that was how it took him, and no amount of good resolutions made it any better.

All through November he ate his lunch by the school fire, and when he looked out it was to see Carmody and Nancy eating theirs outside and Nancy putting up her hand to tidy her hair and breaking into a sudden laugh. Sam always felt the laugh was at him.

One day he came out, ringing the school bell, and Carmody, who had been sitting on the wall, jumped off with such an affectation of agility that the diary fell from his vest pocket. He was so occupied with Nancy that he didn't notice it, and Sam was so full of his own troubles that he went on down the playground and he didn't notice it either. He saw a bit of paper that someone's lunch had been wrapped in, picked it up and crumpled it into a ball. At the same time he noticed the diary, and, assuming that one of the boys had dropped it, picked it up and glanced through it. It puzzled him, for it did not seem like the notebook of a schoolboy. It was all about some girl that the writer was interested in. He couldn't help reading on till he came to a name that caused him to blush. Then he recognized the writing; it was Carmody's. When he turned the pages and saw how much of it there was, he put it in his pocket. Afterwards, he knew what he had done and saw it was wrong, but at the time he never even thought of an alternative. During the first lesson he sat at a desk and read on, his head in his hands.

Now, Carmody was a conceited young man who thought that everything about himself was of such importance that it had to be recorded for the benefit of posterity. Things Sam would have been ashamed even to think about himself he had all written down. Besides, Sam had led a sheltered life. He didn't know much of any woman but Delia. He had thought of Nancy as an angelic little creature whose life had been wrecked by her husband's death and who spent most of her time thinking of him. It was clear from the diary that this was not how she spent her time at all, but that, like any other bad, flighty, sensual girl, she let herself be made love to in motor-cars by cheapjacks like Carmody, who even on his own admission had no respect for her and only wanted to see how far a widow like that would go. 'Anything at all so long as 'tis in trousers,' as Johnny said. Johnny was right. Johnny knew the sort of woman she was. That was all Sam needed to make him hate Nancy as much as he already hated Carmody. She was another cheapjack.

Then he looked at the clock. Dictation came next. Without a moment's thought he went to the blackboard, wiped out the sums on it, and wrote in a neat, workmanlike hand: 'The Diary of a Cheapjack.' Even then he had no notion of what he was actually going to do, but as the boys settled themselves he took a deep breath and began to read.

'October 21st,' he dictated in a dull voice. 'I think I have bowled the widow over.'

There was a shocked silence and some boy giggled.

'It's all right,' Sam explained blandly, pointing to the blackboard. 'I told you this fellow was only a cheapjack, one of those lads you see at the fair, selling imitation jewellery. You'll see it all in a minute.'

And on he went again in a monotonous voice, one hand holding the diary, the other in his trouser pocket. He knew he was behaving oddly, even scandalously, but it gave him an enormous feeling of release, as though all the weeks of misery and humiliation were being paid for at last. It was everything he had ever thought of Carmody, only worse. Worse, for how could Sam have suspected that Carmody would admit the way he had first made love to Nancy, just to keep his hand in (his own very words!), or describe the way love came to him at last one evening up Bauravullen when the sun was setting behind the pine trees and he found he no longer despised Nancy.

The fellows began to titter. Sam raised his brows and looked at them with a wondering smile as if he did not quite know what they were laughing at. In a curious way he was beginning to enjoy it himself. He began to parody it in the style of a bad actor, waving one arm, throwing back his head and cooing out the syrupy pseudo-Byronic sentences. 'And all for a widow!' he read, raising his voice and staring at Carmody. 'A woman who went through it all before.'

Carmody heard him and suddenly recognized the diary. He came up the classroom in a few strides and tore the book out of Sam's hand. Sam let it go with him and only gaped.

'Hi, young man,' he asked amiably, 'where are you going with that?'

'What are you doing with it?' Carmody asked in a terrible voice, equally a caricature of a bad actor's. He was still incredulous; he could not believe that Sam had actually been reading it aloud to his class.

'Oh, that's our piece for dictation,' Sam said and glanced at the blackboard. 'I'm calling it "The Diary of a Cheapjack". I think that about hits it off.'

'You stole my diary!' hissed Carmody.

'Your diary?' Sam replied with assumed concern. 'You're not serious?'

'You know perfectly well it was mine,' shouted Carmody beside himself with rage. 'You saw my name and you know my writing.'

'Oh, begod I didn't,' Sam protested stolidly. 'If anyone told me that thing was written by an educated man I'd call him a liar.'

Then Carmody did the only thing he could do, the thing that Sam in his heart probably hoped for – he gave Sam a punch in the jaw. Sam staggered, righted himself and made for Carmody. They closed. The boys left their desks, shouting. One or two ran out of the school. In a few moments the rest had formed a cheering ring about the two struggling teachers. Sam was small and gripped his man low. Carmody punched him viciously and effectively about the head but Sam hung on, pulling Carmody right and left till he found it hard to keep his feet. At last Sam gave one great heave and sent Carmody flying. His head cracked off the iron leg of a desk. He lay still for some moments and then rose, clutching his head.

At the same moment Miss Daly and Nancy came in.

'Sam!' Nancy cried. 'What's the matter?'

'Get out of my way,' Carmody shouted, skipping round her. 'Get out of my way till I kill him.'

'Come on, you cheapjack!' drawled Sam. His head was

down, his hands were hanging, and he was looking dully at Carmody over his spectacles. 'Come on and I'll give you more of it.'

'Mr Higgins, Mr Higgins!' screamed Miss Daly. 'Is it mad ye are, the pair of ye?'

They came to their senses at that. Miss Daly took charge. She rang the bell and cleared the school. Sam turned away and began fumbling blindly with the lid of a chalk-box. Carmody began to dust himself. Then, with long backward glances, he and the two women went into the playground, where Sam heard them talking in loud, excited voices. He smiled vaguely, took off his glasses, and wiped them carefully before he picked up his books, his hat, and his coat, and locked the school door behind him. He knew he was doing it for the last time and wasn't sorry. The three other teachers drew away and he went past them without a glance. He left the keys at the presbytery and told the housekeeper he'd write. Next morning he went away by an early train and never came back.

We were all sorry for him. Poor Sam! As decent a man as ever drew breath but too honest, too honest!